"What a

"Le Fe's kill

Sloane frowned. "You're a bounty hunter, not a PI."

"So?"

"Why do this?" she asked him warily. "You didn't like who he was or what he did. It's not your responsibility to catch his killer."

"I need to."

"Why?" she asked again.

"The person who killed him is likely a high-level assassin. Someone with a skill set similar to my own. The type of person who won't have too many qualms about taking anyone out who gets too close."

"Including me," she exclaimed. "You're still protecting me."

"I'm asking you to partner with me on this," he said.

"You act like this is personal."

"It involves you, doesn't it?"

She willed herself to be strong. "I'm not going to say no."

"Good."

She sighed. "Stay out of trouble. If you cross the line, I can't protect you."

"No promises."

Dear Reader,

We have come to the end of the Southern Justice trilogy together. Wow! What an intense ride it has been. I knew that I could not wrap up this saga without telling Sloane and Remy's story, both as individuals and as partners.

When I started planning this trilogy, I set out to write about human trafficking survivors. We hear all the time how people wind up ensnared in the trafficking system, but we rarely hear the personal stories of those who escape and find the strength to follow their dreams. Grace, Pia and Sloane are examples of those incredible people.

There are an estimated 49.6 million people in modern slavery worldwide. Twelve million of those are children. Human trafficking is the second most profitable illegal industry in the United States, earning upward of $150 billion. Due to unreporting, the number of people trafficked in the US is difficult to pinpoint. According to a study from the Department of Health and Human Services, estimates range from 240,000 to 325,000 people a year. In 2021, the National Human Trafficking Hotline received 10,360 reports of suspected trafficking cases. In the US, children, teenagers and undocumented immigrants are particularly susceptible to trafficking both in urban areas and small towns.

If someone falls victim to trafficking once, they are more than likely to be vulnerable to the system again due to the dangerous psychological groundwork traffickers lay through the grooming process.

If you or someone you know is a victim of human trafficking, visit www.humantraffickinghotline.org. For immediate assistance, call the 24/7 National Human Trafficking Hotline at 1-888-373-7888.

I hope you enjoy *Vigilante Honor*. If you would like free reads and New Orleans–inspired recipes from Grace's, Pia's and Sloane's books, join my newsletter at www.amberleighwilliams.com!

Amber Leigh Williams

VIGILANTE HONOR

AMBER LEIGH WILLIAMS

Harlequin

ROMANTIC SUSPENSE

Harlequin®
ROMANTIC SUSPENSE™

Recycling programs for this product may not exist in your area.

ISBN-13: 978-1-335-47153-6

Vigilante Honor

Copyright © 2025 by Amber Leigh Williams

For questions and comments about the quality of this book, please contact us at CustomerService@Harlequin.com.

 Harlequin Enterprises ULC
22 Adelaide St. West, 41st Floor
Toronto, Ontario M5H 4E3, Canada
www.Harlequin.com

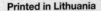 MIX
Paper | Supporting responsible forestry
FSC® C021394

Printed in Lithuania

Amber Leigh Williams writes pulse-pounding romantic suspense and sexy small-town romance. When she's not writing, she enjoys traveling and being outdoors with her family and dogs. She is fluent in sarcasm and is known to hoard books like the book dragon she is. An advocate for literacy, she is an ardent supporter of libraries and the constitutional right to read. Learn more at www.amberleighwilliams.com.

For Rebecca Shedeck—
fellow reader, travel buddy and sister-in-love—
who loves New Orleans as much as I do
(except for that one time our cars got booted).

Prologue

Back in the day, Loup-Garou was blamed for everything from a poor harvest to swamp children gone missing. Though in hindsight the stories were considered an old wives' tale, the Catholic church was purported to have spread the superstition across the land to keep parishioners in line.

Fear of Loup-Garou was no longer commonplace in Louisiana. But when multiple groups claimed to have been attacked around the swamplands by a hooded figure in a black-and-gold wolf mask, whispers of the Cajun werewolf again emerged.

The attacks started with a forced prostitution cell in Mississippi. There, he created a pattern. *Wait for darkness. Disable cameras. Cut power. Move in under the cover of night.*

When the law arrived, they found the perpetrators hog-tied, dazed and bruised but largely unharmed. In place of a vigilante calling card, investigators discovered a data chip containing enough evidence of the cell's wrongdoing to warrant the arrests of the victimizers.

Since then, four similar attacks had taken place in Louisiana. On the scene, nothing was found to identify the masquerading man. Eyewitness statements were enough to fuel talk that if you were holding others against their will, Loup-Garou was coming to get you.

On the night of August 4, the moon was new. Outside the city, deep in the wetlands, light pollution dropped to zero.

The men in the backwoods brothel barely stirred when the lights went out.

Ray de le Fe ventured out into the humid night, bemoaning everything from generators to mosquitos and smacking a flickering flashlight against his palm. A twig snapped under his boot as he rounded the building and saw the shiny golden ears of the wolf mask in the faulty light.

Even as the masked man brought a finger up to his mouth, Ray's jaw dropped, and he squawked.

The spark of a military-grade Taser lit the scene, and Ray dropped like a stone into a bed of wet green pine straw.

The masked man took a few seconds to pat him down, recovering a .457 Magnum from his belt and a pair of oxycodone syringes from the inside pocket of his sweat-washed shirt. The pistol he kept. The syringes he ground under the heel of his steel-toed boot.

As he reached the door to the brothel, it opened to reveal a double-barreled shotgun. "Who's there?" came a gruff shout from behind it.

Knowing there was a finger on the trigger, the masked man went low, taking the man out at the knees with a well-aimed kick.

The shotgun went off like a cannon, and all hell broke loose. Flashlight beams wheeled. The Taser sparked. Another gunshot went off. From the back of the brothel, people screamed.

When the lights came up, the masked man stood, and the traffickers were down. One was bleeding from the stomach.

The masked man used zip ties to restrain the men who weren't mortally injured. As he rummaged through cupboards with gloved hands, he saw the kid out of the corner of his eye.

Fourteen. Maybe fifteen. Fat lip, bruised, too-thin face and scabbed elbows. He wore an ill-fitting T-shirt over his boyish frame, and his eyes were enormous.

The man and the teen stared at each other for several seconds before the boy lifted what he clutched in his hand.

The gun wavered.

The masked man held up a hand. Noting that the safety was on and the kid's finger was outside the trigger guard, he closed the distance to him.

The kid took a step back into the hallway. Behind him, the masked man could see others. Boys and girls in various states of undress. None of them uttered a word when the man gently extricated the gun from the boy's hold.

He broke down the gun. Bullets rained to the floor, rolling toward the body of the moaning, gut-shot trafficker. He took out the .457 he'd taken off le Fe and disarmed it, too, tossing the pieces of the gun aside. Then he took out his Taser.

The kid flinched when Loup-Garou extended it to him, handle first. He didn't move until someone behind him nudged him. Then he lifted his hand to take it.

The masked man gestured to the restrained traffickers.

The kid nodded silently, understanding. The others came forward one at a time, curious, as the masked man again hunted through cupboards, finally uncovering what passed for a first aid kit.

He administered triage to the wounded trafficker, answering his foul curses and cries with studied reticence.

Before he left, he handed the data chip to the kid in charge, then dialed 911 on the bleeding man's cell phone. At the sound of ringing, he offered it to a reed-thin girl with bicolored eyes and a chipped front tooth.

She took it.

The sound of the dispatch operator's voice could be heard in the space between them. "911, what is your location?"

The girl hesitated.

The masked man lifted his chin in an encouraging nod.

She rearranged her feet and said in a voice that was surprisingly strong, "My name's Marie. I don't know where we are, but my friends and me… We need help."

"Okay, Marie. Are you and your friends in any danger?"

Marie eyed the man in the mask. Then she shook her head. "No."

"Are you or any of your friends hurt?"

Marie stared down the trafficker, who was in bad shape. "Not really."

"Good. I'm pinpointing your location now and sending helpers to you right away. Can you stay on the line with me?"

"Yes."

"You're doing great, Marie. I just need a bit more information. How many friends do you have with you?"

As the masked man turned away, he heard Marie's answer. "There were nine of us. Now there's just eight."

The man patted the boy with the Taser on the shoulder before he opened the door. He took a moment to face the room, committing the kids to memory and the searching look on the boy's face. Then he stepped back out into the maw of night.

Chapter 1

"Agent Escarra?"

Santana "Sloane" Escarra stood from where she had been crouched over the slumped body of Terry Booker, a known trafficker, and rotated toward one of the crime-scene technicians on scene, Ed Daily. "What have you got?" she asked, stepping over a pool of blood.

"We found something at the edge of the property," he said. His brow furrowed. "It's a body."

Sloane exchanged a look with fellow FBI agent Pelagie Landry and followed Ed out of the brothel and down the unsanded porch steps that had gone slippery with moss. The smell of rain threatened to speed up the process of evidence collection.

Sloane had been assigned to the New Orleans field office based on her intimate knowledge of the city's neighborhoods, where summer baked the dry streets. Out here in the bayou, however, the debilitating heat was broken regularly by cloudbursts.

The heat clung to her, pasting her blouse to her skin as she and Pelagie trailed Ed through marsh grass to the bank of the murky green bayou. Another smell hit her, familiar in its intensity. When she saw the body half in, half out of the water, she stopped in the semicircle of silent techs and investigators.

Young, she guessed, despite the state of decay. *Too young.*

And the bayou animals had taken their toll. "Has the coroner been here?"

Ed shook his head. "Not yet."

"Get him over here, please," she said to the officer beside her. As he stepped away, a hand balled over his mouth, she took a moment to swallow the knot of bile at the back of her throat.

"The kids said there was another," Pelagie pointed out. "The traffickers dumped her here after her attempt to flee. Guess they hoped the environment would take care of the remains."

Sloane let that sink in, waving away the biting bugs. She wanted to rattle the cage of every victimizer they'd recovered alive from the scene. Surveying the tangled knots of the girl's hair—bleach blond gone dark at the roots—she thought of the dozens of photos from Missing Persons, minors who had disappeared from the area in and around New Orleans. She wondered if the victim was one of them. The chances of identifying her were slim.

Another family would never know what happened to their child.

Pelagie stepped away, her cheeks stamped red. Sloane followed slowly. "This should be priority," Pelagie muttered, hands fisted on her hips.

"Damn right it should." Sloane pulled off the gloves she'd worn inside the brothel.

"Maybe now that we've found the body of the ninth victim, Houghton will let us off the hunt for Loup-Garou and allow us to find out who this girl is."

Sloane frowned at the so-called vigilante's name. Vigilantism was problematic for various reasons. While she could admire Loup-Garou's stand against men who preyed on underage boys and girls, she couldn't uphold her oath as an FBI agent and condone a civilian's penchant to take the law into his own hands.

Traffickers were plentiful in and around New Orleans and often difficult to trace. If Loup-Garou had information about them, he should have brought it to her or any of her fellow agents in the Crimes Against Children unit. Instead, he'd committed assault over the course of six raids. And now they had two dead bodies to contend with. "Wolfman escalated last night."

Brick Houghton, special agent in charge of the New Orleans field office, wanted Loup-Garou bad enough that he'd tasked two of his best agents with apprehending him. Probably because his raids were making the FBI look bad. While Sloane and Pelagie often had to wade through bureaucratic tape to secure warrants or establish surveillance on organized child abductors, Loup-Garou had been rounding them up in droves.

Pelagie clapped her arm where a mosquito hovered. "Damn swamp angels," she said, frowning at the bug residue on the heel of her hand.

Sloane's phone vibrated in the pocket of her slacks. She drew it out and glanced at the screen.

Pelagie tilted her head to scan it. "Who's Thirst Trap?"

"You don't want to know."

Pelagie lifted a penciled brow. "Sounds like I might."

Sloane felt a smile touch the corners of her mouth and stepped away to answer. "It's not a good time," she began. "Can I call you back?"

"If I waited until you weren't busy, I'd die by the phone," Remy Fontenot replied in a deep Southern drawl that was less twang and more slow-burning-whiskey smooth.

"I'm serious."

"Have you heard from any of the other guys you say you'll call back? Cops might want to do a wellness check."

"I'm on an active crime scene, Fontenot," she informed him. "Better be fast and accurate."

"I'm always fast and accurate. You know that."

She closed her eyes because the well of heat in her chest had nothing to do with humidity. "Remy."

"I'm in town."

She frowned. "In the city?"

"I just had a close call with a carriage, so it would appear so."

"Didn't you say you hate New Orleans?" she asked.

"I may have. But needs must."

"And what do you need, Remy?" She caught herself going up on her toes.

In the years they'd known each other, she'd never known Remy Fontenot to ask for anything. She'd always been the one needing the onetime bodyguard, now bounty hunter, for backup.

"Can you meet me for lunch at Willie Mae's?"

"I'm out in the parish," she explained.

"What'd you find there?"

She pursed her lips at the throwaway question. As with all scenes where tales of the wolfman had led her and Pelagie, she was forced to keep it under close wraps. "Nothing good."

"Drinks then. Name the place."

Remy wanted to have drinks…with her? She inhaled and nearly swallowed a fly. "What are you doing?" she asked, lowering her voice.

"What do you think I'm doing?"

"Not in the twelve long, complicated years we've known each other have you ever asked me out to drinks," she pointed out. "As a matter of fact, you spent the better part of the first year pulling me out of bars." Back when he had been *her* bodyguard after a Mexico vacation went wrong in every way imaginable.

Sloane knew firsthand what it was like to end up in sex trafficking. Remy had been there for practically every moment of the ugly aftermath.

"Indulge me."

"You must *really* need something," she weighed. "Meet me at six. Vaughan's in the Bywater."

"Done."

"I'll see you," she said and disconnected the call before she could hang on to the sound of his voice.

Remy had been in her life off and on since being relieved of his bodyguard duties. He'd come into her life when she was at her lowest point. As an agent, she'd called on him most recently to search for her friend, Pia Russo, when she had disappeared to avoid capture from the cartel leader who had kidnapped her, Sloane and Grace Rivera in Mexico. Before that, Sloane had placed him in charge of Grace's safety after she was targeted by the same man. He hadn't let her down.

He'd never let her down.

Which was why her feelings for him were so tangled. He was the man she'd always wanted and the one she knew she could never have.

"Hey, Sloane!"

She looked up to find Pelagie near the back corner of the brothel. Pelagie waved a hand, beckoning.

Sloane walked to her and found the feather-tipped ten-gallon hat lying near an impression in a pine-needle-strewn forest bed. "What's that doing here?"

"Seems your friend Ray may have been here last night."

Ray de le Fe, Sloane's informant, was never seen without his cowboy hat. She fanned away from the impression, searching the ground. A few yards away, she crouched over bits of broken glass mushed into the ground. She squinted to discern the pattern around the shards. A boot print. "These could've been syringes," she said.

Ten yards ahead, Pelagie called, "I've got footprints."

"Me, too," Sloane said. She shaded her eyes with her hand,

then waved over the crime-scene photographer when she caught his eye.

"I think these might've been made by cowboy boots," Pelagie pointed out.

Like the kind Ray found essential for everyday wear. Sloane doubted that the boot print before her had come from those. Two sets of prints. Could this one have been made by Loup-Garou? "If Ray was here," Sloane guessed, "he most likely fled the scene."

"If he got a look at our wolfman..." Pelagie let the sentence trail off with the possibilities.

"Even if he didn't get a glimpse of his face," Sloane said, "if he could identify the vehicle the attacker was driving, that could break our case."

"We confiscated the wolfman's weapon from the boy, Marlon," Pelagie pointed out. "We find Ray, we could have two key pieces of evidence."

"I'll talk to the local sheriff's department," Sloane said. "Have them put out an APB."

"You know Ray," Pelagie cautioned before optimism could take hold. "He scares easy. If he thinks Loup-Garou's out to get him, he's in the wind now."

"We'll find him," Sloane wagered.

"We should interview the victims separately," Pelagie said. "They may have something, too. And they'll likely know the deceased girl's name."

"The data chip's been fingerprinted," Sloane added. "The data needs to be analyzed by our techs as soon as possible."

"Loup-Garou's rounded up more traffickers than anybody in recent months," Pelagie stated. "I hope Houghton's considered the fact that once this guy's off the streets—"

"We can go back to doing our actual jobs?" Sloane interjected. "We can build cases against these predators with evidence gathered through legal channels. Chances are, there's little on wolfman's data chips that will be admissible in court because, besides being a vigilante, he's a hacker or works closely with one. We don't know how many victims will testify against their captors. Not all of them will. I can commend Loup-Garou for freeing dozens of children and young women from trafficking and forced prostitution. But he likely killed a man last night. The world may be better off without the likes of Terry Booker, but his death complicates everything. Loup-Garou isn't a hero."

"We don't know he killed Booker," Pelagie said. "We know the lights went out minutes before the raid. It's pitch-black out here at night. Booker's death could very well have been accidental."

"For the wolfman's sake, it'd better be," Sloane said. "He wouldn't want to wind up in the same detention center as the monsters he hunts."

Despite all statements to the contrary, Remy Fontenot didn't hate New Orleans. The city had been his home once, more than any other. In a lot of ways, it had made him.

But not all men were made of luck or fortune. Some were forged from corruption, abuse and gut-wrenching betrayal.

He kept his sunglasses and black ball cap in place as he wandered through the steam rising off the major thoroughfare. Intense summer heat had morphed into something grim and otherworldly. It was a living, breathing thing—as if hell itself had opened its mouth and swallowed the Crescent City whole. The Mississippi River, which fed its banks and commerce, had plummeted to a historic low. Concerns over heatstroke were coupled with worries over the contamination of drinking water.

Still, New Orleans was primarily a tourist town. People milled about, albeit slowly, as if the heat sat firmly on their backs and they were forced to lug it from one attraction to another.

Jazz still flowed from the streets. Remy passed an underage artist reclining in the shade on a break, trumpet cradled in his lap. Crowds squeezed cheek by jowl in dive bars and restaurants, desperate for AC and sustenance. The smells wafting off the Creole eateries hit him like a fist. They made Remy lust for the spices and delicacies of his native land.

He picked up the pace, escaping the clip-clopping that preceded the approach of carriages. The seductive whisper on the dry, hot wind told him the beignets at open-air Café du Monde were fresh out of the oil.

The threat of messy powdered sugar wasn't the only thing that stopped him from lingering. It was everything about this city that had made him run in the first place.

No one knew he was a lost son of New Orleans. No one had ever guessed the six-foot-six former Navy SEAL had once practically been uptown royalty. If he returned to New Orleans, it was out of necessity and only when called.

The man waiting for him on the Riverwalk faced the red-and-white working steamboat relic, *Natchez*. Torben Ballard wore a short-sleeved cotton button-down in stark white. His gray tie flapped in the hellish breeze. The khaki pants that fit his trim waist where a NOPD detective's badge gleamed were so pressed they could've stood up on their own.

As if sensing Remy, Torben revolved on the spot and watched him come. "Brah," he acknowledged with the regional expression for *brother*. He continued in the New Orleans way with, "Where y'at?"

"Awrite," Remy returned. "Thinking about taking a dinner cruise?"

"Demi and I are coming up on twenty years."

"Congratulations."

"She wants to throw some fancy fais-dodo," Torben explained. "I was thinking something quieter."

"Like a steamboat dinner cruise," Remy concluded.

"I won't get my way," Torben said with a rueful smile. "She'll let me hem and haw till I fall in line and make her happy. How's it feel to be back?"

Like he had a target on his back. Remy shifted his feet and looked across the river at Algiers, the part of New Orleans that lived on the other side of the water. It was connected to downtown via one of the nation's oldest ferry lines. "It'll linger," he decided.

"You hear about our *friends* in the bayou?"

Remy turned his attention back to Torben and felt his careful, neutral expression bow to a frown. "What about them?"

"One of 'em got himself killed last night."

Remy didn't so much as blink. He'd figured Booker would end up dead. "Not by my hand."

"No." Torben took a step closer, eyes sweeping the area as he lowered his voice. "But the blame's on Loup-Garou until they find different."

"Ballistics'll tell," Remy wagered.

"They'd better," Torben said. "What the hell happened?"

"One of his associates got trigger-happy," Remy said. It had been a shot in the dark, a foolish one that could have killed anyone, including one of the kids. That thought hadn't helped Remy sleep.

"You're supposed to disarm first."

"They were expecting a visit," Remy told Torben. "Word's getting around, despite the police's silence."

"There was a write-up in the press this week based on the rumors," Torben said. "Situation's hot now."

"Will there be a press conference?"

"The Bureau claimed jurisdiction over the hunt for Loup-Garou."

Remy's pulse kicked. "Escarra?"

"You've got reach there."

Remy's mind raced. "I've already contacted her."

"What about?"

"Le Fe. He was there last night. He escaped. Might've seen my Jeep parked up the road."

Torben cursed. "We're in the mess now."

"I'll shovel it," Remy pledged. Torben knew he never broke a vow.

"Why'd you contact Escarra specifically?"

"Le Fe's her informant."

"She may know how to find him," Torben added, putting the pieces together.

Remy nodded. His jaw clenched as he considered the situation.

"You know what this means," Torben said grimly.

Torben's understanding went deep, and it didn't settle Remy's anxiety. Remy had changed his identity and disappeared once. He hadn't planned on doing so again. He'd thought—hoped—this time it would stick.

Remy Fontenot's paper trail would end here in New Orleans, just as Baz LeBlanc's had. He couldn't decide if that was sad or ironic.

"You find le Fe," Torben instructed, "then get the hell out of town. You hear me, brother?"

"I hear you."

Torben patted him on the shoulder several times. Together, they started walking. "How soon do you meet her?"

"Tonight. In the Bywater."

"Find out as much as you can. Worse comes to worst, I can maybe get you clemency. But I'll need more than the case file on Loup-Garou. I'll need to know how the Feds plan to prosecute."

The idea of infiltrating Sloane's case made Remy feel more

than a little uneasy. If he had to disappear, she'd never have to see him again, though.

The grief was already there. He shut it off. "It's done."

"Demi will be upset she won't see you at our fais-dodo."

"Let her think I'm a coldhearted bastard who skips town without saying 'bonne chance,'" Remy replied. He'd meant to make the request offhand. It sounded dull. "It's better that way."

"She knows the truth," Torben offered as they followed the banquette back to the noise and bustle of the French Quarter. Demi DeLacy Ballard might be the one person other than Torben who knew Remy at all.

Then there was Sloane, whom he'd kept close tabs on since her abduction twelve years ago. Not because she was a federal agent. Because she mattered.

She'd always mattered. And not because she was the lone daughter then-Senator Horatio Escarra and his Hollywood ex, Iza Diaz, had trusted him with. Guarding Sloane had been more than a job. When he'd looked into the insouciant dark eyes of the nineteen-year-old survivor, he'd seen fifteen-year-old Baz LeBlanc punching back at him.

Unlike Torben and Demi, however, Sloane had never known where Remy came from.

The thought of putting the life of Remy Fontenot behind him, as he had done once before with Baz LeBlanc, hurt more than he anticipated. Because of the connections—to Torben, Demi, Remy's military family made up of brothers-in-arms. To Sloane, Dr. Grace Rivera, Pia Russo and their families.

He'd been careless with his connections.

Connections were what made the past catch up with him. As a hacker—as a victim and a runaway—he knew that better than anyone. But a man needed allies. And on some damning level, Remy had still needed a family.

He hadn't considered that it would hurt them every bit as much as it would hurt him to break ties and disappear again.

"I'll want to say goodbye," Torben noted.

Remy kept his head low, making sure his expression was cloaked in the shadow of his ball cap. "I'll be in touch," he assured him before they went their separate ways.

Chapter 2

What Vaughan's Lounge in the Bywater lacked in ornamentation, it made up for in coziness. It was a low-key, no-pretense kind of place. The price of drinks was reasonable. Sloane sank into a chair with her back to the wall and a view of the entry door. When the server arrived, she ordered crawfish and a hurricane.

Sloane was sipping the rum and fruit medley when "Thirst Trap" Remy walked through the door. Tall, dark Cajun intrigue wrapped in an unassuming black T-shirt, ball cap and shorts. He would've looked like any other tourist if not for the sleeve of tattoos down both arms, which were delectably roped in muscle. His calves were particularly impressive.

Ay, Dios mío, she loved his calves.

He wore danger like Ray-Bans and was frickin' mysterious to boot. She'd known him over a decade and still found herself perturbed and enthralled in equal measure. She wanted to swim in his mystery, just dive in and coat herself in it. He'd earned the "Thirst Trap" moniker she'd hung on him when she was nineteen, whether he liked it or not.

His black eyes were shaded under the bill of his hat, but she knew the moment they found her because the hairs on the back of her arms stood on end, and she felt a frisson of excitement.

He hung his sunglasses in the neckline of his black tee as he wove his way toward the corner where she was posted.

She'd waited twelve years for this man to come at her as more than a friend. Sloane liked a challenge, but she didn't like waiting.

She felt the low simmer of blood beneath her navel and heard her heart tapping a high cadence on her eardrums. *Keep it together*, she chided as she rose to greet him. "Remy."

He smiled, his gaze roving over her face, assessing her. The individual attention was disconcerting. It was intoxicating. His eyes gripped her. The skin at the base of her spine drew up in earnest, and her skin grew dewy in anticipation. "Sloane." After a second's pause, he leaned in.

She closed her eyes. It was automatic, as was the hand she laid on his biceps. She turned her cheek because that was what he was going for.

Not your mouth, she told herself sternly even as her lips tingled at the promise of what would never be.

His large hand fit into the space on her spine above her waistband. His lips skimmed her cheekbone. They lingered long enough for her to get high on the scent of him. He smelled like Nawlins—a slight tinge of exhaust, spicy foods, river and something extra. An old bay rum scent that was all his.

He stepped back, and she made herself sit, watching him mirror the motion. He sat beside her, close. He, too, wanted a view of the door and the surrounding patrons. "Nice dive."

She looked around so she wasn't looking at the long slide from his jaw to his neck. Still, she licked her lips...and tasted his skin, the vague presence of salt there. Remy was many things, but he wasn't a flirt. Or a tease. Or any of the things she had been in the past. He was honorable, stupidly so.

She sucked on the straw of her hurricane. "People keep to themselves here."

He grunted and gave a quick forward roll of his shoulders as if to adjust his shirtsleeves. The restless movement brought his shoulder into contact with hers and she cursed inwardly at the warm tug from her midsection. "You need to quit drinking alone," he said knowingly, picking up the drink menu. "What's good here?"

"Depends," she said. "What's your pleasure?"

He turned his face to hers. With his shoulders hunched over the tabletop, it nearly put him at eye level with her. His eyes pinged from her left to her right and back again. His five o'clock shadow peppered the lower half of his face. Otherwise, his skin was golden bronze with the slight undertone of red brought on by summer.

His gaze dipped over her mouth, and she was suddenly very aware of his breathing.

Want me, her mind bleated. *Want me enough once to mess up my lipstick.*

He looked away, scanning the people at the table of regulars next to them who were laughing over afterwork bloody marys. His profile was severe. "I'll have whatever you're having," he replied.

Sloane lifted a hand for the server, who approached with a tray. "We'll have another hurricane. And can you bring an extra basket of crawfish?"

"Sure thing, chère," the server returned. She gave Remy a long look, taking in everything between his ball cap and tennis shoes before walking off.

"You haven't eaten."

Sloane stirred her drink. "I've been putting in some overtime."

"What's going on?"

"It's not up for discussion."

"The Sloane I know never lets work get in the way of an empty stomach."

"The Sloane you know doubled her caseload over the last six months," she volleyed back.

"It's as bad as that?"

"It's New Orleans." She rolled her shoulders, too, because they felt tense under his unblinking stare. "I just got back from the hospital, where eight kids between the ages of fourteen and eighteen are undergoing recovery. They were found in a brothel near Abalone."

Remy was silent, but she felt edginess rolling off him in waves.

Sloane took another hit from the hurricane. "They're strong. More so than I was."

"No." The word dug deep into her bones. "No one's as strong as you."

"Not even you?" she tossed back, because her nerve endings were trilling incessantly. She swore her scalp was tingling. "Mr. Navy SEAL-Bodyguard-Bounty-Hunting Fontenot?"

"That's right," he said without having to think about it.

What was he doing? What *the hell* was he doing? "What do you want, Remy?"

"Who says I want anything?"

"I read people for a living," she reminded him. "You only call to check up on me. But that's not what this is."

He remained tight-lipped.

"What do you need from me?" she asked.

A band was setting up nearby. He watched them and muttered a "thanks" when the server brought his drink and two baskets of red boiled crawfish.

"Anytime," she said, smiling long from under her lashes. She touched his shoulder before moving along.

Sloane wondered vaguely if he was even aware of his effect on women.

Picking up one basket, he heaped the crawfish from it on top of the other, leaving it empty except for the film of parchment paper on the bottom. "You still suck on the heads?" His bare knee nudged hers under the table.

Sloane grabbed a crustacean, squeezed the tail and head

then twisted, pulling them apart. She inserted the crawfish head into her mouth and sucked the juices out.

As he reached up to wipe his mouth with a napkin, his hand paused in midair. When she was done and reached for the next, he released a low laugh.

"You next," she ordered, peeling off the first few rings of the tail section and pressing the base so she could extract the meat.

He'd already pried the head from the tail. He lifted the crawfish head to his mouth. The hollows of his cheeks shrank inward as he sucked.

She might've moaned. It was a near thing.

He licked his lips and nodded as he placed the head in the empty basket. "That's *fine*."

"Damn right it is." The art of eating crawfish was considered an essential New Orleans skill. "When was your last crawfish experience?"

"Too long ago."

"You deprive yourself, Fontenot."

"I know it."

"State your business."

He peeled another crawfish. "Ray de le Fe."

She paused with a head halfway to her mouth. "What did you say?"

"You know him?" he asked casually.

She thought of the hat left at the crime scene in Abalone. "Why?"

"I've been looking for him."

"What for?"

He dug into his pocket and produced a folded piece of paper. He unfurled it and set it on the table.

It was a printout of her informant's details, complete with picture and priors, age, last registered address, known associates...

Remy spoke again. "He skipped out on his parole officer three weeks ago."

She knew this. There wasn't a lot about le Fe she didn't know. "You're hunting him?"

"Word is he likes talking to the Feds when it serves his purpose," he said. "Particularly a tall Latina based here in New Orleans."

She didn't cop to that. Not even when he leaned back, expectant. She reached for her hurricane. Sipping, she considered the situation. "What are the chances you'd come looking for le Fe the same day he goes off radar?"

"He's *been* off radar."

Le Fe was likely so far off radar now there was no recovering him. "He's involved in what happened in Abalone. Did you know that?"

"No."

She tried to get a read on Remy. He made it near to impossible. She noted, however, that he was no longer eating. Taking another sip, she thought it through. "You know anything about what he's involved in?"

"The drug trade, primarily. Oxy. He supplies to traffickers. Hence your interest in him. It's rumored that his intel has led to several arrests and convictions. Now he's back on the streets, doing the same thing he was doing before you sent him up. You've got to be miffed he's mixed up in this brothel business."

He had no idea. "If I knew where he was, he'd be in a holding cell."

"Not much incentive for him to pop his head aboveground. Especially if he knows how great a shot you are."

"His informant status just got an upgrade to key witness," she revealed. "He testified for me once."

"You think you can get him to take another deal?"

"I need to find him," she stated, "before someone else does."

"Who?"

Unwilling to drag the wolfman into this, she placed her elbows on the table. "You're strapped."

He didn't reach for the P226 he had sheathed at the base of his spine. "So are you, Agent Escarra," he tossed back. "Your off-duty weapon is riding your right hip. And if I know you well enough, I bet you've got a lethal little sidepiece in that high-priced bag of yours."

The Louis Vuitton had been a gift from her mother. Sloane didn't like to flash her family's wealth around, but she had a weakness for handbags. The sidepiece, a switchblade, was nestled right up against her pepper spray. She loved her hometown. But she knew its crime rate was significantly higher than the national average.

"I'm a federal officer," she reminded him.

His expression remained unchanged but for a there-and-gone hint of irritation that bolted across his eyes. "You want to read me my rights, boo?"

"You really shouldn't call me that," she warned, letting her voice go low and slow.

His arms folded across his chest. The muscle and ink threatened to distract her. "If you don't want me to ride along, just say so."

"I didn't say no," she told him, "but you've got to understand. We need le Fe's testimony. I won't have you putting the fear of God in him."

"I'm not God," Remy replied and moved toward her just enough to make the next words sizzle. "I'm Old Nick's friend. If your guy's going to keep messing around supplying oxy to traffickers, he's better off scared."

"Remy," she said, unwilling to give an inch on this. She

knew what kind of man Ray de le Fe was, and she wanted him off the streets as much as the next officer of the law. But she needed to catch the wolfman, or Houghton would have her and every other agent at his disposal siccing Loup-Garou through the bayou until the rapture. That wasn't what she'd signed on for.

The faces of those kids at the hospital came back to her, as did the image of the girl lying on the shore of Abalone. It was her job to return them to their families.

They deserved better than the battery of questions she'd been required by regulation to ask them this afternoon. She shouldn't be spending her day-to-day crashing through palmettos, trying to untangle a silhouette from shadows or fact from urban legend.

Sloane knew because of what he'd seen her go through that human trafficking was every bit as serious to Remy as it was to her. He'd fought as much as she had to bring her back from the edge of trauma. This was every bit as personal to him as it was to her.

"If I let you do this," she said, starting again, "you're under my orders. Can you live with that?"

It took a second for amusement to bleed across his face, not so much softening his features as honing them. He sniffed, reaching for the hurricane he had yet to touch. Raising it, he toasted her. "Looking forward to it, chère."

The tension broke as the MC announced the evening's entertainment and the band started off with a dreamy rendition of Fats Waller's "Louisiana Fairytale."

She eyed his glass a moment before deciding to lift her own. "Here's to—what—hauling scumbags off the streets?"

He thought about it. "To bon temps," he offered.

She tipped her glass to his. "Bon temps." As they raised

the hurricanes for a sip, she added, "I swear to God, if you call me 'boo' out in the field…"

Rewarded by the sound of his quiet laughter, she drank and settled into his company.

Chapter 3

Despite the rum in her system, Sloane didn't sleep a wink. The sight of Remy filling the space inside her Creole-style maisonette had sobered her rapidly.

Remy's staying. In my house.

What the hell had she been thinking? His shoulders barely fit in the tight stairwell to the second floor. He was too long for the spare bed. He looked ridiculous amid the frilly accoutrements her abuela and tías had insisted on installing for her.

The bed squeaked every time he turned in the night. She lay in hers on the other side of the wall, thinking about him between her flower-patterned sheets.

What does a badass wear to bed? He just turned again. Is he uncomfortable?

Is he thinking about me—in bed, just a heartbeat away...?

Her skin flushed with heat, and she had to toss the blankets off. When she heard the bed squeak again underneath him, she covered her head with a pillow and prayed sleep would take her.

He was already up when she finished showering and dressing the next morning. She found him standing in her kitchen over her coffeepot. "This thing must be a hundred years old," he said with a groan.

She eyed her old percolator, the one she was fond of when it wasn't being a pain in the ass. Reaching around him, she hit the button…and came up against a hard wave of his scent. *Dear baby Jesus.* Forcing herself to turn away, she went to her retro-style Frigidaire unit. Its minty color complemented the sunny yellow kitchen walls. "How did you sleep?"

"Fine," he obviously lied, watching the percolator distrustfully. His stare was moody and lethal enough to make the machine shrink behind the rack of mugs and cower.

Right, Sloane remembered. Remy was *not* a morning person. That made him almost…human.

She would've smiled if her eyes didn't feel so gritty. She opened the door to the fridge and stared blankly at her options. Her hands and brain made contact long enough for her to choose yogurt, a basket of berries and a jam jar. She juggled them as she took them to the butcher-block table.

Remy had his hips back against the counter now. His mouth was folded in a stern line, his arms, folded across his chest. "I can make eggs."

"What kind?" she asked.

"Any kind you want," he claimed.

Eggs à la Remy. She sighed, regretting the impulse to invite him to stay with her instead of him forking out the cost for a hotel. He looked more absurd in her small living space by the moment.

The bottom floor of the maisonette consisted of a parlor, kitchen and a linen-closet-size entryway hardly big enough for her umbrella stand. The bathroom was upstairs, along with two bedrooms. There were no closets, and a lot of it was still true to the period of the eighteenth and nineteenth centuries, down to the baseboards. At some point, the house had been wired for electricity, and window units now supplied cool air. On the roof were terra-cotta tiles, and a wrought-iron balcony hung off her bedroom.

Sloane's favorite thing about the maisonette was its private courtyard, especially this time of year, when the bananas trees were full and the nighttime jasmine opened on the arbors. The noise from busy Bourbon Street wasn't bad, either.

Remy had bumped his head on both the entry door casement and the chandelier in the parlor. And, for whatever reason, being inside her living quarters seemed to unsettle him. Was it the *Alice in Wonderland* feeling the rooms must be giving him or the fact that he was here with her?

She marveled over the slant of light across his unshaven cheek. She'd never seen him bearded, but now his stubble burned red under the sun.

When he moved to the fridge behind her, she tried draining her tension with her morning routine. She layered berries, yogurt and oats in a mason jar before spreading an indulgent layer of jam over the top. Settling into a chair, she licked the jam stuck to the butter knife.

He bumped into her chair as he shut the fridge and cursed. "Sorry."

She shrugged as he carried the carton of eggs to the stove. They hadn't slept in the same bed. Why was her kitchen full of awkward morning-after booty-call energy? He was here to work. If his collar wasn't her informant, they wouldn't be doing this.

If she hadn't stupidly invited her longtime crush to bunk in her doll-size house, they wouldn't be doing this, either.

She rued her own stupidity as he located her lone frying pan. Peering at the stove's burners, he asked, "When was the last time you used this?"

She thought about it. "I cooked for Pia and Babette once."

"How'd that go?" he asked cautiously.

"The fire marshal showed." When he gave a startled laugh, she added, "I'm the world's least domestic person."

Experimentally, he switched the burner on. When nothing caught fire or spontaneously combusted, he was optimistic enough to place the pan over the heat. "You're eating healthy."

"So?"

"Last time we cohabited, you thought French fries and a Wendy's Frosty were the best part of waking up."

Good times, she ruminated. "If I don't eat a balanced diet, my hips expand."

"Your hips are fine."

A warm feeling twined around her heart. "Don't talk about my hips," she said, jabbing her spoon in his direction.

He raised his hands from the stove. "My bad."

It took her a moment to settle—to get her head right.

"What else is off-limits?" he wondered.

"What do you mean?"

"Is there something else I shouldn't talk about?"

"You're my guest," she pointed out. "I won't police you." *Just don't talk about my body in any way that makes me want to use it on you.* He ramped up her sexual frustration one hundred degrees just by being here. Just by *being* at all. Why couldn't he understand that?

He cracked the eggs with one hand, letting the insides run into a bowl. Was this his morning routine? Did the morning-after with Remy come with protein and chivalry?

How many mornings-after did he have on his roster?

She groaned at her rogue inner monologue. Being around this man was a minefield.

He discarded the shells and ran water over his hands from the sink. "No harm in having some ground rules."

Don't look at me. Don't smile at me. Shave that ridiculously cute scruff off your diamond-cut jaw. Don't do or say anything that makes me remotely think about sexing you up. And, for the love of God, stop making the bed squeak at night so I don't think of you alone over there with or without your drawers on...

She chose not to say any of that. Instead, she kept her

tone neutral. "I think we've already established that you're a frickin' choir boy. Also that you're resistant to my charms."

He snatched his hand away from the stove eye with a hiss, shoulders high.

"Do you need help?" she drawled.

He grunted an answer. Using a fork, he beat the eggs in the bowl. "What's the plan?"

"Have you run down le Fe's known associates yet?"

"The ones who aren't serving time," he confirmed, spooning a butter pat into the pan from the butter keeper on the counter. He picked up the pan and rolled it around so the melt spread evenly across the bottom. "Same old routine with them. 'Haven't seen him. Wouldn't tell you if I had.'"

Sloane narrowed her eyes, wondering how the business side of Remy would've taken that kind of lip.

He poured the eggs into the pan. They sizzled. "There's no information about his family."

"There wouldn't be." Not in an accessible database. "He does have a sister, though."

"How did that not come up in the background check?"

The muscles in his arms popped as he stirred, and she was enjoying the display despite her better judgment. She sucked a dollop of yogurt off the end of her pinkie finger. "It's not known whether they're actually related. Her name's Delta Bean. He's looked after her through the years, as best he can."

"Is she in some kind of trouble, too?"

"She's been homeless for the past eight years," Sloane revealed. "I haven't been able to determine her age, but she's at least ten years his senior."

Remy aimed his thoughtful frown at her. "He's looked after her, but she's still on the streets?"

"You can only help someone as much as they'll let you."

"Do you know where she is?"

"This time of year, she's normally found under the I-10 overpass in Tremé."

"Why there?"

"She grew up in Tremé," Sloane ruminated. "She gravitates toward areas she has a personal connection with."

He shoveled the eggs onto a cooling plate and brought them to the table, carrying her small antique caddy with the salt and pepper shakers with him. Straddling the seat next to her, he set them down between them. Then he drew a line in the eggs with the side of his fork. "That side's yours," he said before digging into his.

Gathering her wet hair over one shoulder, she picked up the pepper shaker and sprinkled it over her half. Then she cleaned off her spoon before taking a bite. "Thanks for this."

He jerked a shoulder, brows low. "I'm not paying room or board. You need a new frying pan, by the way."

"What's wrong with the one you used?"

He eyed her moodily over a forkful. "The bottom sticks to whatever you cook. You're lucky this is fit to eat."

"Chalk it up to your expertise," she granted. "And, as I never use it, I'll pass."

"How the hell am I supposed to cook you anything tomorrow morning?"

She liked that he was thinking about being here with her the next day. It made her feel all warm and fuzzy inside. "I told you," she whispered and sent him a saucy wink. "Takeout."

He stopped chewing, his jaw knotting. Dropping his fork, he reached for her.

She froze as his thumb swiped the corner of her mouth. Unbidden, her lips parted at his touch, and her chin dipped with the movement of his finger, following it.

He pulled back and, unthinkingly, brought the jam dot on the tip of his thumb to his mouth.

He. Did. Not. Heat flooded her. The corner of her lip burned with guilty pleasure.

He knew he'd made a mistake, too, because he went still, his hand close to his mouth.

She cupped her palm over her lips, wishing she could cover her cheeks. *It doesn't mean anything,* she schooled herself. He'd done it thoughtlessly. Really, it was a testament to how comfortable they'd grown with each other through the years. As friends and associates.

The heat was going nowhere, and her thoughts continued to spiral.

The percolator choked.

Remy looked away, trying to find the source of the noise. "Coffee's ready," she murmured.

He pushed his chair back and rose.

She'd survived weeks in trafficking with a badly broken leg, then the year of hard partying that had followed. She'd come through nine years as a field agent with hardly a scratch. But Remy's ride-along today might be her undoing.

Chapter 4

Remy walked to the public parking lot near Jackson Square. He needed a minute away from Sloane.

She hadn't had this effect on him when she was nineteen, that was for damn sure.

He was aware that she was a woman, that he was staying in her house and that these were likely the last days they would spend together. He owed her more than half a plate of eggs.

Ruminating over that instead of what the soft brush of her mouth against his thumb had felt like and the way her face practically glowed before she applied makeup, he located his blacked-out Rubicon with a Hemi V8 and mud tires. He'd had the Jeep lifted six inches, so he had to step up onto the running board to seat himself behind the wheel. He reached for the duffel bag on the passenger seat.

Then stopped.

Le Fe had been at the scene the night before last. Had he escaped by road or water? If he'd gone by road, then there wasn't much doubt he'd seen the Jeep parked on the shoulder of the swamp road to Abalone.

Remy considered his options, watching people pass. A streetcar clanged cheerfully by.

If Remy and Sloane found le Fe, she would take him in for questioning as a witness to Loup-Garou's raid. Sloane would then most likely have a description of the Jeep. It wouldn't take her or her team long to run down vehicles matching its description.

Remy needed to know what she had on Loup-Garou. If he couldn't wait for the ballistics report that would clear him of Terry Booker's death, he at least had to inform Torben what the FBI planned to charge Loup-Garou with.

Parking the Jeep outside Sloane's maisonette wouldn't be wise. She was trained to believe there were no coincidences. Nothing he could say could convince her that he'd come seeking the bounty on le Fe the night after a Jeep identical to his had been seen at the brothel.

She'd see right through him. She'd know the truth...or some of it.

Would she arrest him right away? Or would she let him explain what he could?

His identity didn't matter anymore. Remy wasn't his given name. He had to cover up Torben's part in it. In order to do that, Remy had to get out of New Orleans as soon as suspicion swung his way.

Even if Sloane arrested him, it would be hard to connect Remy's past to Torben's, considering that the two had met before Baz LeBlanc went missing twenty years ago.

The lot near Jackson Square was too public. He needed to park somewhere more discreet before meeting Sloane on Bourbon for their venture across town.

Sloane's phone rang on the dash where she'd clipped it. She drove with one hand as she answered, letting it go to speaker. "Hola, Abuela," she greeted. "Que bolá?"

Her grandmother's quiet, gracefully accented voice smoothed through the car speakers. "Hola, Santana. You're coming this evening. Yes?"

"Ah..." Sloane glanced at Remy in the passenger seat when

he sent her a curious look through dark sunglasses. She cleared her throat. "What for?"

"Enrique's engagement. You remember."

Sloane closed her eyes briefly. "Right. The party. It depends on when I can wrap things up with work—"

"Not everything is about work, *pequeña*."

Abuela still called Sloane *pequeña* even though she now stood head and shoulders above her grandmother. "I'm aware of that," Sloane said, grimacing at the coming lecture.

"Family needs family. When was the last time you came to a gathering? All your primos will be here. Your tíos. Your father's bringing his novia…"

Sloane pressed her lips together, carefully refraining from saying anything about the woman her father was dating. Abuela clearly disapproved of her, just as she'd disapproved of Sloane's mother.

"And I've invited Miguel."

Sloane fumbled the phone out of its holding, punching the button to take Abuela off speaker. Bringing the phone up to her ear, she kept her voice to a murmur. "That wasn't necessary."

"Why not? You two have been seeing each other for months now."

"I never said we were…" She glanced at Remy and found herself under his acute attention. Fighting the urge to cringe, she cleared her throat. "I thought you said this was a *family* gathering. Miguel hasn't met everyone. Why would you invite him?"

Abuela's voice was quietly stern. "Santana Escarra. Is he a nice man?"

Sloane felt herself deflate. "Yes."

"Is he good to you?"

"Sí."

"Does he come from a good family?"

What Abuela clearly meant was, *Is he Cuban?* And the answer was yes. At least partially. Enough, apparently, to satisfy her grandmother. "I haven't met *his* family, either. This is too soon—"

"You are coming to the party," Abuela decided for her. "Wear the white dress I bought you. The one with the bell sleeves. You look so ladylike in that one. Oh, and I have a gift for you."

"I…" Sloane struggled with what to say and settled, as always on, "Okay."

"Good," Abuela said, pleased, and hung up.

Sloane held the phone for a few seconds longer before clipping it back into its holder.

Remy cleared his throat. "Who's Miguel?"

"No one." She said it too quickly.

"Right," he said, unconvinced. "And when is the wedding?"

She whipped her head sideways. "*What? What* wedding?"

"If Abuela likes him, and it appears you're catering to her wishes now, I hear wedding bells in your future."

"I'm not… Miguel and I aren't even…" Sloane reached for more words, but they'd abandoned her. "We've been on *two* dates…"

"Did you sleep with him?"

Ire took over. It was irrationally hot. "That is *none* of your business."

He offered her something of a smile. "That's the Sloane I know."

She saw what he was doing. Bringing her back to herself. Just as he'd done all those years ago when they barely knew each other. She released a breath, letting go of the strain. "Abuelo died two years ago. We've all been trying in our own ways to help Abuela through it."

"And for you, that means saying *yes* to everything she assumes is right for you?" he asked.

A headache was building behind her temples. "Mostly."

"Even the white dress with the bell sleeves?"

He'd heard every word of her conversation with Abuela. She wanted to slap him a little. "Maybe."

"Times," he said, turning to face the passenger window, "they are a-changin'."

"It's not forever," she said, making herself believe it. "She's upset with my dad."

"Because he's dating a real estate agent from Shreveport instead of the good Cuban woman Abuela wants for him?"

"You know too much," she accused.

"Did she set Enrique up with his fiancée?"

She gritted her teeth. "Yes." Just as Abuela had set up Sloane's once-bachelor uncles and most of her other cousins with their current or future spouses.

"And you're next on her radar?"

She sighed, knocking her head back against the headrest. Abuela's attempts at getting her to settle down made her feel like she was in the crosshairs of a heat-seeking missile. So far, dodging had worked. "It would seem so."

The silence that followed was as thick as bacon grease. Not for the first time, Sloane wished she could get a bead on Remy's thoughts. He was always in control. When he'd been assigned to her protection, she'd made it her singular focus to crack his impassivity. She could blame that mission for the panties she'd left him on the dash of his car, as well as all the times she'd offered herself to him. *What do you say, Saint Remy? You want a taste?*

The memories did nothing to quell her heat or embarrassment.

She still wanted to open him up, but she wouldn't resort to flirtation again. Not for the wide world. "You should come," she offered.

"To your cousin's engagement party?"

"Sure," she said, angling her vehicle onto a side street. "Dad will be happy to see you. And the tíos."

"Your tíos hate every man who rubs elbows with you," he pointed out. "If anything had happened to you on my watch, I'd have been shot."

That was true. Her father's four brothers—Nestor, Juan, Vincente, and Ramon—were the collective reason none of her high school boyfriends had stuck around for long. It didn't help that Sloane was the lone girl born to an Escarra man.

She changed tactics. "Abuela will want to see you while you're in town."

He had no rebuttal for that. Sloane's mother may have been responsible for Remy's hire, but without Abuela's blessing, he wouldn't have made it through the door of Casa Escarra.

Slowly, Remy released a breath. "Okay."

She bit her lip to hide a successful grin. There wasn't a man alive who could say no to Ezmeralda Escarra. Her tough-talking sons practically bent over backward for her. Her grand-sons were putty in her hands, hence Enrique's engagement to Lola García. The Cuban community in New Orleans wasn't as extensive as Miami's. Abuela's ability to successfully pair off every member of her extended family with someone of strong Cuban descent made her matchmaking prowess that much more impressive.

And terrifying from where Sloane was sitting.

She liked Miguel. She'd enjoyed his company. But marriage wasn't in the cards. Having Remy at her side at the party might impede Abuela's efforts to throw her and Miguel to-gether for one day.

And because she was evil, Sloane jumped at the chance to see Remy fend off her tíos.

"Tell me more about le Fe's sister," Remy said.

"First things first," she began, "she doesn't need to see you."

"Why not?"

"She's skittish," Sloane pointed out. "If she gets a bead on you…" She gave him a pointed once-over, noting the banded muscles underneath his array of tattoos. His long, level stare would be enough to make Delta Bean clam up on sight.

"What if she doesn't talk?"

"Bringing her in for questioning won't work," she warned. "A colleague made that mistake the last time we went looking for le Fe. You take Delta Bean off the streets, and she regresses."

"Even for a free meal and AC?" he asked. "The heat index will be a hundred and ten degrees before noon."

"She's been known to frequent a shelter in cases of extreme weather," she replied.

"You brought water," he said.

The twenty-four-pack of chilled Dasani wasn't all Sloane had brought. She'd chosen one of her brightest handbags—a large embossed leather Brahmin tote in a stunning cyan. She'd loaded it with hydration packets, a small cordless fan and batteries to operate it. Delta Bean was drawn to shiny things like a bee to flowers. She'd carry the bag with her until bartering it became inevitable.

"You shouldn't talk to her alone."

She rolled her eyes. "You're not my babysitter anymore."

"Something happens to you, your family's still coming after me."

"I'm responsible for my safety. I think I've earned that."

"Undoubtedly," he said, his even tone unhindered. Still, his jaw knotted. "But I need you alive."

"So you can get your bounty?"

She felt the singe of obsidian eyes through his Ray-Bans. The chords of his neck were rigid.

She'd pissed him off. "That wasn't fair," she acknowledged. "I apologize."

The glower didn't level off. "Do you know what it would

do to me," he questioned, "if anything happened to you?" She *felt* the low register of his quiet voice.

She prayed like crazy he wouldn't see the flush rising to her cheeks. Staring daggers into the center of the road, she gnawed her lip.

"That's not a purgatory I'm keen on visiting," he warned. "Not in this lifetime."

He'd follow her into the next one, wouldn't he? Just to keep her out of trouble. "You know what I am," she told him.

"I know *who* you are."

She closed her eyes briefly because she felt that, too. She felt him and wished she didn't—wished he'd take his laser focus and his deep cuts somewhere else.

"I know what you've come through," he continued. "I know what you carried from that hellhole in Mexico. I saw that place with my own eyes."

She stilled. "What do you mean, you *saw it*?"

He wavered for the first time in indecision. "I went there."

"Where?"

"To Mexico," he revealed. "The Solaro compound where they held you, Grace and Pia after they kidnapped you. Then the house where you were kept the next few weeks—the one you escaped from."

She wanted him to stop, but she couldn't make herself say the words. Her breath backed up in her lungs. Her chest felt tight.

"I walked the miles from it to Jaime Solaro's hacienda," Remy continued. "Just like you did." His voice cracked with tension, and she had trouble meeting his gaze as the words roughened. "I stood where you stood against him—where you tried to get Pia out of his hands. I know exactly where he hurt you for trying."

She shook her head automatically. "Remy—"

"And that cell he put you in," he went on, undeterred. "I saw the inside of that, too."

Sloane looked away, turning to face the side window. There was a mess inside her that threatened to come unleashed. "Why would you do that?"

"When your father told me my services were no longer required—that the family would take care of you from that point forward—I went to see for myself what you came through. It was the only way I could let go."

"All those hours of self-defense training you put me through?" she ventured. "They weren't enough?"

"No."

She gave in, scrubbing her hands over her face. He wasn't the only one who'd had trouble letting go. Remy had been her lifeline after Mexico. "Anything else I should know?"

He was silent for what felt like a small eternity. Then he said, "I met them."

Sloane gripped the steering wheel as she turned to face him. "Who?" she demanded, afraid she already knew.

"Jaime. Pablo. The whole Solaro family. Or what was left of them after you, Javier Rivera, Grace and Pia led the wolves to their door."

"How?" she asked, shocked. Then it hit her, and she closed her eyes. "Dad."

"He was no longer senator then," Remy recalled. "But he still had strings to pull."

"What did you say to them?" she wanted to know. "The Solaros?"

"Nothing."

"Nothing?"

He shook his head. "I didn't need to say anything. I just needed to look into the eyes of the men who tried to chain you down and failed."

She felt her scalp tingle. Jerking the wheel, she pulled over, letting the tires jounce over the curb. She put the car in Park and aimed the AC vents at her face.

He reached over to flip the knob for the fans to high. "I was right not to tell you before."

"I'm *fine*," she gritted through her teeth. She opened the neck of her unbuttoned blazer wider.

She wasn't fine. She was the furthest thing from fine. If the mere mention of the Solaros and the locations where they'd held her and the others could affect her this much still, she wasn't brave or strong or even capable. She was still a victim.

She would *not* be a victim to anyone. That was what had brought her out of her post-Mexico spiral. That had been what *she'd* carried forward.

She saw the victims from yesterday as if they were before her now. Some were glassy-eyed; others, haunted. A lot of them were scared. She'd seen herself in all of them, and that feeling alone had made her want to weep for them and the lost pieces of her eighteen-year-old self.

"Damn it," she cursed. The dash beeped as she shoved open the driver's door.

"Where are you going?" he asked as she stepped out of the vehicle.

"Don't follow me," she warned before slamming the door.

Chapter 5

Remy gave her a ninety-second head start. He hadn't meant to make Sloane run. He'd only wanted to...

What? he wondered. To remind her of the hellstorm she'd barely survived in Mexico? To bring her face to face with old trauma if only to prove a point?

Remy cursed himself viciously. No, his feelings had been far too close to the surface—things he had bottled for years in order to remain objective. He'd felt her vulnerability brushing up against old memories, of her, of himself...or at least the old version of himself...the one with enough trauma to identify with her and every child she had ever saved.

Those feelings weren't helpful, not when he would more than likely have to say goodbye to her soon.

Being hard on her wasn't the answer, however. He would need to make it up to her.

He yanked the keys from the ignition before leaving the comfort of the cab for the baking street. Cars whizzed by, drivers leaning on their horns as they passed.

He hadn't seen which direction she went, so he locked the car and scanned the area.

The I-10 Claiborne Expressway, in the seventh ward, had long been a subject of controversy. Built over a corridor of marginalized communities, it had not only brought economic decline, but it caused more than enough noise and air pollution to be considered a public safety issue. Residents of the Tremé neighborhood had been campaigning for its removal since its development.

Claiborne Avenue had once been an oak-lined street and a thriving cultural center. Now the ramps made it dangerous for residents to walk, and there were only a couple dozen small businesses left.

As Remy strolled, he could distinctively hear the scream of passing engines and the rhythmic *cuh-clunk, cuh-clunk* of tires passing over the interstate deck. He spotted Sloane on the corner, talking to a man sitting on a stoop of a building with faded graffiti. She'd removed her blazer, revealing the white shell she wore underneath. The man pointed. Sloane nodded, straightened and started across the street.

Remy sprinted to catch up.

She flicked him an irritated glance. "I told you not to follow me."

For a man who'd made a habit of letting people, places and things go, Sloane Escarra was not one of them.

She approached the line of tents under the overpass.

He'd have to let her go eventually, wouldn't he? Once she found out the truth about Loup-Garou, goodbye was the only recourse. The sting of that was getting hard to ignore.

For now, he shadowed her.

She stopped, eyeing the people laboring under the shade of the viaduct, and placed a hand flat against his sternum. "Wait right here."

"How 'bout no?"

"You'll do it," she asserted and patted him harder than necessary where her hand rested.

He took her wrist, drawing her closer. There was a smattering of infinitesimal brown freckles across the tops of her cheeks, if he looked closely enough.

He looked and did his damnedest to ignore the slight widening of her eyes, the rise and fall of her chest under the shell and the stir in his blood that caught like the pistons of a well-oiled crankshaft.

Not now, he thought belatedly. He was backed up to the end of his tenure as Remy Fontenot and his time with her. The worst thing he could do was damn them both and lose his heart. However easy he knew that would be. However much he'd always known on some level that it would be inevitable.

He grazed her hip and felt the shape of her government issue Glock.

She bristled. "I'll be back in five minutes. You can hang out here or go smolder somewhere else. Those are your choices."

"Is this you ordering me around?"

"Is this you taking orders from me?" she volleyed back. "Because you suck at it." She stepped off the curb.

He watched her cross to the overpass, scooping her hair off her neck. He saw the little damp curls on her nape as she secured her ponytail with the hair tie on her wrist, red nails flashing. There was no sense in following the sway of her determined walk with his eyes, so he didn't.

His phone rang, and he answered it without looking at Caller ID. "Yeah?"

"Remy," Torben hesitated before continuing on. "What's all that noise? Are you at the airport?"

"Claiborne Avenue," Remy corrected.

"Oh." Torben's tone alone said *say no more*. "What're you doing there?"

"Looking for le Fe," Remy said.

"Have you reached out to Escarra?"

I slept in her bed. And that, Remy determined, would be his last intrusive thought of the day. "She's running down his sister as we speak."

"Has she said anything about Loup-Garou's visit to Abalone?"

"Nothing definitive," Remy admitted. "She's being cautious with me."

"You'll need to hack into her case files if this continues."

Remy knew what his job was and hated himself for it. "My equipment's upstate."

"If there's something you need to get the job done, you know who to call."

Remy's scowl deepened as Sloane crossed from light to shade. "Yeah."

"Take care out there, brah," Torben said.

"You, too," Remy replied before ending the call. He slipped the phone into his pocket and counted all the reasons he should step off the curb and follow her.

"I brought you something."

Sloane had the pleasure of seeing Delta Bean's eyes go wide with wonder at the sight of the purse. "Ooh," she said, reaching with hands tipped by yellowed fingernails. Her chin dropped as she expelled air, admiring. "That's right pretty, right there."

Before her fingers could close around the strap of the bag, she froze. Her face fell, her nose hanging low over the thin line of her mouth. "I can't take this one off your hands, Miz Sloane."

"Why not?" Sloane asked. She kept her voice soft. Delta Bean was easily startled, which was one reason her living on Claiborne Avenue, with its endless stream of noise, was so strange.

Delta Bean shook her head as her arms crossed over her blouse of faded red. She'd done up the buttons wrong so that there was one more at the top than there was at the bottom. Sweat circles drenched the fabric under her arms.

Sloane reached into the bag and held out a bottle of water. "At least take what's inside. I brought a case of water for you. And a fan for the heat."

"You went to too much trouble," Delta Bean said in a sad mumble.

"Not at all," Sloane said, relieved when Delta took the bottle and instantly raised it to her heat-stained cheek. She checked the inclination to lay her hand on Delta's arm in comfort, well aware that skin-to-skin contact set the woman on edge. "Do you need something to eat?"

"I got some ice cubes from the corner store," Delta Bean said. "Mr. Jemison. He give me some. He a nice man."

"That he is." Sloane wished there were more people who cared for Delta Bean. She was thinner than the last time Sloane had found her, and her color was worrisome. "Do you need something else? I can get you a cold drink and a sandwich. Or we could go to the Mission. Remember? I introduced you to the sisters there?"

"You lookin' for Ray again. Ain't you? That's why you came out this way."

Sloane refused to lie. "I'm afraid I am."

"He said he wasn't gonna do bad no more. He said he was done with that life, that he was gonna take care of me."

Was that the reason le Fe was involved in what had happened in Abalone? Had it been one last job to get him and Delta Bean by—at least for the time being? "It's important that I find him."

Delta's pupils jerked, and she almost looked Sloane in the eye. Her breathing quickened. "You ain't the only one looking for him. Are you, Miz Sloane?"

Sloane swallowed. Delta Bean knew her brother was afraid, which must mean he'd found a way to make contact with her. "I need to find him first."

Delta Bean's chin dropped to her chest. Her eyelashes were so light, they were nearly diaphanous. "He told me not to tell, even if you came looking for him. And I don't want him to go away again. You put him away before. He couldn't take care of me then, neither."

"He's strictly a person of interest at this point," Sloane said. "I can protect him. You know I can."

Delta Bean shuffled restlessly. Traffic thundered over their heads. The noise was incredible. It seemed to add to her consternation. A movement caught her attention. She clutched her elbows. "Who's he?"

Sloane glanced over her shoulder and groaned. It was Remy, carrying the rest of the bottled water from her back seat. "He's my friend."

Delta Bean took a step back, shaking her head. "I don't know him."

Sloane advanced carefully. "He's not here for you. He's… He protects me. Just like Ray protects you."

Delta Bean's rabbiting feet shuffled to a standstill. They both watched as Remy stopped under the shadow of the overpass. He set the case down and backed away slowly.

"See?" Sloane said as he fell back at a safe distance. "He's not here for you. He's here for me."

Delta Bean cast her gaze at Sloane's beltline. Concern webbed across her brow. "You got people coming after you, too, Miz Sloane?"

"It's always good to have somebody at your back. Isn't it, Delta Bean?"

She gnawed that chapped lower lip of hers, still clutching her elbows. Casting her fearful eyes up to the underside of the overpass, she seemed to ask for help from somewhere. Then she mumbled, "He took himself off to Jazzland."

Sloane tilted her head. "Where?"

Daisy Bean gave a frustrated huff. "He *took himself* to Jazzland. You know? With the rides?"

Rides? Sloane racked her brain and came across a scattered memory. Jazzland had been the original name of the New Orleans branch of… "Six Flags," she realized out loud.

Delta Bean neither agreed nor disagreed. She simply rocked herself back and forth over the same spot.

Again, Sloane wanted to soothe her, but she settled for closing the distance and laying the bag at her feet. "You sure you won't let me drive you to the Mission? Just for a day to get you out of this heat?"

"Ray won't know to look for me there."

"I'll tell him," Sloane swore. "Please, Delta. The sisters will take care of you until he comes."

Delta Bean pegged the shadow that was Remy in the distance, worrisome. "Your man friend'll come along. Won't he?"

"I can take you and come back for him, if need be," Sloane offered. "It's up to you."

Delta Bean thought about it, then shook her head. "You shouldn't be without protection neither, Miz Sloane. Do you think I could bring my new purse?" she asked tentatively.

"You bet," Sloane said. She watched as Delta Bean gathered it to her, then rooted around in her tent for what she wanted to take with her.

Sloane left the case of water for the others under the overpass until she could pass word on to the Mission that there were other lost souls under the deck of Claiborne Avenue.

In its heyday, Six Flags New Orleans was the lone theme park in New Orleans, complete with thrill rides, wet rides and a Ferris wheel. Built in New Orleans East, it backed up against the swamplands of Lake Pontchartrain. During Hurricane Katrina, its carefully constructed drainage system failed spectacularly. The park was submerged in brackish water for over a month after the storm. Because of prolonged immersion and wind damage, its owners declared bankruptcy and closed the park permanently.

The property had been evaluated by several companies, but no one had ever felt that the monumental task of breaking down the park's dilapidated attractions and cleaning up the defunct site was tempting enough to build something new in its place. As a result, Six Flags had been left to rot, and nature was slowly taking the site back for itself.

The sign on the barred entry gate read NO TRESPASSERS. PERPETRATORS WILL BE PROSECUTED. The park's once-bright welcome sign looked faded and hole-punched. It sagged over their heads, like an exaggerated smile gone sinister and wrong on a clown's face. Sloane used the bar cutters from her trunk to sever the chains. They slumped, and Remy unwound them enough to part the gate with a shrieking protest, admitting them into the forbidden playground.

"You ever been here before?" Sloane asked. Her hand was on her sidearm.

"Long time ago," Remy said, reaching around his spine for his piece. He and his sisters had eaten fried carnival food and ridden the roller coasters until they puked. He felt a twinge. He didn't allow himself to dwell on memories of his sisters or his childhood, happy or otherwise. He'd left that life behind.

This wasn't the Six Flags of his youth. The information booth had collapsed in a defeated sprawl, its carousel-like mirrors broken and oxidized. The buildings that lined the alleyway to the attractions stood shoulder to shoulder, flood damage evident. Trees hulked over each, wild with summer splendor. Not a breeze stirred them or the leaves of kudzu vines that had snaked their way through broken windows and open doors and woven together over the broken banquette.

Maybe it was the invasive vines that had kept Six Flags from sliding out onto Lake Pontchartrain altogether—like some oversize, unhinged parade float.

Sloane took the first door, her weapon in front of her in a two-handed hold. She swept the room. "Clear," she said.

Remy repeated the motion with the first door on the other side of the alley. Arcade, he found, and again memories stirred.

SpongeBob plushies crowding the interior of a claw machine. His youngest sister, Gabbie, spending all her quarters to win it. Her crushing disappointment when she came up empty-handed...

Remy burning through the rest of his snack money until the machine yielded what she wanted...

Her face sticky from ice cream and her smile broad as she held SpongeBob in one hand and Remy's hand in the other as they left the park...

Remy stared at the walls where standing water had made its mark and mold damage was still visible. He made himself back out of the room. "Clear," he tossed out before moving to the next entryway.

He'd been right to assume that the places of his youth were best avoided. Fighting against glimmers of the past, he shouldered through the half-closed door of the next building and found empty deep fryers and rusted sinks. There were no places to hide, only a partially cracked back door.

Remy crossed the room and reached for the latch.

A gunshot rang out. Its reverberation went clean through him. He raced through the door to the alley.

Sloane was down.

For a split second, her body on the broken ground was all he saw.

Then she raised her head, her hand clapped above her elbow. Her face was red and tight with pain, but her eyes... They were furious. "He got the jump on me!" she shouted, pointing. "That way!"

He followed her motion and saw the skinny, retreating form of Ray de le Fe fleeing farther into the park.

Remy saw the man who could tie Loup-Garou's whereabouts to him escaping. And all he could think about was

Sloane on the ground. There was blood on her arm. He took a step toward her, his weapon lowering. Images flooded him again, but these were cold and black and white, like the worst of his nightmares.

A school crossing. Gabbie on one side of the thorough-fare, her bright grin flashing when she saw him on the other.

She didn't wait for the light to change. She started running toward him...

"No!" he called. "Go back!"

She couldn't hear him over the clangor of the streetcar or the horns of vehicles bearing down on her...

"Stop!" *he yelled, as if his voice alone could freeze time...*

"I'm fine!" Sloane told him, snapping him out of it. "Go after him!"

There was enough surety and authority in her voice to break through his haze of worry and recollection.

"Goddamn it," he ground out before he left her there.

Chapter 6

Anger blinded Sloane. Nothing pissed her off more than a fleet-footed runner.

"Son of a bitch," she growled as she retrieved her weapon, which had gone flying. She had nothing to cover her wound so she kept her hand closed over the broken skin and pursued the others.

Le Fe and Remy had disappeared into the maze of trees and cumbersome steel structures. She pressed her teeth together, hiding the noise of her own tearing breath behind her lips so that she could listen for shouting or footsteps.

In the distance, she saw the shadow of le Fe hurdling over the rail of the loading platform for the wooden roller coaster. Close behind, Remy's larger figure followed.

She broke into a run. They were headed toward the wet part of the park where a man-made canal snaked its way in from the swamp. Wiping the blood from her palm, she locked her gun in a two-handed hold again as she rounded the side of the loading platform. She could see the canal and le Fe splashing his way across it.

Before he could get to the far side, something stirred in the water behind him. Sloane watched in horror as it barreled closer, revealing the shape of a large bull alligator. Before she could scream, it clamped down on le Fe's retreating leg.

He went down, shrieking.

Remy raced into the canal. He picked up his knees, try-ing to get across the waterway as swiftly as possible, his gun hand high.

The gator tugged le Fe into the watery alley, fighting to keep his leg while le Fe paddled backward with his arms, squalling.

Remy didn't shoot. Instead, he balled his hand into a fist. His arm arced, and the jab caught the gator in the eye.

The reptile didn't let go. Remy struck again.

The gator's jaws scissored open, and it slunk back, free-ing le Fe.

Remy grabbed le Fe underneath the arms and dragged him back from the shore. He raised his gun and pebbled the edge of the water with shots.

The alligator hissed and lunged, threatening. Then it slowly slunk back into its shallow belly of water, eyes rippling above the surface, watchful.

Le Fe wept as Remy dragged him farther away from the canal.

Sloane saw a covered bridge intact downstream and fought her way through a forest of cattails to get to it. Her phone was at her ear before she made it to Remy and le Fe's position. Remy had laid the man underneath the frame of the flying carousel. As soon as Dispatch picked up, she reported, "We have a man down at Six Flags New Orleans. We need an am-bulance right away."

Remy was already tending to the wound, trying to stop the bleeding.

Le Fe's gaze seized on Sloane. His face was stained with tears. He sobbed.

Sloane had promised Delta Bean she'd bring her brother to her. She crouched next to Remy and gripped le Fe's knee to hold him still.

Remy's eyes flickered to her arm. "You good?"

"I'm in better shape than he is," Sloane said, holding the phone between her chin and shoulder. "We have to stop the bleeding, Remy. Ambulance won't be here for another fifteen minutes or more."

"I know." His hands were covered in blood and that singular focus of his was intent on the injury. "Is there a first aid kit in your vehicle?"

"On it," she said and took off running back the way she came.

"You need to get checked out."

"I'm fine, Remy," Sloane said. "The paramedics fixed me up."

He hooked his hand underneath her elbow and torqued it slowly toward the light to examine the bandaging. At her quick wince, his jaw flexed. Still, he tilted his head to examine the area. "You're bleeding through."

"I said I was fine," she snapped. The biting pain of the graze wasn't something she wished to talk about. She knew it was making her punchy, more than she would've been without it.

Hospitals had never been her favorite place. Ever since what had happened in Mexico and the surgery that had followed the injury to her leg, she did her damnedest to avoid them.

"At least let Grace take a look," Remy insisted, letting her go.

"She's busy trying to save my witness." Luckily, Dr. Grace Rivera had been on duty in the ER when they brought le Fe in.

"Witness," Remy repeated. "He deals oxy to traffickers."

She closed her mouth, wishing she'd left it shut.

"He also shot a federal agent," he pointed out. "When he wakes, I hope you'll read him his rights."

"He grazed me. More because I surprised him than anything," she corrected. When Remy's brow furrowed, she sighed. "Look, you'll get your bounty. That's all that matters, right?"

That iron jaw of his hardened. "I'll ignore that because I know you're hurting and because we're in a hospital."

"So?"

His eyes gleamed knowingly. "I brought you here once. Remember?"

"No." The memories she had of that night were fuzzy.

He loosened a breath and shook his head. "You sneaked out again. I followed you to the dive bar after you thought you'd given me the slip. I kept my distance. You danced, you drank with the help of the fake ID you didn't think I knew you had, and you smoked. It soon became clear you'd gotten a little more than you bargained for. One of your dance partners put roofies in your drink."

"And Prince Charming saved the day," she muttered.

"Consider what would have happened if I hadn't followed you," he said.

"You did your job," she granted. "However much I resented you for it later."

"Because you begged me not to tell your family you sneaked out again," he added.

"You did anyway."

"And you thought I betrayed your trust."

"Your checks weren't written by me," she continued. "They were written by them."

He scowled. "It doesn't matter who paid me. Anyone with a shred of decency would have gotten you out of that situation."

She narrowed her eyes. "Would a decent citizen have tracked the perpetrator down and threatened to blow off his kneecaps if he ever tried to take advantage of another woman again?" she wondered.

His face blanked. For the first time, she seemed to have chipped away at his stern front. "What are you talking about?"

"You know exactly what I'm talking about," she threw back at him. "The guy in the club I danced with that night. I ran into him several months later. He told me all about my bodyguard's visit to his private residence and the promises you left there."

"Did he mess with you again?"

"No. He acted like I was the Mind Flayer from *Stranger Things*."

One shoulder lifted. "Then I did my job effectively."

"You kept tabs on me, too," she stated, "after your body-guard services were no longer required. Why? Because that's what decent citizens do?"

"No," he said.

"Then why?" she wanted to know.

"Because I cared about you."

She stilled. *Well.* He'd said it, hadn't he? And that did nothing for the vortex of flame he brought about every time he was within shouting distance.

He held her gaze steadily as silence closed around them, shutting out the frenzied bustle of the ER waiting area. She tried to breathe through it. Between the bite of pain from her elbow, the licks of heat inside her and the environment of the hospital hanging over her, she felt like she was about to come out of her skin.

"I need to walk," she said at last.

"I'll go with you—"

"No," she argued. "You wait. I'll be back before le Fe gets out of surgery."

"Are you going to get looked at?" he asked.

"I'm going for a walk," she told him again and veered into a corridor she knew would take her to the atrium. Being in the open-air chamber allowed her to take several steadying breaths.

The man knew better than to say things like that—how much he'd cared. The lengths he'd gone to in order to keep her safe. Would he have gone to the same lengths for another client?

Of course he would have. He was Saint Remy.

She had to stop reading into every gesture and hanging on his every word. Those things were dangerous. Especially with him staying in her house.

It didn't help that she'd watched him punch an alligator in the face to save a man he could argue wasn't worth saving.

She came to the front desk. "I was here yesterday," she told the person behind it. She showed the man her badge. "A group of kids was brought in early that morning. From Abalone. Are they still in Recovery?"

"Hold on a second," he said, typing quickly on his computer. He scanned the screen. "They're still here. Doctors transferred one to the psychiatric unit."

"Which?" she asked.

The keyboard clicked busily under the clerk's fingers. "Marlon Thomas."

"Is he allowed visitors?"

"Is this an official visit?" the man asked, nodding toward her badge.

She could've played that card, but she chose not to. "I'm here as a friend."

The clerk pursed his lips. "Kid likely needs all the friends he can get right now, huh? I'll put a call through the psychiatric desk, see what they say. Hold on a minute."

Sloane did just that, clutching her badge so tight the tips of her fingers numbed before the clerk called her over again.

"Take the elevator to the fourth floor," he advised. "Hang a right when you get there. They're expecting you."

Chapter 7

Dr. Grace Rivera emerged from the OR, still wearing her mask, covered shoes and scrub cap. "Remy," she said warmly when she saw him. "Sloane's not with you?"

"She went for a walk a while ago," he said, pushing off the wall. "You know how she is with hospitals."

"Don't I just," Grace said, widening her eyes for emphasis. Wearily, she tugged the mask down to reveal her unpainted mouth. "I'm told you helped her bring in the patient?"

"He's a person of interest in her investigation," he explained, "and someone I was tracking." He tried to read her expression. "What's the verdict?"

"He's stable," she said. "The leg... Time will tell whether he needs to worry about infection. I don't imagine the water at Six Flags is sanitary."

"No," he agreed.

"We tend to see a high frequency of soft tissue infections with alligator bites," she went on.

Remy wondered fleetingly how many alligator bites Grace saw in her day-to-day.

"At this time, I'm unable to release him into your custody," Grace revealed. "Nor can he answer questions Sloane has regarding her investigation."

"What's the time frame look like?" Remy asked.

"He'll still be groggy tonight," Grace estimated. "I'd suggest holding off on interviewing him until tomorrow afternoon at the earliest. As for when he'll be ready for transfer, I can't say. He lost a fair amount of blood, and it's important we keep checking for infection."

Remy nodded. "You work miracles, Gracie."

She smiled, some of the weariness sliding away. "I heard you gave that alligator the heave-ho."

"I did what I had to," he dismissed.

"You always do," she mused. "You and Sloane are working together?"

"For the time being," he said. Though with le Fe no longer at large, Remy wouldn't be able to stick around. If le Fe was up for questioning tomorrow afternoon, Remy could be in the wind by tomorrow night.

He frowned as something constricted in his chest. He didn't want to leave Sloane alone with this. Sure, she was on the hunt for Loup-Garou. But if she knew more about the greater trafficking web in the Louisiana-Mississippi area he'd been peeling back the layers from for months, her boss might allow her to shift her focus from unmasking the vigilante.

Traffickers were difficult to trace. But when small sectors were brought together by a powerful third party, they became more difficult to single out.

Remy had employed all his hacking powers to find out who the third party was. He was close. But it wasn't enough. *He* wasn't enough.

Sloane was an expert in trafficking. Moreover, she came from a family with both political and business connections. If he could steer her in the right direction, she could back off Loup-Garou long enough to help him find the central power.

If the hunt for Loup-Garou took a back seat altogether, Remy might not have to disappear.

"Her birthday's in a few days," Grace mentioned.

Remy lifted his chin, remembering. Sloane and all her Leo energy culminated in August. "That's right."

"Has she mentioned the party her family's throwing her?" Grace asked.

"No," he said. Jerking his thumb over his shoulder, he added, "We're going over to her abuela's tonight. Something about her cousin's engagement."

"Enrique," Grace said with a nod. "He and I dated for a little while back in the day. It didn't last long."

"Who got to you—Abuela or the tíos?"

"The matriarch," Grace answered. "Even then, she was terrifying."

"He missed out," Remy asserted. "How's Javier?"

Wistfulness touched her. "Adjusting, still. It's culture shock, going from life on a cattle ranch to life in New Orleans."

"I imagine it is," Remy said.

"Sometimes I miss it, too," she revealed. "I have a rotation that night, but you should go to Sloane's party," Grace suggested. "It's at the salsa club. Maybe you remember it. Salón Tropicana."

God, did he remember. He'd never been her dance partner. Relegated to the corner, he'd been forced to watch, intervening when men got too close. Salsa was an intimate dance. They always got too close.

She'd resented him for that. He'd resented her for putting him in that position. She'd returned to the salsa club at least once a week, determined to ruffle his feathers.

He'd comforted himself with the notion that he was immune to her flirtations. He could laugh off her pointed offerings to take their relationship beyond professionalism. He could even move past the delicate undergarments she left for him to find.

The salsa club, however, had been the place where he'd felt it the most. He remembered clearly the flick of her long legs, the sensual sway of her full hips, the fall of her hair across her face. Even now, his body tightened in reaction. He shifted from one foot to the other.

Sloane was never so tempting as she was when she danced.

He couldn't hide a grimace. "Would I have to dress up?"

"Maybe," Grace hedged. "But it would make her happy to have you there. Pia won't be able to make it, either, for obvious reasons."

"Yeah, isn't she like sixty-three weeks pregnant at this point?" Remy drawled.

Grace belted a laugh. "The baby isn't due until the end of the month. Don't forget I have your number, Remy Fontenot. I'm not going to stop bugging you about it," she warned. "Now, go find Sloane. I want to look at her arm before she escapes."

"Will do," he replied.

He searched the atrium and several other waiting areas before he remembered the kids who had been brought in from Abalone. After talking to Information, he thought he had a pretty good idea where to find her.

When she emerged from the psychiatric unit, he was there.

Sloane spotted him before she could close her emotions inside her usual vault. Before she could speak, he wrapped his hand around her uninjured arm and tugged her into an empty exam room.

"What are you doing?" she asked wearily when he sealed the door behind them.

"Quiet, and look at me."

"You don't need to do this, Remy."

He knuckled her chin and angled her face up to his. He took a good, hard look. "You're lying."

Her dark eyes blazed. "I don't want this," she continued. "Not right now."

He'd let it go. But he saw what he'd seen when they first met—when he recognized himself in her. He'd known her.

He'd been able to taste her pain, feel her trauma. He'd known her anger like it was his own.

It had become his own—all of it. *She* had become his own.

His hands moved up to her cheeks, framing her face between them. His thumbs grazed the prominent ridge of her cheeks.

Her lips parted, and her lashes lowered. "Don't do this," she said in a whisper.

He was too far gone now, damn it. He pulled her against his chest, wrapping her up tight.

She remained stiff, stubbornly refusing to let go.

"You're not made of iron," he murmured, tucking his chin against the crown of her head. "The rest of the world may not see that, but I do. Stay," he added quickly when she jerked against his hold. "Just stay."

She lasted for another handful of seconds before caving. She pressed her face into his shirt and made a noise—a plaintive little mew that reached down his throat and pried his heart open.

Her hands balled in the back of his T-shirt. "I hate this," she moaned.

"I know," he murmured, rocking now. "Let it go, boo."

It was a testament to how much she trusted him when he heard her sniffle. She shuddered, and he felt the front of his shirt grow wet in small increments.

Sloane's strength was everything to her. Yet here, with him, she knew she could be vulnerable.

She hiccupped. "I hate you."

"That's right," he murmured, flattening his cheek against her hair.

Her words were small now. "He tried to harm himself. He said he couldn't look his family in the face, not after what happened at the brothel, what he was forced to do."

Remy closed his eyes and struggled to breathe evenly.

"I told him none of it was his fault—that his family will know that. That they'll love him through this. I don't think he heard me. So I told him about me, Grace and Pia. Everything."

She'd taken herself back to Mexico. "Christ, Sloane." Remy exhaled and tightened his hold.

She hiccuped again. "I don't know if it helped…"

He dropped his cheek to hers now, his mouth near her ear. "I'm certain it did. He'll get help. There are people who'll be looking out for him, who specialize in this. You've been where he has." So had Remy. He could never tell her that. He'd left that disillusioned tale behind, along with everything else to do with Baz LeBlanc's existence.

He, too, hadn't been able to look his family or friends in the eye. He felt the breath of that hopelessness and inquietude on the back of his neck. It itched along the soles of his feet.

There'd been no one he could talk to after he disappeared. No counselor or specialists. No kickass FBI agent who spoke for those who struggled to speak for themselves—who agonized over their fates every bit as much as they did.

"He gave me her name," she told him, her face still mashed against his sternum.

"Whose?"

"The girl we found in the bayou. The traffickers left her there, like debris, after she attempted to flee."

"Tell me," he said, knowing she would need to speak it out loud.

Sloane turned her cheek against his chest so she was no longer muffled. "Esther. From Natchitoches. She had planned to go to school there at Northwestern State. She wanted to study biology."

"Esther," Remy repeated. Sloane would need to hear it spoken as well, just as she'd need to see it in the papers and on the news.

She'd make it happen, wouldn't rest until she did. Esther had a fighter in her corner.

"Now she's lying on a slab at the coroner's office," Sloane said. "And I'm going to be the one who tracks down her parents and delivers the news."

"You have a partner," Remy reminded her. "You don't have to take on everything."

She stiffened again. "I need to do it. I don't expect you to understand—"

"I told you, Sloane. I know who you are. I know what it is you go through with these cases. And I know you still choose it every morning." She saved as many victims as possible from the predators who hurt them because it was the only way she knew how to live with what had happened to her and her friends.

Remy ran his palm up her spine to her neck and back down until she relaxed once more. "Take another moment to reassert yourself in the quiet. Before you go back out there and kick ass."

She sighed, releasing her fists. Her hands fell to his waist. "You were the one who kicked ass today."

"Grace wants to look at your wound."

"Fine," she relented. "But only because we're stopping by Abuela's. I'll need to go home first."

He frowned. "For the white dress with the bell sleeves?"

Tipping her chin up, she studied him. Under the fluorescent lights, her eyes looked as liquid and cavernous as uncharted waters. "You don't like me dressing up for another man?"

Tread carefully here, Fontenot, he warned himself. Her emotions were close beneath the surface. He chained his feelings down when they leaped for her. He reined them in by the skin of his teeth. "You flirtin' with me, Agent Escarra?" he asked.

Her gaze took a turn about his features, touching on his brow, the length of his jaw...

The breath backed up in his lungs when he realized her attention had seized on his mouth.

It would be easy to cross the point of no return, to take her mouth. To know exactly how she would respond, how she would taste...

He took her by the shoulders and eased her back to arm's length. "We don't want to be late." He raised a brow. "You good?"

"If I said I wasn't," she murmured, studying him closely, "what then?"

He felt stripped under the glide of her knowing stare. "Abuela's waiting."

Disappointment slithered in. The wall came up, placing him in pointed opposition on the other side. "As you wish."

When she moved to the door, he took a second to reassert himself, too.

Her dark eyes were too much for him.

Chapter 8

The party could be heard from the street where Sloane parked—voices, laughter, music. She reached for the gift in the back seat. "Don't be tense," she told the man beside her. "This isn't your first time facing the firing squad."

"Just tell me where your abuela keeps the rum, and all will be well," Remy said.

He'd cleaned up. Showered off a day's worth of wear and the grime from Six Flags' canal. He'd had le Fe's blood on him, just as she had. He'd again chosen a T-shirt—this one charcoal—but had softened the palette halfway with olive-toned shorts that set off those tan calves of his. His tennis shoes were white, heightening the effect of the colorful wave of tattoos on his legs.

She didn't tell him she'd likely be right there with him, shooting rum while the family gushed over wedding details and babies. There had been three born to the family in the past year alone. The idea of helping to plan another baby shower or trying to keep up with conversations over the best car seat brands or the pitfalls of diaper rashes made her bandaged arm twinge in sympathy.

Rum was the answer. Abuela and Abuelo's own Escarra Cuba. One of the fifty años bottles.

Abuela had been a rum princess from the moment she was born outside Havana. She hailed from master rum makers.

The industry was the legacy her father had left her. Legend was that she could trace their heritage back to Pedro Diago, the father of Cuban rum.

Not much of a legacy, considering the dark history between rum and the slave trade.

When Fidel Castro overthrew Fulgencio Batista's government in 1959, he nationalized the sugar cane and rum industries. Abuela, then a freshly minted bride, lost the family business and immigrated to the United States with Abuelo to avoid his imprisonment.

They'd had to start over. It took some time, but they developed a new label under Abuelo's name. Escarra Cuba had built a standing in the rum community, one that wasn't easily swept aside. They'd established a big enough business empire to nudge their eldest son, Horatio, into political office when the time came.

The dissolution had started slowly, first with the very public scandal surrounding Sloane's mother's affair while her father was still a senator. Then came the IRS's seizure of family assets when Abuelo was accused of tax evasion. Over time, the Escarra name lost its luster. Abuelo and his lawyers, his sons Ramon and Vincente, had fought for Escarra Cuba's holdings in court. They lost, and the company had been dissolved.

Sloane wasn't the only one who suspected Abuelo's decline in health was linked to the loss of another legacy.

She smoothed her hand over the long skirt of the white dress. It fell to her ankles, and there was no slit. With its sweetheart neckline and bell sleeves, it felt demure and uncomfortably bridal.

"Too late to back out now," Remy said knowingly. His hand went to the small of her back.

She let him usher her up the driveway to the historic mansion built in the Queen Anne style, complete with lush landscaping and a cast-iron cornstalk fence. With its white stories stacked like a cake, it looked like a bride, too, peering out from behind the green veil of verdant oaks.

The light pressure of Remy's hand above Sloane's hip did well to distract her from the expectations that would be heaped on her from the moment she stepped through the door. "You know what'll happen to you if my tíos see you touching me."

"Does this Miguel have a gun?" he wondered idly.

"No." She knew because she'd looked into him. Abuela didn't need to know how Sloane had searched Miguel's background, combing for something—anything—to make marriage to him distasteful to her family. She'd found nothing. He'd never fudged his taxes. He wasn't registered for a handgun. No priors. No parking tickets. Hell, he'd probably never had a cavity. "I know for a fact, though, that Nestor does."

Remy made a noise.

The door opened, and Vincente's wife poked her head out to frown at them. "Santana, is that you?"

"Hola, Tía Rosa," Sloane greeted, holding the present out to her. "Como—"

"You're late!" Rosa said, taking her by the hand and pulling her inside. "Who's that with you?" she asked, squinting.

"You remember Remy," Sloane said. "He was my—"

"Remy!" Tía Rosa shouted, throwing her arms around him warmly. "What a surprise! Bienvenido!"

"Mil gracias, Rosa," he said, smiling.

She touched his face. "Eres tan guapo! Wouldn't you say, Santana?"

Handsome as a descriptor was far too watered down for Remy, but Sloane wasn't going to debate that with Rosa. "Is everyone here?"

"The ladies are in the kitchen with Ezmeralda," Rosa reported, "and the men are in the backyard, teasing our poor Enrique mercilessly."

"And the rum?" Sloane heard Remy say under his breath.

"Look who's arrived!" Rosa announced, all but pushing Sloane into the room. "It's Santana and Remy Fontenot!"

The home's furnishings had been curated carefully. The antique sofa and chairs had been reupholstered. It was a room from another era. The house smelled faintly of cigar smoke, sandalwood and sofrito. If Sloane didn't know any better, she'd have thought she'd stepped through a time warp back to the Escarra's palatial 1950s casa.

As one, the women turned to look at the newcomers. The tías raised their arms in greeting. The primas hung back, openly curious as both Sloane and Remy were showered with love and solicitations. Remy's cheeks were covered in kisses by the time the tías parted for Abuela.

In a flowing emerald green summer dress, she stood smaller than anyone in the room—even twelve-year-old Elena. Her gray hair styled in a tasteful coiffure, the softness around her chin held strictly in place by a discerning mouth, Ezmerelda held out her hands.

Sloane took them and bent down to press a kiss to one cheek and then the other. "Abuela. Te ves bonita."

Ezmeralda waved dismissively. She stepped back to scrutinize Sloane's appearance. "You wore the dress."

"I did," Sloane replied, hoping her grin didn't look as wooden as it felt. "Did it turn out like you expected?"

Ezmeralda's gaze seized on her face. "Perhaps. Perhaps not." Sloane got the impression she was no longer speaking about the dress.

Remy seemed to sense her unease. "Buenas tardes, señora," he said.

She stilled, observing Remy standing tall at Sloane's shoulder. "You've returned," she noted.

It wasn't the effusive greeting the tías had extended. Nor was it the one Sloane had expected. When the tíos had threatened to drive Remy off years ago, Abuela had vouched for him after several quiet sit-downs between them. Not only that, she'd started setting a place for Remy at the dinner table, silencing anyone with questions. She'd been his biggest supporter in his quest to keep Sloane out of trouble in the wake of Mexico, sure he'd be the one to straighten her out.

Her faith had been well-founded. When Remy left the Escarra house after being released from his contract by Sloane's father, Abuela had thanked him effusively, embraced him and graciously wished him luck on his journey.

So few people had the wherewithal to charm Abuela. Saint Remy had worked his magic there.

This chilly welcome wasn't at all congruent with how Abuela and Remy had left things. Sloane fought the protective urge to reach for him. The last time she'd seen that look on Abuela's face, a primo's date had been sent on her way, demoralized.

Abuela scanned Remy thoroughly, lingering on tattoos he'd added to his collection—the binds around his wrists Sloane had thought were coiled ropes but were really serpents; a grim visage in a gas mask leering out from under his sleeve; the line of belt-fed bullets marching up the opposite forearm. The standing rifle underneath a helmet on his leg, an homage to a lost SEAL teammate.

Abuela didn't appear to be impressed. "I don't believe you were invited."

"I invited him," Sloane asserted. When Abuela lifted a discerning brow, she forged ahead. "I thought he'd be welcome again at your table."

Abuela considered this. Finally, she lifted her chin. "Of course he is welcome."

Those around them seemed to breathe a collective sigh. The tías started chattering again, touching Remy, bringing him forward, offering him food.

Abuela seized the opportunity to escort Sloane to the door to the patio. "Have you seen Miguel?" she asked.

Sloane glanced over her shoulder and saw that Remy was being forcibly detained by women and empanadas. Their eyes met briefly. He lifted his shoulders helplessly.

She returned the gesture.

"He'll be fine," Abuela stated. An arm around Sloane's waist, she guided her outside.

The backyard had been lit with vintage lanterns. Citronella candles infused the air while holding mosquitos at bay. Colorful patterned tiles graced the patio floor and walls with a palette of yellow, turquoise and jungle green. A fountain burbled at its center. Tropical plants flowed out of terra-cotta pots. Hibiscus flowers bloomed pink and red.

With the swamp heat lending to the atmosphere, it looked and felt like a Havana night.

It helped that the tíos and primos were wearing straw hats and had gathered in a cloud of Cuban cigar smoke with Enrique at their center.

The lone man without a hat wore a pressed blue pin-striped suit. He was clean-shaven, as always, his crop of dark hair combed just so over his brow. His strong nose set him apart from Sloane's relatives.

"Miguel," Ezmeralda said, extending her hand to him. "Santana's here. I told you she would come."

Miguel smiled from a wide mouth. He was shiny and handsome in the polished way that Remy wasn't. The way he took Sloane's fingers in his and bent his head slightly, his eyes never leaving hers, was perfectly correct. "Hola, Sloane."

"Hola, Miguel," she replied, letting him keep her fingers because Abuela was beaming.

"Ya hace tiempo."

"It has been a while," she acknowledged.

Abuela touched her elbow. "Shall I get you a drink?"

"Rum, please," she said decidedly.

As Abuela left them, exchanging words with her sons and grandsons, Sloane let her hand drop from Miguel's.

He cleared his throat and stepped closer. "She's got her eye on you."

"I've been trying to dodge it for a while now," Sloane explained.

His mouth quirked, amused. "Are you in some kind of trouble?"

"I'm the eldest grandchild and still single," she pointed out.

He clucked his tongue. "I've heard worse."

"I've done worse," Sloane revealed. "But now that I'm on the straight and narrow, she's determined to see me settled."

Miguel nodded, aware of Abuela's matchmaking ways. "She invited me to your birthday party."

Sloane fought the urge to close her eyes in exasperation.

"This is all right with you?" Miguel asked cautiously.

It made Sloane smile slightly. Miguel had never forced his hand or taken advantage of Abuela's attempts to give him a leg up. Sloane admired him for that. "I'll save a dance for you."

He grinned, his eyes shying from hers.

She could think of a good many women who'd consider themselves lucky to have Miguel by their side as Abuela wanted him by hers. Sloane neither blamed them nor wanted to be one of them. They'd gone on two dates, per the matriarch's request. Friendship had blossomed and little else.

He was clean-cut and sophisticated, the way Abuelo had been. Sloane was all angles and edges. While it touched her that Abuela would think a man so like her own would suit Sloane as it had suited her, Sloane hadn't been able to find any common ground between Miguel and herself beyond the fact that they were both descended from aristocratic Cubans in exile. Sloane's family was made by rum. Miguel's had been built on the back of the sugarcane industry. Yet Sloane had known from their first date that he was meant for someone else.

Hell, they both were, weren't they? She belonged to someone, regardless of whether that someone wanted her back.

The scene in the exam room at the hospital came back to her, unbidden—Remy's hands on her face; his mouth inches from hers. She'd felt so close to making the connection, to surging up to her toes to kiss the man. He'd pulled away, just like all the times before. And, once again, she'd felt the jab of rejection.

She could continue to see Miguel. She could string him along simply to satisfy Abuela's wishes. But she refused. In the end, she knew who she was. Not the woman Abuela saw her as or wished she could see. She wanted to be seen for what she was—the way so few people did.

Remy came through the back door, and her focus centered on him.

He saw her more clearly than Abuela did. Even if he didn't want her, that was enough.

It's enough, she thought and did her damnedest to smile as the tíos descended on him.

"Remy's back, I take it."

She turned at the sound of her father's voice. Sloane had seen Horatio Escarra in every state of emotion. His expression rarely changed. It had driven her crazy as a teenager. She'd wanted to push him beyond composure. But the former senator was unflappable—something the constituents of Louisiana had liked after decades of politicians with too-big personalities and even bigger scandals to their names.

He'd gone silver through the years. He was the eldest of Abuela's sons, and he looked like it, though his signature smile still brought women around by the flock.

His carefully accumulated wealth didn't hurt.

"We're working together," she told her father. Though with le Fe's capture, that seemed uncertain now.

"Should I ignore the way he looks at you?"

"I ignore the way the real estate agent looks at you," Sloane noted, gesturing to the window where a buxom blonde peered out from behind the curtains. "Though that may be less a look of love and more a cry for help. Abuela's still giving you crap about dating her?"

"Of course she is," Horatio said. "Judith's not what she pictured for me."

"Neither was my mother, and your marriage lasted twenty years."

"It wasn't a success."

"Twenty years," Sloane repeated. "That's commendable."

"Your mother and I seem to have given you a poor understanding of what marriage is."

"Be sure to tell Abuela that. She might take some of the heat off me."

He chuckled, a quiet, contented noise. "She wants what's best for you. She wants what's best for all of us."

"I've watched no fewer than six of my cousins marry over the last three years," Sloane pointed out. "Only half of them seem happy about it."

"They don't know how to fight for what they want," Horatio explained. "Not like you."

Her affection swelled. Sloane still had contact with her mother in Los Angeles. However, it wasn't the same as the relationship she'd built with her father. Her childhood and teenage years had been nothing less than turbulent, with their fighting and his political ascent. Much had needed to be repaired between her and her father. They had since reached a level of understanding she hadn't thought possible.

She touched her lips to the smooth skin of his cheek. "Don't

bow to pressure," she advised. "If you like Judith, see where
it goes."

"I'm the one who should be giving you sage advice, hija de
mi corazón," he mused, dimples flashing. He touched the flat
of his brow to hers, closing his eyes. He lowered his voice. "I
won't if you won't."

She sensed something in him—strain he so rarely let on.
"Is everything all right, Papá?"

He kept his forehead against hers for several seconds more,
the skin between his eyes folding. Then he blinked and pulled
away, rubbing a circle over the space between her shoulder
blades. "Por supuesto."

"Santana."

Sloane flinched at the sound of Abuela's voice. She stood
at the door to the kitchen, hands linked at her waist and mouth
pursed.

"I must go," Sloane whispered to her father. "Try to keep
Tío Nestor from wringing Remy's neck."

"No promises," he returned, watching her go.

Abuela led her upstairs, taking it slow on the stairs and
leaning heavily on the banister.

On the landing, Sloane braced a hand underneath Abuela's
forearm because her breathing sounded labored. "Estás bien?"
she asked.

Abuela jerked her chin in an impatient nod. "I'm stronger
than I look."

Sloane removed her hand, wishing Abuela would give in to
suggestions that she sell the family abode and buy something
smaller—a one-story that would be easier for her to navigate.

Abuela was no more willing to acknowledge the realities
of aging than she was to understand why Sloane didn't want
to marry Miguel.

"In here," she said, moving into her bedroom. "I laid this
out for you."

Sloane studied the gown draped across the bed. "It's stunning," she said, touching the embroidery of the tea-length skirt. "Wait. I've seen this. Weren't you wearing this—"

"When Arturo and I had our grand opening, sí," Abuela said affectionately. She sat on the bed next to the dress, running her hand over its layers. "That was 1964."

Sloane loved that picture of Abuela. There were no photographs of her and Abuelo's life in Cuba. Even their wedding photographs had to be left behind. In the picture from Escarra Cuba's grand opening gala, Abuelo had looked dashing in his white suit. Abuela's dark hair had been perfectly rolled and pinned around her face. There had been a large flower tucked behind her ear. The gown had made her elegance in motion.

Sloane let her hand trail away from the skirt. It felt too delicate for handling.

"You'll wear it," Abuela said.

Sloane's eyes widened. "Me?"

"For your birthday," she added.

Sloane stared at her in shock. "Abuela, I can't wear this."

"Why not?"

"I bought a dress for the party," Sloane said. "A dress that I love."

"You can take it back."

Sloane shook her head. "This dress won't fit me. You're shorter than me."

"The hem can be altered."

"I'm bigger here," she said, planting her hands on her hips.

"These things can be adjusted. I've already made an appointment for you to see my tailor. The day after tomorrow. Ten o'clock."

"But my work," Sloane said. "My cases—"

Abuela's expression closed. "Santana. The world does not hang on your work."

Sloane gaped at her. "Children's lives depend on it."

"It takes a toll on you," Abuela accused. "It takes a toll on the family."

"That doesn't make it not worth doing," Sloane told her.

"At what cost?"

Sloane pressed her lips together. She was tired. So tired of fighting her on this. "It's important to me." Why wasn't that enough?

Abuela's eyes narrowed. "Is this about Remy?"

"Remy?"

"He came back."

"Sí. Temporarily."

"Is he the reason you're keeping Miguel at arm's length?"

Sloane brought her hands to her face and scrubbed. "Ay, Dios mío."

"I don't understand you, Santana. How can you love yourself and love a man who doesn't love you at the same time?"

"Wow," Sloane breathed. After a moment, she dropped her hands, unable to meet Abuela's gaze. Striving for understanding and patience, she reached for Abuela's hands, linking them. "Look, I know what this is," she said slowly. "You've had a good life, and you want me to have one, too. You've always wanted me to be some version of yourself. But you and I are different. Maybe that's why you can't make yourself see what being a federal agent means to me."

It didn't help that the US government had taken away Escarra Cuba's assets. It had in essence destroyed everything Abuela and Abuelo had built together here in America. The company's demise had taken Abuelo away too soon.

"I'm sorry if that upsets you," Sloane said. "But this is who I am."

Abuela's grip doubled. She squeezed Sloane's hands. "It's just a dress, pequeña."

It wasn't. That was clear.

"You'll wear it," Abuela said, patting Sloane's hand before

letting go to gather her shawl closer around her. "Ten o'clock Thursday. I'll meet you at the tailor's."

As she rose from the bed, Sloane stayed where she was, feeling too big, too loud, too out of place and not at all herself.

Chapter 9

Sloane had been unnaturally quiet on the drive home, then again at breakfast at the maisonette this morning. She'd had a meeting with her team early and then had to report to her SAC before noon.

Remy checked his watch. She'd been gone for several hours. And he figured le Fe had had enough time to recover from surgery.

At the hospital, he caught Grace in the corridor between the ER and the recovery ward, about to go into surgery.

"You're early," she announced. "Where's Sloane?"

"She got caught in meetings," he said. "I know le Fe's not ready for transfer, but if I could have five minutes with him…"

Grace considered his request. "Fine," she said. "But just five minutes."

"Thanks," he said. "Which room?"

"Keep walking. Once you reach Recovery, he's in room 106."

Le Fe was right where she said he was. He looked three shades paler than the pillow behind his head. When he opened his eyes, they were glassed over. That didn't stop him from reacting to Remy's sudden entry. He sat up. "You ain't the nurse."

"Nope," Remy said.

"What d'you want with me?" Le Fe asked. "You ain't a cop, either."

"You've got that right."

"You one of Booker's boys?"

"Booker's dead."

Le Fe looked as if he'd been slapped. He slumped on his pillow. "Well, somabitch."

Remy watched him, waiting.

Le Fe's eyes flew open. "It wasn't me that killed him. I was laid up in this here bed the whole time, see?"

"Does the name Loup-Garou mean anything to you?"

Le Fe stared for several seconds before something clicked. He blew out a laugh. "They catch that asshole?"

"He's still at large."

That shut down le Fe's amusement abruptly.

"You saw something out there in Abalone, didn't you, Ray?" Remy asked.

"Who's asking?" le Fe wanted to know. "Where's Escarra? She's the one what usually asks the questions."

"She sent me instead," Remy lied smoothly. He took a step toward the bed.

"You ain't got no badge," le Fe observed.

Remy took the printout from his pocket and unfolded it before dropping it on le Fe's blanketed lap. "You violated your parole."

Le Fe groaned. "You're a bounty hunter."

Again, Remy waited.

"I'll get off with a warning," le Fe dismissed, tossing the paper away.

"There's evidence to suggest you were at the brothel before it was raided," Remy told him. "You left your hat and prints."

"You don't know those belong to me," he said, though he was beginning to twitch.

"If the judge finds out you were supplying traffickers again with oxy," Remy continued, "they'll revoke parole and toss you back in jail where you belong."

Le Fe swallowed. "They cain't do that."

"The law says different."

"The law ain't seen what I've seen," le Fe asserted.

"What did you see?" Remy asked, feeling a frisson of unease.

"I can give you an address."

"For?" Remy prompted.

"You people…you run around trying to catch smoke. But Loup-Garou ain't the one you should be worried about."

"Is that right?" Remy asked.

"This is bigger than him. It's bigger than the handful of pedophiles you've scooped up over the last few months. You want the people responsible? You got to think bigger. Outside the box."

Remy wrapped his hand around the bedrail. "Elaborate."

"The last time things got this serious, it was the Guidrys," le Fe explained, down to a confidential whisper. "You remember Gretchen Guidry. She had all the traffickers in lower Louisiana, Mississippi and Alabama in her pocket. They worked for *her*."

The name made Remy's pulse miss a beat. To hear it after so many years… It was like taking a haymaker to the face. "Guidry's dead."

Le Fe lifted his chin. "Got herself killed. Turf war. The sectors split. Nobody's had the know-how to bring them back under one hat."

"Until now."

"I don't know who's replaced Guidry," le Fe said. "But I know where Booker and his fellas were getting their crop."

"Where?"

"A warehouse," le Fe revealed, "on Carondelet Street right here in Nawlins."

Remy searched his face. "Is that all?"

Le Fe raised his hands. "I'll do anything to keep from going back inside. I got people depending on me. Cain't take care of them if I'm in the pen. If I knew more, I'd tell you."

"Escarra's going to ask you questions about Loup-Garou," Remy pointed out, "and whether you saw anything that night."

"I didn't see nothing but a freak in a mask. When I came to, he was already in the house. I lit out of there fast. Took my boat back the way I came."

He left by boat, Remy told himself. "If I have any more questions…"

Le Fe lifted his hands from the bed. "Hell, ain't like I'm going anywhere. Not with this busted leg."

"I'll be back later with Agent Escarra," Remy told him, tapping the bed rail before backing off.

"Hey, if you see the nurse—the one with the braids—tell her ol' Ray could use another hit of morphine." He grimaced as he shifted his leg underneath the covers. "Wound's acting up again."

Sloane read the profile on Loup-Garou for the dozenth time while rubbing the space beneath the bandage on her arm.

…between 6'3" and 6'6"…size 12 boots…most likely wealthy or hired by a wealthy entity…his ability to avoid detection and disarm targets effectively suggests a background in crime, perhaps even law enforcement or special ops training…a skilled hacker with intimate knowledge of computers and the black web or works with a partner who is a hacker…

Her eyes kept coming back to the words *law enforcement or special ops* repeatedly.

On the board across from her desk, she stared at the map where she and Pelagie had pinned the locations of Loup-Garou's raids. Headshots of the traffickers he had apprehended marched up the left side and photos of the victims he had freed lined the right.

In the center of the board was a mugshot of Terry Booker, a photo of the custom Taser that had been recovered from the brothel and a sketch from a police artist of Loup-Garou's wolf mask.

She stared into the blank eyes of that mask. Ballistics from Booker's fatal shooting were still with the lab, no results yet. The Taser was being analyzed for fingerprints.

There wouldn't be any. Though if Loup-Garou was responsible for Booker's death, perhaps he was starting to slip. Every criminal made mistakes if they stayed in the game. The perfect crime was as mythical a concept as the Cajun werewolf itself.

She wanted to close this case. She wanted it so badly she could taste it.

This morning, she'd traced Esther back to Natchitoches and had placed the phone call no parent ever wanted to receive. With or without the information from the data chip that Loup-Garou had left at the scene, the men from the Abalone brothel would be incarcerated for the death of Esther Fournier. Sloane would make the case file on her abduction, trafficking and death so airtight, no jury would think twice about convicting.

Of course, that didn't take away Esther's suffering or the pain her family was facing. Sloane glanced up at the board where Esther smiled from her last school portrait. Pain swelled behind Sloane's ribs, and she tried taking a deep breath to ease it.

It didn't work. She was angry and raw. Her conversation with Houghton earlier hadn't helped. Apparently, the media now had a hold of Loup-Garou's story and would run it in all the local papers. It would be picked up by nationwide syndicates, too, most likely.

Pelagie rushed in, out of breath. She tossed a file onto Sloane's desk. "I think I've got it."

Sloane frowned at her partner's flushed face. "Yeah?"

"I went to every custom mask shop in the city," Pelagie said. She leaned against the desk for support, pointing questioningly at the bottle of water on Sloane's desk.

Sloane passed it to her, then opened the file. "Did you find the one who designed Loup-Garou's mask?"

"Maybe," Pelagie revealed. "After striking out at a dozen different places, I came across a designer who said he might know who makes masks like that. I asked for a name. He gave me a website." She held out her phone.

Sloane took it, rotating it so that the screen was right side up. "Bonhomie Masks—Mardi Gras, Halloween, cosplay," she read from the website's banner.

Pelagie wagged a finger. "Scroll down."

Sloane did so. There was a heading above a series of eye masks, typical of Mardi Gras. Then another over a section of full-face masks. She paused at the third.

Pelagie nodded. "She makes custom animal masks. And look here…" She took the phone, toggling the *Show More* feature that took them to another page. She scrolled and turned the screen back to face Sloane. "Bingo."

Sloane couldn't have said it better. The wolf mask exhibited on the page looked almost identical to the one from the police sketch. She sat up straighter. "Where's this company based?"

"This is the part you won't believe," Pelagie explained. Her brows lifted behind her bangs. "The designer is Célestine Clairmont."

The name rang a bell. Sloane narrowed her eyes. "Remind me…?"

"Her former husband, Sebastian LeBlanc, ran for governor twenty some odd years ago. He had all the sleaze and charisma to put him ahead in the polls. Until word got around that he liked underage girls."

Sloane lifted her chin. "Right. He did some time."

"On charges of child pornography and exploitation. The guy served ten years before he was released. Célestine Clairmont was his first wife. She served him divorce papers after the disappearance of their eldest child, Sebastian LeBlanc II—known to family and friends as Baz."

Baz LeBlanc's vanishing had been headline news, Sloane remembered. The rumors had been wild. Some believed his father was behind it. Others believed it was blackmail related—an attempt to secure leverage against LeBlanc Senior gone wrong. "No one ever found him."

"Célestine and his surviving sister never stopped looking for him," Pelagie revealed. "His youngest sister died after a hit-and-run accident a couple years before he went missing. Célestine's lived her life out of the spotlight. She runs her business out of Baton Rouge."

Sloane glanced at the clock on the wall above the board full of pushpins. Baton Rouge was a little over an hour's drive away. "She should be interviewed face-to-face."

"We could drive up tonight or tomorrow," Pelagie suggested. "Your choice."

Sloane's phone pinged. "Hold on," she said and answered the call. "Escarra."

"Sloane, it's Grace."

Sloane heard the threads of distress in her friend's voice. "What's wrong?"

"Your witness," Grace said, "Ray de le Fe. I don't know what happened. We had a guard posted at his door. But someone sneaked in and…"

Sloane shook her head. "He's not."

"Dead," Grace said thinly. "He's dead. I'm sorry, Sloane. I'm so sorry."

"What about the kids in Recovery? Are they—"

"I checked. They're safe. I've got them under guard, but you'll want to take further precautions."

A guard hadn't been enough to protect le Fe. "I'll be right there, okay? I'm coming." As Sloane hung up, she stood and swung her blazer off the back of her chair. Punching her arms through the sleeves, she met Pelagie's curious look. "Le Fe's dead."

Pelagie's eyes bugged. "What the hell?"

"Somebody got to him," Sloane said. She grabbed her badge and weapon from the desk drawer.

As Pelagie followed her out of the field office to her vehicle, she asked the question that was rolling around Sloane's mind. "Could it have been Loup-Garou?"

"That's what we're going to find out," Sloane said. "Call ahead. Have security ready for us when we get there. I want the guard on the door questioned, and I want to see the security footage from his floor. The kids from Abalone should be transferred immediately to a safe house. Le Fe's killing may not be isolated."

As she got behind the wheel, she shut the door and wrapped her hands around the leather until her knuckles whitened, thinking of Delta Bean at the Mission, waiting for her brother.

Chapter 10

Remy met Sloane on the corner of Josephine and St. Charles in front of the Pontchartrain Hotel. One look at her and his stomach sank.

"I've got questions for you," she said in greeting, her frown a mile long.

He tried searching her, but her gaze was hidden behind a pair of aviators. The only read he got off her was his own carefully blank face in their reflection.

Hell, should he have followed his better logic and skipped town overnight, knowing she would interview le Fe this afternoon? He knew she'd been by the hospital. And he was starting to doubt that what le Fe had told him was the truth. "You want to go someplace cooler?" he asked, waving at their surroundings.

She thought about her answer for a minute before she nodded toward the entrance to Bayou Bar. After speaking to the hostess at the door, she snagged them seating toward the back.

Remy vaguely catalogued the exposed wood, shotgun bar and Steinway piano. He could focus on little more than the dull thump of his pulse.

The table for two offered them plenty of privacy. Neither of them glanced at the menu. When a server came by, Sloane ordered them both an ice water. "I'm on duty," she said, waving off a laminated drink list. Taking off her sunglasses, she shot Remy a dark look. "You?"

He shook his head, passing up a serious beverage—however much he might need one.

"I'll give you a moment to go over the menu," the server said before leaving them.

Sloane waited until she was out of earshot. "What'd you do today, Remy?" she probed.

She was leading him. He tried anticipating her. Treading lightly, he folded his arms over the table and leaned over them. "I left your place around eight, went to feed the meter at public parking so they wouldn't tow my vehicle and took a walk."

"Where?" she asked pointedly.

"I went to see our friend," he admitted.

"Le Fe," she guessed.

"Yeah," he stated, unwilling to pretend anymore. The idea of pretense was exhausting at this point.

"Why?" she demanded.

He'd seen her like this before. In February, when Jaime Solaro, the man responsible for a lot of what had happened to her in Mexico, had escaped capture after nearly killing Grace's then-boyfriend, Javier Rivera. "What happened?" he demanded.

"You tell me," she shot back.

He didn't respond because the server was back with their waters. "Thanks," he said.

"Would you like to hear the specials?"

"No," Sloane and Remy said as one.

When the server blinked in response, Remy cleared his throat. "We need another minute."

The server nodded and retreated.

Remy felt Sloane's stare boring into him, but he took a second, taking stock of her mood. The truth struck him like a thunderbolt. "He's dead."

She gave away nothing.

He shook his head. "It wasn't me."

"I have footage of you leaving his room no less than half an hour before the nurse found him choking on his own blood," she explained. "Hell of a coincidence."

"Sloane," he said. "You know me. I wouldn't do this."

"Then explain."

"I had an obligation to inform him he was in custody," he reminded her.

"If you'd waited for me like you agreed, you wouldn't be in the middle of this hell storm."

"What else did you see in the footage?" he asked. "There was a guard at his door."

Slowly, she let a long breath out through her nose. Her shoulders seemed to deflate. "He stepped away. Then there's a brief time lapse in the footage. I'm told power went down at the hospital. The generators immediately went into action, but the cameras didn't reboot until several minutes later."

"Did you question the guard?" he asked.

She tilted her head dangerously. "Are you telling me how to do my job?"

"I'm following the only logical place this leads because you know I didn't do this," he challenged. "The only reason you'd go down that road for even a second tells me le Fe's killer knew what he was doing. A professional hit of some kind. One that could be construed as a military skill set. Such as mine."

Again, she remained silent.

She couldn't tell him how le Fe was killed. But her reticence told him he was on the money. He shook his head. "You know I don't kill people."

"You have," she pointed out.

"In the name of my country, yes," he granted. "Not since I left the service."

She studied him for another simmering minute before, finally, her gaze fell away.

He tried to swallow the knot in his throat, but it didn't budge. He couldn't be upset or angry her mind had gone straight to him. He had no right, because she didn't really know him, did she? He'd been hiding the truth since the day they met.

"Did he say anything?" Sloane asked.

"He gave me an address."

"What address?" she wanted to know.

"He said a warehouse on Carondelet supplied Booker and his men with victims," he explained. "I scoped it out after I left the hospital."

"Why would he tell you that?" she asked.

"He didn't want his parole revoked."

"Did he tell you anything else?"

"The traffickers have organized. They're being led by one kingpin. It explains why they've been so hard to catch over the last few years. Someone high up the chain's been calling the shots."

"Did le Fe give you a name?"

"He said he didn't know it." When Sloane made a disgruntled noise, he pressed on. "But the warehouse could be a link."

"Take me there," she told him. She took a sip of water, put money on the table and stood.

Sloane cursed as she hung up with Pelagie over an hour later. "The warehouse is owned by a business in Delaware."

"Bad news for us?" Remy guessed.

"Delaware allows anonymous LLCs that protect owner identity." She brought her first two knuckles up to her mouth, scanning the exterior of the warehouse for the umpteenth time. "We can't search without a warrant, and a warrant won't come without just cause."

"We have le Fe's word."

"Doesn't mean much to a judge when the man's dead and had a criminal record as long as my leg," she pointed out.

"Is your wound hurting?"

She dropped her hand from the space above the bandage. "It's fine."

He crossed his arms. "So what's our move?"

She considered. The warehouse had two access points from the street—a door she'd tried and failed to open and a garage meant to process deliveries.

It would be easy to get victims in and out of the warehouse without detection. A vehicle would pull in, the garage would close, and the driver could load or unload as needed. Plus, there were no street cameras on this part of Carondelet. She thought about doing a canvass to determine if any of the neighbors had security feeds or could provide intel into what went on at this location.

"One victim from the brothel remembered coming here by night," she thought out loud. "The boy, Marlon, confirmed it—only he came in a separate vehicle weeks later."

"There's no activity during the day," Remy surmised, "because they operate by night."

"Most every address on this block is business, not residential," she added. "The traffic around here decreases after dark."

"Less chance of discovery," he concluded.

She nodded. "The best way to catch on to whatever they're doing in there is to sit on the place. In the meantime, I can have our cybersecurity team take a run at the Delaware company, see what they get back."

She thought about what she'd said at Bayou Bar and the accusations she'd made. She closed her eyes. "I'm sorry."

He turned his head away from the window to stare at her. "Are you?"

"You're right," she admitted. "I do know you."

He looked away again swiftly.

She licked her lower lip, wishing she wasn't fumbling her way through this. "You wouldn't have killed le Fe."

"Who do you think did?" he asked quietly.

She held on to the only other avenue she could see at this point. "Loup-Garou knew le Fe was at the brothel."

Remy went stiller than stone, but he still didn't turn to face her.

"Could be he was trying to silence anyone who could identify him," Sloane went on.

"You believe that?"

"It's plausible," she answered. It was the best lead she had. Though it didn't fit the vigilante's MO or his behavioral pattern. His work was clean and efficient, minus the gun discharge that had killed Terry Booker.

What she'd found in le Fe's hospital room had been cut-throat and messy. It'd even felt a touch personal.

"Doesn't it strike you as odd," she asked, "that le Fe was killed before the FBI could formally question him about what happened the night of Loup-Garou's Abalone raid?"

After a minute, he said, "I think you're chasing a ghost."

"This ghost leaves footprints."

"You don't want this one found," he assumed. "Not really. He's on the same side of this fight as you are."

"I want him found so I can go back to doing what I joined the FBI to do. What I was *made* to do. What saved me."

Remy remained silent.

She wanted his control wrecked. She wanted him unleashed, just to know who and what he was like—really like—underneath the surface. What kind of dynamite did she have to throw at him to make that happen?

She remembered what they'd shared outside the psychiatric unit. She'd made herself vulnerable. He'd bowed out.

Because the subject felt loaded, she changed it. "I need to have a word with Delta Bean."

"Is she still at the Mission?"

Sloane nodded. "It's not something I need to put off. The news of le Fe's death should come from me."

"That's a lot for you to take on yourself."

"I'm responsible for her now," she pointed out. "I'm not sure if that would have been what le Fe wanted, but… I feel responsible."

"You're a good person, Sloane."

"No one should be alone in this world."

His silence felt weighted.

Quickly, she looked for something else to say. "You handled yourself well last night."

He shook his head shortly. "Your tíos took it easy on me. I suspect your father got to them. Miguel seems like a nice guy."

"You think so?"

"Too nice."

Wasn't he just? "He deserves better."

"The hell he does."

If Remy didn't want her, why did he have to say such perfect things?

"Abuela looked at me like I was Castro's insurgents rolling up on Havana."

She blinked at how intuitive he was. "She still likes you."

"Then why does she see me as a threat?" he wondered.

She couldn't tell him why. Not without revealing how deep her feelings for him went. Remembering the conversation with Abuela didn't help her relax.

In this light, she could see the thin layer of gold around the outside of his pupils. It made her breathless. Her heart skipped. She felt wrapped up and need bound.

She swallowed, breaking their eye contact. "I'm going to Baton Rouge tomorrow afternoon," she decided.

"What's there?"

"A lead," she said. "I should be back before dinner."

"I'll order in," he offered.

"Thanks," she returned. "The family's throwing me a party on Friday. You should come."

"I should?"

She nodded and tried not to dwell on the vintage dress she'd hung in the closet next to the one she'd bought for the occasion. "My family will be there. All of them."

"Miguel?"

"Yes," she admitted. "But I need you there, too."

"What do you want?"

"Want?" she asked, breathy.

"For your birthday."

She let false laughter fall from her. "You don't have to get me anything. Just show up."

A beat of silence. Then, "I'll do my best."

She smoothed her lips together. She told herself that was enough. "I really am sorry—about before."

"It's forgotten," he dismissed.

She opened her mouth to speak again but thought better of it.

They resumed the stakeout in taut silence.

Remy had avoided Torben's phone calls throughout the day. Once Sloane's partner, Agent Landry, took over their shift outside the warehouse on Carondelet, he had her drop him off a few blocks from his Jeep. From there, he drove to Bayou St. John.

The narrow, raised-basement Victorian had been painted a stately yellow. Its postage-stamp yard was a verdant green despite the heat wave. The heavy hydrangeas at each corner of the house were a prize-winning blue.

When Remy reached the door, he stared for a moment at the magnolia wreath hanging there before lifting his fist to knock.

After a few seconds, the door opened. A woman smiled at him from the parting, opening it wider. "Remy Fontenot, is that you?"

"Demi," he greeted warmly. She looked good. Wide, warm, dark eyes in a sweet, round face. She wore a White Lily apron over her professional black dress. By day, she taught history at Tulane. By night, she kept her husband religious by way of her kitchen. Remy didn't miss the fact that her feet were bare. Without her high heels, she was five feet tall.

Still, those eyes could wound, he knew, and her tongue could scald. She was the pillar of strength Torben needed at the end of his long hours at the local precinct.

"Come in, come in," she said, stepping back into the foyer so he could enter.

"Thanks." Remy caught himself shoving his hands in his pockets as he looked around. "You've changed things."

She closed the door and locked it. "A little. The house has good bones. And we left the historical details—hardwoods, mantels, stained glass and such. But it needed sprucing up."

They'd done more than that, he noted. "It looks great. And something smells delicious."

She touched his arm. "Stay for dinner. I'm making Cajun cassoulet with bread pudding in bourbon sauce."

"If Torben ever leaves you, I'll kick his ass."

She leaned in, lifting a brow. "You'll have to find the body first."

He laughed. It was easy with her. "How is he?"

Her smiled tapered off. "I'm worried about him. Something at work…" She shook her head. "Those poor kids up in Abalone. They're doing a number on him. More so than usual. I'm worried about him burning out. Or worse, working himself into an early grave. Like my daddy."

Remy blinked several times. "I wish there was something I could do," he said honestly. Wasn't that why he transformed himself into the elusive Loup-Garou every thirty days? He knew the burden his friend shouldered, just as he knew that the numbers of missing people in New Orleans were staggering.

Remy and Demi both knew why Torben had gotten involved in Missing Persons in the first place—particularly cases involving minors. Nearly half of all underage kidnapping victims were sexually assaulted. The stats haunted Torben, just as his and Remy's history haunted them both.

That history was part of the reason Torben and Demi had yet to have kids of their own.

Her long fingers circled his wrist. "You being back here… That's something."

He didn't have the heart to tell her he didn't plan on staying long. "How are you doing?" he asked, scanning the bone structure of her face. Several years ago, she'd had a brush with breast cancer. During treatment, those bones had gone from prominent to stark. She'd lost her hair, and though it had grown back since, she kept it short.

She beamed at him. "Right as rain, cher. Can I get you a beverage?"

Before Remy could answer, a voice called from the stairs, "I didn't know we had company." Torben descended, freshly showered and wearing relaxed slacks, a New Orleans Pelicans T-shirt and no shoes.

Demi placed her hand on Remy's arm comfortably. "I asked Remy to stay for supper. Help me twist his arm."

Torben's eyes went soft on his wife as he drew her close. His palm passed over her cap of hair before coming to rest on the nape of her neck. He bent to touch his lips to hers. "I know from experience, darlin', that you are more than capable of bringing a man to his knees."

Seeing Torben's open affection and easy intimacy with his

wife made Remy feel many things. Relief beyond measure that his friend had found Demi...that despite everything, he'd built this life with her. Wonder at it, too. It was a life Remy didn't dare dream of. Too many secrets. Too many lies. Too much hidden.

He also felt that he was intruding and cleared his throat. "Sorry I missed your calls."

"You've been difficult to get ahold of," Torben said, sliding his arm around Demi's shoulders. "You'll stay for dinner. Then you and I can have a long talk on the porch afterward."

As they both looked at him expectantly, Remy realized there was no refusing them though he feared dinner wouldn't go down easy knowing he had brought bad news with him. "All right."

Chapter 11

"You know about le Fe," Remy said.

Torben stared across the yard. The lights on the screened-in porch were off. His face stood out in stark relief against the fragile blue cast of the darkening sky. "You were there. Did you see anything?"

"Guard on the door. Staff circulating throughout the corridor. Nothing out of the ordinary, though Escarra tells me the guard got called off shortly after I left. There's a time lapse in security footage."

"Power outage," Torben confirmed. "Takes something big to knock out a hospital grid."

"It was professional," Remy said darkly.

"I'm surprised you haven't fled."

Remy chewed over that in silence.

"Escarra knows you were there."

"She does."

"She question you?"

"She knows I wouldn't kill him," he said, though the conversation with her earlier weighed on him.

"You sure about that, brah?" Torben asked, turning his gaze away from the night. It narrowed on Remy's profile.

"She knows me."

"Like I know you?"

Remy bit back a curse. "I'm not going anywhere. Not for the time being."

"You've never had this much trouble leaving something behind," Torben pointed out. "Or someone."

"Le Fe's dead. He can't identify me. And Loup-Garou stays underground—at least until the heat backs off."

"Our friendly neighborhood werewolf was on the nightly news last night," Torben pointed out.

"I thought the police were keeping this quiet."

"I thought I told you it's out of our hands," Torben rebutted. "It's with the Feds now."

Once more, Remy retreated into silence.

"There's something else you're not telling me."

Torben did know him—all too well. "Le Fe confirmed that all the major trafficking cells in the area have merged."

"Did he tell you under whose authority?"

"No." Remy wished he had. He wished he would have pressed le Fe harder for that information. "He brought up the name Gretchen Guidry, however."

Remy didn't have to see Torben clearly to know the man had tensed. He felt it. Their past was filled with many ghosts. The one that they shared was Gretchen Guidry. She'd left her mark on both of them.

"Guidry owned this town," Torben bit off. "Judges, bankers, prosecutors, city council members. The mayor himself. That's why nothing she did ever came to light. She's dead, and people are still holding up her good name. You know what they say? That she had more sway in this town than Marie Laveau herself."

The same people debated whether the voodoo queen Marie Laveau was a devil-worshipper or altogether evil. But there was no doubt in Remy's mind that Guidry had sold her soul… and those of a good many others along the way. Including his.

Torben's voice was barely above a whisper. "Why would

le Fe speak her name if not to suggest that someone just as influential has taken her place?"

Remy didn't have an answer, and the implications were enough to make him perspire.

"What the hell's going on in this town, Remy?"

"I'll find out," Remy swore. The hell if he was going to allow another Gretchen Guidry to profit off the exploitation and trauma of others.

"I'm not convinced you should," Torben warned. "I'm worried about you."

"It's mutual. Demi says you're burning yourself out." Remy wouldn't allow that, either. "She deserves better than to watch another man she loves work himself to death."

"I'm not the one being pursued by Feds at the moment," Torben replied.

"You have everything," Remy heard himself say. When Torben stilled, he felt like shrinking into the woodwork. "Good home. Good name. Good standing. The woman of your dreams who happens to adore you. Never mind that she serves the best frickin' bread pudding I've ever tasted. You let me worry about the Feds and Loup-Garou. Whether I go down for this, none of it traces back to you. I made sure of that—for you and for Demi."

"You go down," Torben countered, "I'm not letting you sit in a cell alone for the rest of your life. We both conceived of this. We both pay the price. We're brothers, you and me. We fight the same people, the same demons."

"If you leave your wife to martyr yourself for what I've done, she'll never forgive you for it," Remy replied. "And neither will I. You want the two people you love most in this world to turn their backs on you?"

Torben's scowl was far too entrenched, too comfortable on his face. "You'll go down for manslaughter if they have their way. Escarra won't fight for you when she finds out what you've been doing. Who you are."

"Maybe not," Remy acknowledged. But he couldn't leave her. Not with this. "I'll find out who ordered the hit on le Fe. I'm going to find who's behind all this and take them out at the knees. There is no Gretchen Guidry anymore, and there'll never be another like her, if I have anything to say about it."

"How do you plan on doing that?" Torben asked.

"Same way I've been doing."

"Loup-Garou's gone to ground."

"Yeah, but I'm still here," Remy pointed out. "I need tools."

Torben raised his chin, understanding. "If anyone can hack their way around this, it's you." He took a moment to consider that. "I'll get you what you need. Just promise me one thing."

"What's that?"

"If you do come to your senses and want to disappear, you'll let me help you."

Remy fought a sigh as Torben put his hand between them. It was odd how hard they struggled sometimes to understand one another when they felt the same way. Torben felt responsibility for Remy's fate every bit as much as Remy felt responsibility toward him. He'd forged bonds in military training and on the battlefield, but nothing as strong as this.

"You're the only family I've got left," Remy told him. He gripped Torben's hand and didn't hesitate to let the man pull him into a hard embrace.

"Ay," Sloane groaned as her phone dinged for the tenth time. The notifications had started before her five thirty alarm. Texts from her tías had piggybacked on top of each other.

The close-knit nature of her family was the security blanket she hadn't known she needed until after Mexico. She would never forget how they all rallied around her, trying to help her convalescence each in their own way. Their methods hadn't always been effective. Tío Nestor had offered to kneecap each member of the Solaro crime family, despite the fact most of them had been in prison at that time. The tías had brought her dish after dish of authentic Cuban soul food. Abuelo had quietly ushered her into his study once a week to sit in silence and sip illegally imported rum with him. Abuela had brushed her hair every night before her vintage trifold vanity mirror.

Her mother, though by that time forbidden in Abuela's household, had hired Remy and thrown him into the mix, and the rest was history.

The Escarras operated on open avenues of communication. Secrets never stayed secret, and as a rule, there was no shame in meddling. As Sloane descended the stairs to the kitchen, she held up her phone. "The tías have spoken. You will be at my birthday party this weekend."

Remy peered over his shoulder from where he stood at the stove, doing something magic in a pan.

Goddamn bedroom eyes again, she observed, her heart clenching in reaction. Either he or her tías would be the death of her. It was a toss-up at this point.

"How do they plan to enforce this?" he asked warily. He looked as if he hadn't slept. Fatigue was stamped in lines around his coffee-dark eyes.

"The usual way," Sloane mused. "Bribery. Guilt. Then the tíos, if you let it go too far."

He turned back to the stove. As tired as he was, his spine was straight. She could see the dip of it through his T-shirt. His packed muscles tapered to a lean waist. He already had on his shoes. Above them, his inked calves popped. Under the pockets of his cargo shorts, his ass was perfect. Round enough to make her want to bite down.

She wouldn't drool over him. Not before coffee. She veered toward the counter and then stopped. "Who is this imposter?"

she asked, pointing to the shiny new apparatus sitting where her old percolator had been.

"The old one spat at me," he told her. "It was a hazard. You're lucky it didn't burn this place to the ground."

"So…you bought me a new one?"

"Consider it an early birthday present."

It took some effort to close her mouth.

She felt him at her back, close. "If you ask nicely, I'll show you how to use it." His words vibrated along the tiny hairs inside her ear. His hands closed over the counter on either side of her waist, bricking her in. "Did you change your bandage?"

She closed her eyes, absorbing the ready warmth of him. "You need to quit worrying about me."

"Never," he murmured close enough to her ear that his breath moved the hair around it, and she was suddenly fully awake.

Fighting intrusive thoughts that commanded her to turn into him, wrap around him and press against the hard steel line of him, she gave herself a hard pinch on the inside of her wrist. It did nothing to stifle the nibbles of lust along the lengths of her thighs.

Her heart flung itself haphazardly against her sternum when he reached around her to plug the coffeemaker into the wall. He imparted instructions, following them up with a demo.

She heard nothing but the beat of her own blood. Saw nothing but his large, sun-bronzed hands going through the motions in sure strokes. She wished he would stroke her.

His hand came to her hip. "Sloane?"

She jerked out of her stupor. "Yeah, yeah. I got it."

"It's simple, just like the other one. But safer and more efficient. I also bought you a fire extinguisher."

"What? Why?"

She could practically feel his eyes boring into the top of

her head. "Because you don't have one. God knows how old the wiring is in this house. It was the first thing you should've bought when you moved in. How it never occurred to you to get one…"

"It's lucky I have you then," she muttered.

His hands gripped the counter again. She thought she felt his head lower over hers. He lingered, the sound of his long, indrawn breath filling her like air. At the end, she heard an almost imperceptible groan.

Was he…smelling her hair?

Hell. He'd done it now. This was worse—far worse—than rubbing jelly off her mouth.

She gave in to the sweeping impulse and turned to face him.

He backed away, sidestepping to the stove. His gaze didn't touch hers as he grabbed the dish towel next to the hot skillet and tossed it over his shoulder. Picking up the spatula, he went back to cooking.

He was a tease. A prude. Both. And now she needed another shower—this one cold and bracing like the reality of him and her. It was a shame she wasn't the old Sloane anymore, that girl who hadn't hesitated to make her needs clear.

As she poured her coffee and contemplated sweetening it with rum instead of sugar, her phone vibrated on the counter. A reminder from Tía Rosa via Abuela to meet her for the dress fitting this afternoon. Feeling low, she studiously took her coffee to the table, keeping her head down and her gaze off the man at the stove.

The old Sloane would have begged. She would not.

The old Sloane would've put her foot down and worn the dress she'd bought to her own birthday party.

A container of peanut butter sat on the table in front of her. She'd gotten the munchies while sitting around waiting for Remy to come back last night and going over and over her visit with Delta Bean at the Mission. She'd sat with the woman while she wailed over her brother's loss. It had been late into the night when the Sisters had assured Sloane they would see to Delta Bean's care.

He set a plate down silently in front of her. For a moment, she just stared at it. When he thrust a fork in front of her, she frowned. "What is this?" she asked.

"Fried green tomatoes," he said, pointing to the green things on her plate, lightly breaded. "Eggs benedict. Hollandaise sauce."

She'd told herself she wouldn't drool. The Lord was testing her. "Why did you make this?" she asked.

"You're hungry," he said simply, serving orange juice in the mason jars she kept in the cupboard.

"I didn't have any more eggs," she pointed out. "Or tomatoes, red *or* green. I sure as hell didn't have hollandaise."

"I did the shopping."

How could the man look like sin and be her angel? If he didn't want her covering him like pure cane syrup on pancakes, he had to stop.

"Eat up," he advised, dropping into the chair next to hers.

She scarfed, hoping to stifle her moans of pleasure with expediency. When she was done, she drained the mason jar and patted her mouth with the napkin he'd folded next to her plate. She had to get out of here before he did something else that could be construed as thoughtful or sweet.

The fatigue around his eyes caught her attention again. "You aren't sleeping. Are you?"

He dropped his fork, chewing. "It's fine."

"If it's the bed, we can switch," she heard herself offer.

"It's not the bed. There's a lot on my mind."

That made two of them. "Le Fe?"

He grunted.

She nodded. "Will you still get the bounty?"

"The bounty doesn't matter," he said, waving the notion away.

She studied the tension coiled in the edges of his face. "So... you're not going anywhere, then?"

Finally, his eyes rushed up to meet hers. A line threaded across his brow. He shook his head. "No. I'm not going."

The relief was shocking in its intensity. She did her best not to show it. But there it was—that snowball of need rolling down the hill again.

"What's next for you?" he asked.

"The family of the victim from Abalone will be here today to identify her," Sloane said. That was enough to make all the warm, fuzzy feelings disappear. "I want to meet with them, offer my condolences and assure them I will do whatever it takes to keep the men who did this to her behind bars for the rest of their natural lives."

"Rough day for you all the same," he murmured.

"It'll be an even harder one for them," she added. "I need to arrange teams to stake out the warehouse on Carondelet. We need to keep it under twenty-four-hour surveillance. Then I need to meet with the tech team, find out if they have anything more on the company that owns it. After that, it's a trip to Baton Rouge. What are you going to do?"

"Le Fe's killer is out there," he said.

She frowned. "You're a bounty hunter, not a PI."

"So?"

"Why do this?" she asked him warily. "You didn't like who he was or what he did. It's not your responsibility to catch his killer."

"I need to."

"Why?" she asked again.

"The person who killed him is likely a high-level assassin. Someone with a skill set similar to my own. The type of person who won't have too many qualms about taking anyone out who gets too close."

"Including me," she realized. "You're still protecting me."

"I'm asking you to partner with me on this," he said.

"You act like this is personal."

"It involves you, doesn't it?"

She willed herself to be strong. "I'm not going to say no."

"Good."

She sighed. "Stay out of trouble. If you cross the line, I can't protect you."

"No promises," he murmured, eyes fathomless in the morning light. He reached into his pocket. "Here."

He slid the folded piece of paper across the table. "What's this?"

"The name of the LLC."

She gawked. Carnival Antiquities, she read after unfolding it. "How did you get this?"

"Friend of mine," he said. "He's good with that kind of thing."

"He didn't get this through legal channels," she assumed.

"If it comes from an anonymous source, does it matter?" he asked.

She searched his face, something tingling along her spine. "Is this source a hacker?"

"He gave us a name. That's all you need to know for now."

Chapter 12

Bonhomie Masks was wedged between a thrift store and a taxidermist. The sign over the purple-and-green-striped awning looked less tired than those around it, the window display more appealing.

Célestine Clairmont's corner of the market might be small, but the curb appeal of her physical store likely kept her in business.

Sloane had done a deep dive on Clairmont, her family and her store. She hailed from the town of Charenton, home of the Chitimacha Tribe of Louisiana. She was Chitimacha by her mother, who had been a master of rivercane basketry. Her mother had clearly passed an eye for craftsmanship on to her daughter. Célestine had left high school early to attend a fine arts school in New Orleans. From there, she'd branched out into costume design and had become so adept at it that she'd been hired by several prominent theater companies.

At twenty-two, she met the infamous Sebastian LeBlanc, a native of New Orleans. A good-looking glad-hander, Sebastian was following in the family footsteps by getting into politics. His father had been a judge, his mother a city council member. His great-granddaddy had been a state senator. Even then, Sebastian had had an eye for the governor's office and conspicuously young ladies. Célestine was twelve years his junior.

His and Célestine's courtship ended with what many suspected to be a shotgun wedding. She gave birth to their first child, Sebastian "Baz" LeBlanc II, seven months later. Their first daughter, Emmanuelle, had followed eighteen months after. By the time their third child, Gabriella, was born several years after that, the marriage was on the rocks.

LeBlanc's affairs had been as numerous as they were public. His mistresses trended young, most of them barely of legal age. Then Gabriella had died in a hit-and-run accident on her way home from school.

In the run-up to realizing LeBlanc's dream of governorship, the first stories had broken about his alleged ties to child pornography and exploitation. His opponent had used the stories to openly campaign against him. It wasn't until the disappearance of Baz LeBlanc, then sixteen, that Célestine finally divorced him. With the dissolution of his image and marriage, he lost the governor race in spectacular fashion. Formal charges and a public trial followed on the heels of that failure.

Célestine and Emmanuelle slipped away from the spotlight. Emmanuelle received her bachelor of science in social work and worked to improve the lives of vulnerable people, groups and communities. Célestine drifted away from New Orleans to Baton Rouge, where Bonhomie Masks took off. The bulk of her client base was built through online marketplaces, such as Etsy and her website storefront.

As Sloane left the car and joined Pelagie on the sidewalk, she secured her badge on her belt. Despite the heat, she fixed her blazer into place, tucking the shield out of sight. Pelagie did the same. With a history like her ex-husband's, Célestine might be resistant to talking to officers, however much she may have cooperated with authorities during the time of LeBlanc's arrest.

Bells over the door chimed as they moved into the shop. Like the online store, the shelves and displays were organized by theme. Mardi Gras was the headliner, the classic feathered half masks prominently featured on the head table along with a sign extolling the history of Mardi Gras masking. There was another sign about other masked celebrations throughout the world—Carnival in Brazil and Carnevale in Italy—along with examples from both. African masks hung alongside a wall of cosplay coverings.

Toward the back of the shop, Sloane located the subject of their visit among a small rack of animal masks. She raised the wolf mask from its stand.

It was less cumbersome than she'd thought it would be. Facing the nearby mirror on the wall, she lifted it to her face, peering at her reflection through the eye slits.

A woman appeared over her shoulder. "May I help you?"

She lowered the mask and visually identified Célestine Clairmont. She was a tall woman, rail thin and poised. Long elegant neck, shoulders drawn back in excellent posture, hands folded at the waist of a wide-leg mulberry jumpsuit. Her long dark braid was streaked with silver and hung over her left shoulder.

"You must not have read the sign," Célestine stated, raising an arm so that the bangles she wore clacked together.

Sloane glanced over to where Pelagie stood next to yet another sign—this one stating plainly that customers were to wait for an assistant to try on masks. Her partner handily pointed to it in untimely warning.

"My mistake," Sloane said, replacing the wolf mask on its stand.

Célestine's eyes never left her. "You are not here to shop for masks. Are you?"

"How can you tell?" Sloane asked.

Célestine let out a small laugh through her nose. Her lips didn't bend from their severe painted line. "I have seen my share of police."

Sloane parted her blazer to let her badge catch the light. "Agent Escarra. FBI. This is Agent Landry."

Célestine scanned the shield. Something kindled in her expression. She raised her stare to Sloane's once more. "What is the reason for this visit, Agent Escarra?"

"We believe a person of interest bought one of your custom products," Sloane said and drew the police sketch of Loup-Garou's mask from her bag. She extended it to Célestine.

Disappointment flickered in her expression. Célestine blinked several times before stepping forward and taking the sketch. After a moment's consideration, she said, "This is one of mine."

Sloane exchanged a glance with Pelagie. The latter raised her brows before Sloane fixed her attention once more on Célestine. "You're certain?"

"Quite certain," Célestine said with a nod. "The customer contacted me via the portal on my website. Their specifications were very clear. They wanted a product similar to this one," she said, gesturing toward the mask Sloane had handled. "But with some alterations. Black, not gray. The gold detailing…"

"When was this?" Sloane asked.

"I received the order during the Christmas rush," Célestine recalled. "It was one of the few orders, however, that wasn't requested before the holiday. The customer asked that it be completed for New Year's instead."

"Do you have a record of the exchange?" Pelagie asked.

"Perhaps," Célestine said. "I'd have to check."

Sloane looked around for cameras and didn't see any. "Did they pick it up in person?"

"No. It was shipped by my shop assistant. She takes care of shipping. I have a bookkeeper who handles accounts and purchases."

"Do you know how the mask was purchased?" Pelagie asked.

"I don't," Célestine said with a shake of her head. "Again, I have a bookkeeper who handles that end of things. I'm not efficient with a computer."

"How long would it take to get a copy of the invoice?" Sloane asked.

Célestine pursed her lips. "Is this a matter of urgency, Agent Escarra?"

She felt a breath away from Loup-Garou. "It is."

"Both my assistant and my bookkeeper are off today," she said. "Halloween, Christmas and Mardi Gras are our busiest seasons. The shop draws few customers between. This time of year, they're only required to come in twice a week. I can handle things without them in the meantime."

"If you could contact your bookkeeper to access that information, we would be grateful," Pelagie told her.

"All right," Célestine said cautiously. "She's visiting her sister in Lake Charles, but she should be back tomorrow morning."

"I can come back," Pelagie suggested. "Tomorrow around noon?"

"That should work," Célestine calculated.

"Thank you," Sloane said. Before Célestine could lead them to the door, she felt the tingle along her spine, remembering the woman's disappointment. "Initially, what did you believe we were here to discuss with you, Ms. Clairmont?" When the woman's lips wove together, mute, Sloane pressed, "Was it your ex-husband, Sebastian LeBlanc?"

Célestine gave an almost imperceptible sigh. Weariness coated her as she looked toward the light from the shop windows. "No."

"What then?" Sloane wondered out loud.

The woman was silent for so long Sloane didn't think she

would answer. Then her mouth parted, and she said quietly, "I thought you were here about my son."

Sloane's stomach clutched. "Baz LeBlanc."

Célestine's eyes lowered from Sloane's. "You know the story, then."

"Not all of it," Sloane admitted.

"That's the trouble, Agent Escarra," Célestine said, folding her arms across her middle. "No one seems to know all of it."

"Yet you're still looking for him," Sloane pointed out.

"What kind of mother stops looking for her child?" Célestine wondered. Grief was inlaid in the lines of her face, so apparent that Sloane wondered how she'd missed it before. "I've had to say goodbye to one child. I refuse to close the book on another."

"His missing persons case is still active?" Pelagie asked.

Célestine managed to make a snort sound dignified. She rolled her eyes. "The police. They stopped looking for him almost as soon as they started."

"Why would they do that?" Sloane asked.

Célestine's cheerless smile chilled Sloane. "Why indeed?" Moving to a display, she straightened the headdress of an elaborate Mardi Gras mask. "We could go into all the theories, but that's not why you're here. And the therapist my daughter arranged for me to see says that going down this rabbit hole is no longer a healthy avenue for me."

Sloane chose her words carefully. "Is there evidence to suggest your son is still out there?"

"I think what you're asking me is how I know my son is still alive," Célestine replied.

Sloane waited, practically on tiptoe.

"Shortly after Baz disappeared," Célestine began slowly, "my daughter, Emmanuelle, had a nervous breakdown. One could hardly blame her. She'd lost both her siblings in a short period. Add in all of Sebastian's misdeeds and the publicity that followed… She was forced to leave school to recuperate. During that time, she became pregnant. Her child, my grandson, Azael, was born the next year.

"I signed a prenup when I married Sebastian, so he took everything in the divorce," she revealed. "What was left, anyway, after the authorities came in. His family nearly took Emmanuelle and the baby before she turned eighteen. She had dreamed of going to college and furthering her education. In high school, she had the highest GPA in her class. Colleges started recruiting her early. But after she was forced to leave school, that stopped. I didn't have the means to pay for her tuition, and Sebastian was wrapped up in his own demise. She was working as a server, and I was working several jobs to pay the mortgage and daycare.

"And then, one day, out of the blue, a package arrived in the mail." Célestine stopped to gather herself briefly, straightening her spine. "It was addressed to Emmanuelle. Inside were several thousand dollars in cash and a note."

"What did it say?"

"'For Azael.'" Célestine again had to blink several times before continuing. "There was no return address, but I recognized the handwriting."

"Your son's?" Pelagie asked.

Célestine nodded. "I showed the detectives working his case. They said they tried to trace the package's origins but hit yet another roadblock. It was the same with all the ones that followed."

"How many were there?" Sloane questioned.

"They arrived randomly. There was no discernable pattern."

"When did they stop?" Pelagie asked.

Célestine raised a brow. "I never said they did."

Sloane's eyes widened. "How much money have you received from this source, total?"

"Upwards of eighty thousand," Célestine said. "There were

no more notes, after the first one. But I knew. It was enough that we could pay for Azael's preschool, then private school tuition. That allowed Emmanuelle to save up enough to attend college. I started Bonhomie. Had it not been for Baz's gifts, none of it would've been possible."

Sloane had a hard time believing that not one package had been traceable. "Police still have no leads as to his whereabouts? There've been no sightings? Nothing?"

"The detective in charge informed me five years ago that the case was no longer active."

"They closed the case?" Sloane asked, shocked.

"I gave up on the police a long time ago," Célestine told her. "After that, I hired a private investigator. He was certain Baz was alive and living under an assumed name, but that was all he could ascertain."

"Why do you think Baz hasn't come forward?" Pelagie asked. "What's stopping him?"

"The same thing that stopped the police from looking for him in the first place," Célestine answered.

It hit Sloane suddenly. "Your ex-husband."

Célestine nodded. "I believe Sebastian was behind Baz's disappearance. Further, I think he made absolutely sure Baz could never return. My ex-husband's criminal affairs go further than anyone has been able to prove. Blackmailers shadowed him. We received threats to our person, our livelihoods, our family through the years because of his nature and proclivities. Perhaps Baz discovered something. Perhaps Sebastian made him go away to stop him from revealing the truth."

"Why would he do that to his own son?" Pelagie asked. "And why wouldn't Baz come forward after LeBlanc's fall from grace?"

"Sebastian and Baz never saw eye to eye. They fought constantly. More, Sebastian made it very clear his family wasn't a priority. He was never interested in the children and only offered them affection or praise when he had something to gain from it. Whatever made him disappear, I know my son is still alive. There's nothing anyone can say to convince me otherwise."

Sloane thought it over, nibbling the inside of her lip. Baz LeBlanc had once been a missing child, just like all the victims in her caseload. Just as she had once been. "With your permission, I'd like to look into your son's case."

Célestine stared at her for a moment, stunned. Then she said, "I would appreciate it, Agent Escarra. More than I can say. And I'll call as soon as my bookkeeper returns."

She wasn't the only one who was surprised. Pelagie waited until they left the shop before saying, "Why'd you do that?"

"Had to."

"It's not just the police and PIs who've been looking for Baz LeBlanc. The media have, too. Hell, your father got involved when he was a senator. He went on television and announced he'd do everything in his power to bring Baz home."

Sloane stopped, seating her hands on her hips. Looking back at the shop, she analyzed that feeling along her spine. "I believe her."

"If he's alive, he clearly doesn't want to be found."

"She and her daughter deserve to know why," Sloane said. "Once we wrap Loup-Garou's case, I'm going to look for him."

"A lot of ants under that hill," Pelagie cautioned.

"I'll buy bug spray," Sloane assured her.

Chapter 13

"Who's your friend?"

Remy looked across the front seat of Sloane's car. "What friend?" he asked.

"The hacker," she said, not looking away from the warehouse entrance.

Night had fallen. The traffic on Carondelet had grown sparse. He'd offered to sit through the night watch with her since sleeping at the maisonette was damn near impossible. He'd spent the night before with the tools Torben had provided him. Even when he uncovered Carnival Antiquities's name, he hadn't been able to close his eyes. Not with the name Gretchen Guidry echoing through his head.

If Sloane was up against someone of Guidry's caliber, she wasn't safe. Before the morning light hit the windows, he'd known he wasn't going anywhere, even if running meant saving himself.

He'd see this case through with her—whatever the fallout meant.

He faced the warehouse once more, considering her question. "Why do you want to know?"

She'd changed from her peacock-blue pantsuit combo to black jeans and a black tee. Over her hair, she wore a Tulane Green Wave baseball cap. Her apparel may have been casual, but her lips were still painted poppy red to match the tapping nails on the steering wheel. Under the brim of the ball cap, her eyes pierced the dark night. Eyes that spurred him.

His response was as involuntary as it was inconvenient. He fought not to fidget in the passenger seat.

"Hackers leave a footprint," she explained, choosing her words carefully. "Sometimes, it's easier for one to find another's."

"Easier than the FBI's cybersecurity team?"

"I've considered bringing in a consultant."

"On le Fe's case," he asked cautiously, "or something else?"

She didn't answer.

Remy propped his elbow on the window ledge. He couldn't tell her he was the one who uncovered Carnival Antiquities. At least…not yet. Nor could he let her hire a consultant to assist with the hunt for Loup-Garou. "I don't know his name." The lie crammed in his throat like a bone, leaving him feeling more than a little raw.

"You're protecting him."

Was it frightening how well she knew him?

No, he weighed. If anything, it was comforting. Deep down, he struggled with another inconvenient truth. He wanted someone to know him—all of him. Remy Fontenot. Baz LeBlanc. Loup-Garou. All the shades of gray in between. Moreover, he longed for *her* to know him—to accept him for all he was.

There would be peace… *Christ*…so much peace in that. He hadn't known peace. Not since he'd had both his sisters next to him. Certainly not since he was forced to leave home.

But acceptance of all of it, all of him, was inconceivable. As honor bound as she was to her badge—and the purpose she got from it despite the toll it took—he knew she wouldn't be able to open her arms to him, and he couldn't blame her. Her identity and the Crimes Against Children unit were interwoven. He admired that and her, more than he could say.

She'd gone through so much. Yet here she was. Not just ambitious and unswerving but devoted to the victims—those she saved and those who had parted from this world before she could. Did she know how incredible she was? She was gunpowder running riot with his code of ethics, a constant inner battle that pitted secrets and preservation against friendship and need.

She made him hungry—fiercely hungry—for the hunter in her and everything else. The salsa dancer, hell-raiser, friend, victim, fighter, hero, sinner, saint.

He wished someone like her had been there to fight for Baz and Torben and all the other young souls Gretchen Guidry had scooped into her net.

"You know anything about the LeBlancs?" she asked out of the blue.

His head swiveled in her direction as a feeling overcame him. A slow-motion, underwater kind of feeling. "What did you say?"

"LeBlanc," she said again. "The would-be governor whose kid went missing."

Sweat gathered between his shoulder blades. He held himself still, trying to think through the noise in his head. "Why?"

She jerked a shoulder. "He came up today in conversation."

"Conversation with whom?" he probed.

"Does it matter?" she wondered out loud.

Yes, if that conversation involved her trip to Baton Rouge. He knew it had something to do with Loup-Garou. He knew because she'd been reluctant to tell him the details before departing. "I've heard of him," he said simply.

"Did you know Papá LeBlanc didn't serve a full sentence?" she asked. "He got out on good behavior. He lives here in the city still. Not as a public servant. He'll never hold office. But he's a power player. Followers fawn over him. They pay him to speak at conventions, grease their hands, kiss their babies…"

Remy knew it all. The idea made him weary. "You don't have to have decency for people to worship you."

"I get that he's charismatic," she stated. "But how do people see anything but the child exploitation?"

"A lot of people saw it as a smear campaign," Remy explained. "They think his chances for governor were foiled by his opponents. LeBlanc had enemies."

"Do you think they started the rumors about his son's disappearance?"

The sweat down his back turned cold. "What rumors?"

"That LeBlanc was behind it? That he made his son disappear?"

He struggled to breathe steadily. If she looked at him now, he wouldn't be able to hide it from her. "Maybe."

She sat up straighter. "Check out these guys."

He zeroed in on the subjects, two men walking at a brisk pace down the banquette. One scanned the street, then reached into his pocket.

"Keys," Remy said. When she reached around to check the weapon on her belt, everything inside him clenched in apprehension. "You're going to approach?"

She gave a slight shake of her head. "That'll alert their employers. We watch. No approach unless it's to shadow anyone exiting the building."

He nodded, relieved. He'd bet Larry and Curly were stacked and ready.

Remy and Sloane watched as the two unlocked the door. When it parted, a light flickered on, but the door closed before Remy could gain any impression of the entry layout. Silence hung heavy in the cab as they waited.

"Door," Remy said as soon as the large cargo door began to rise.

Sloane gripped the steering wheel in both hands as the door

rolled away to reveal the headlights of a large black BMW van. As soon as it had clearance, it started to move.

"And we're rolling," Sloane said, hitting the ignition switch.

Remy checked the van's rear suspension. "It's riding heavy."

"They're loaded down," she said, shifting the car into gear. "It's likely a transfer."

Meaning that there were victims inside the van. Remy lifted his hand to the grab bar above the passenger window instead of doing what he wanted to do—leave Sloane, beat the van to the corner, yank open the driver's door and haul the traffickers into the street for a bare-knuckled brawl.

Sloane dialed her partner with the phone on the dash. Pelagie's greeting came through the car speakers. Sloane replied urgently, "A black BMW van has departed the warehouse on Carondelet. Remy and I are in pursuit."

"I'll get dispatch on the line. Any idea what their destination may be?"

"No, but we believe they're carrying cargo."

The airport. Sloane hung back at a discreet distance as the van paused at the security gate. The driver's window lowered as the security guard left the booth, flashing credentials. The guard stepped back and waved them on. The gate parted, the driver's window went up, and the van rolled forward again.

Sloane cursed. "They're letting it onto the tarmac."

"It's likely a private plane," Remy said, painted with readiness. She saw it in the rigid line of his cheek and jaw and the coiled muscles of his arms. A spring waiting to be released. "Which means the pilot could be fueled and ready."

Sloane relayed all this to Pelagie, who was still on the line.

"Backup's right behind you."

"No flashing lights," Sloane warned. "Not yet. We don't want a hostage situation on our hands." She pulled up to the security booth. When the guard stepped out, she held up her badge. "Agent Escarra. FBI. Who's in the van?"

The guard's eyes flickered from her to the van's disappearing taillights through the chain-link fence. "The driver comes through here regularly. He's always cleared through security."

"Name," she demanded.

The guard, whose ID badge read PERRY, lifted his clipboard. "Westcott. PJ Westcott." He glanced up as a NOPD cruiser slowed to a stop behind Sloane's bumper, followed closely by a second unit.

"Open the gate, Perry," she advised.

"Do you have a—"

"Perry," his fellow security guard said from the booth, holding a phone to his ear. When Perry turned, he signaled. "They're clear. Let 'em through."

Perry lowered the clipboard as the gate whirred.

"Did you see how many people were in the van?" she asked Perry.

"Two white males, driver and passenger. I couldn't see anyone in the back. The windows were tinted."

"Any weapons?"

"Not in sight. Could have been concealed. They looked like the enforcer type."

"Which hangar?"

Perry checked the clipboard again. "Seven."

She gave a single nod before tapping the accelerator.

Remy took his SIG Sauer out and checked the chamber. "What's the plan?" he asked.

"For you not to shoot anyone," she pointed out. When he angled his head toward her, she added, "More paperwork."

"What's the real plan?"

"Avoid a hostage situation," she explained.

"Draw the sons of bitches out in the open," Remy agreed with a nod. "Have backup circle around and secure the hanger."

"Keep the plane on the ground," she added. "I've got a couple of vests in the back."

He unlatched his seat belt restraint and reached into the back seat.

She parked a marked distance away from hangar seven. Together, they strapped the bulletproof vests around themselves. She pulled her jacket on and buttoned it so the FBI letters across the front were obscured.

Before Remy could reach for the handle of the passenger door, she gripped his arm, urgency slamming into her. "Remy."

He turned back to her, frowning deeply as if he expected her to tell him to stay behind.

She lifted her hand to his face. "Don't get shot," she ordered.

A muscle in his jaw jumped under her palm. The low dash lights shone lovingly over him, casting half of him in shadow. His eyes glimmered at her. A thousand unspoken words crisscrossed between them.

Her heart flipped over. She didn't stop the impulse. Not this time. Giving into the ever-present tumble of inertia between them, she leaned across the console.

He didn't move as her mouth skimmed lightly across his. But his eyes closed tight. She hooked her hand around the nape of his neck, wanting to be closer, to share this space, this breath with him.

When still he didn't move, she shied away. She waited until his eyes opened before offering an explanation. "I just wanted to do it once," she whispered. She forced a smile when he only stared at her, every muscle in his face drawn tight. He hadn't taken a breath since she leaned in. The stillness unnerved her.

She stroked the back of her knuckles across his rigid cheek before turning away to push the door open. Taking several gulps of thick night air, she took out her weapon and greeted the officer of the K-9 unit with a nod, recognizing him. "Sergeant Seller."

"Agent Escarra," he returned. He scanned Remy, who braced himself behind her. "Me and Officers Pachette, Isaacson, and DiMonte will be your backup this evening. More squad cars are en route. Dispatch advised no lights and sirens."

"I appreciate it," Sloane said. "You've been brought up to speed on who we're dealing with?"

"At least two white males, likely armed and dangerous with possible human trafficking victims in tow."

She nodded. "This is Mr. Fontenot. He and I will approach the hangar from the front. I'll ask that two of yours proceed from the sides and back us up if the subjects fire. Two others can circle around back and secure victims inside the vehicle or plane."

"There's a private jet in that hangar," one officer said, pointing. The ID tag on his NOPD vest identified him as DIMONTE. "Pilot may be armed."

"The plane will need to be swept, like the vehicle," she pointed out. "This is all the intel I have for the time being."

Sergeant Seller wrapped his hands around his gun belt. "We're with you."

As Sloane and Remy advanced toward the hangar on foot, she asked him to walk behind her to the left. He ignored this, choosing to position himself at her hip instead.

"Let me do the talking," she told him in no uncertain terms.

"You can do all the talking you want, boo," he said, his voice low. The van was parked underneath the wing of a small, streamlined white jet. "We both know how this is gonna end."

One subject came into view. He saw them, and his body pivoted, primed to meet them. His stance told Sloane everything she needed to know about how equipped he was to do so. "Can I help you?" he barked.

She held up her identification quickly before lowering it. "Airport security. We're going to need to check your paperwork once more."

"We've already been through security," the man said. He had wide-set eyes and wore a leather jacket over impressive shoulders. He looked like he could take down a bull. Behind him, his partner peered around the van. He stepped out but didn't walk to them.

She made a gimme motion with her hand. "The tower can't authorize takeoff until we double-check," she said.

He narrowed his eyes. "What's this about?" he asked, reaching around his belt.

Sloane tensed, doing the same.

Remy's gun was already in his grip, one foot in front of the other. "Show me your hands!" he commanded.

"You're not airport security," the man barked. "You're a cop."

Over his shoulder, Sloane saw the other assailant move forward. He stepped from the hangar.

Officer DiMonte took him out on a flying tackle. The man's grunt winged into the night.

The first man turned. Sloane moved quickly, grabbing one wrist, then the other. "Down on the ground," she ordered, ignoring the bite of pain from the wound on her arm.

He struggled, cursed.

With one hard kick to the side of his knee, Remy made him buckle over sideways with a shout. As Sloane restrained him, Remy disarmed him.

"Pat him down," she requested. She moved forward, low to the ground, as DiMonte did the same to the other assailant.

Sergeant Seller stepped out of the plane. "Clear," he called.

Officers Isaacson and Pachette were checking the van. One of them shouted an all-clear.

Sloane sprinted the rest of the way to the van as they opened the back doors.

The first victim was female. She was wearing a blindfold, but her arms were free.

"It's all right," Seller said as he assisted her. "New Orleans Police. You're safe."

"How many?" Sloane asked as Isaacson took off the girl's blindfold.

"Six," Pachette said, going around to the other side of the van.

As the girl blinked in the bright lights of the hangar, Sloane took her hand. "I'm Agent Escarra. What's your name?"

She wasn't any older than fifteen. She swallowed, her lips dry and chapped. "Corrine. My name's Corrine." Her eyes slammed shut, and she grimaced. "I'm sorry. I think… I think they put something in my Coke."

"It's okay," Sloane said, patting her arm and drawing her forward as others disembarked from the van. God, they were all so young. "We're going to get you out of here, Corrine."

Corrine's chin trembled. "They said they would give my friend Keesha and me a place to stay and comp our meals while we were volunteering for them. They said it would look good on our college applications. They won't tell me what they did with Keesha." A tear rolled down her cheek. Her shoulders shook with sobs. "I talked her into this, and I don't know where she is…"

"We'll find her," Sloane said and gathered Corrine in a hug as she continued to shake. "I promise we'll find her. Are any of you hurt? Is anyone injured?"

"I don't think so," Corrine said, her voice dropping to a whisper.

"Okay," Sloane murmured. "I'm still going to transfer you to the closest hospital."

"I don't want to go. I'm scared."

"It's just routine," she vowed. Then she swore under her breath. These men had promised Corrine, Keesha and likely the other girls enough. They didn't need more words dressed up as promises. "I'll go, too."

"You will?"

Sloane nodded. As she put her arm around Corrine's shoulders, leading her out of the hangar, she caught sight of Remy.

He was standing at the door to a squad car, having assisted DiMonte with loading the two traffickers. He stepped forward. "Everyone okay?"

Sloane rubbed Corrine's arm. "I'm taking them to the hospital."

He gauged the girl's condition. Then his gaze shifted to Sloane. "Want me with you?"

She would've sighed over him and his knowing eyes if they'd been anywhere else. "Affirmative."

He gave a solitary nod of understanding before he fell in step with her.

"Thank you," she murmured, wanting to reach for him.

He didn't turn his head. She heard the low rumble of his answer, regardless. "Always."

Chapter 14

"Happy birthday, niña!"

Sloane rubbed the sleep out of her eyes. Her mother might live two thousand miles away, but she never failed to call the morning of Sloane's birthday. At the exact moment of her birth.

5:02 in the morning.

"Thank you, Ama," Sloane replied.

"I have a surprise for you!"

Is it five more hours of sleep? Sloane wondered, blinking at the windows where the light was only at its first blush. She had been at the hospital with Corrine and the five other girls—Sofia, Amaya, Luna, Amelia, and Genovie—until two in the morning. She'd known it would be an early one. The traffickers had been IDed as Elias Caldwell and Jermaine Olivante. PJ Westcott had been an alias, the papers, falsified.

Excellent fakes, Pelagie had said when she arrived at the hospital to see the victims. *Just like Carnival Antiquities, who own the private plane, too. It's a shell company.*

They both would take a run at Caldwell and Olivante this morning before Pelagie's trip back to Baton Rouge to retrieve Loup-Garou's purchase information from Célestine Clairmont's bookkeeper and to interview the woman about what she remembered about the purchase and the specifics of the custom order. Sloane planned to spend the better part of the day trying to find out more about the shell company, the murder of Ray de le Fe and anything Caldwell and Olivante knew about Loup-Garou. All before the party her family had arranged tonight at Salón Tropicana.

As she rose, she crossed to the closet and pulled out her robe. She couldn't go walking around in her nightie with Remy next door.

Not with the taste of him, dark and forbidden, still on her lips.

She suckled her lower lip as the sensation took hold. Warmth swept her, wakening her in ways she couldn't afford to be. He was likely up, dressed, cooking…

She needed to put it all back in the box before she had to confront his bedroom eyes once more. "A surprise?" she asked her mother, touching the garment bag with Abuela's dress inside. It had been altered. As she'd donned it in front of the tailor, it had felt too delicate for her skin. It was stunning, yes, but it belonged to another time. Another place. Another person.

It and the smile on Abuela's face had made her feel like an imposter.

She toyed with the silk skirt of the salsa dress she'd bought, the one she'd seen in a boutique window. The one that had fit when she tried it on. It had made her feel like that girl again— the one before Mexico, alive, fierce and free. The one who'd known how to have fun without letting it go too far.

She'd lost that girl. Nothing could bring her back. But the dress… Seeing it in the mirror had made Sloane feel light inside again.

It was the kind of dress Abuela wouldn't be caught dead in.

She sighed and closed the closet, belting her robe.

"Go downstairs," her mother told her. "It should have arrived by now."

"What delivery person did you bribe to get up this early?" Sloane wondered fondly as she padded down the stairs.

Remy wasn't at the stove—or the sink. She listened to the house for a moment, hearing nothing.

He was gone?

She felt a jab in the ribs and pressed the heel of her hand over the space.

Was it because she'd kissed him? They hadn't spoken after they left the hospital. Not a word. No mention of the kiss or the events of the night. She could blame it on fatigue. It was better than what she feared it was.

Regret.

She strode to the door and opened it.

A thundering wave of music hit her. She was startled back a step at the sight of two drummers, two trombonists, two trumpeters, a tubist and two saxophonists, all wiggling in shimmering gold Speedos to the beat.

As her mother's laughter spilled into her ear, Sloane endured a zippy blast of the birthday song.

At the end of the rendition, the band dove straight into "When the Saints Go Marching In" and, one by one, filed out of the courtyard, scantily clad man buns swinging as they went.

"Did you like it?" her mother chirped.

"It was wonderful," Sloane said, closing the door. She slid the bolt into place and leaned against it. "Gracias."

"I had to do something special. I'm tied up on set. That new telenovela I was telling you about. But I couldn't miss my baby's birthday. You know how much I love you."

"I do," Sloane assured her. "I love you, too."

"Have fun at your party, niña. I'll call you later."

"Okay, Ama," Sloane agreed and let out a long breath, sinking to a chair at the table after her mother hung up.

She confronted her empty house.

She'd knowingly crossed a line last night. It wasn't any wonder he split. She'd gambled right for wrong. But she gained something she'd always wanted. The feel of his mouth. The taste of his lips.

She closed her eyes. Other than not having the sight of him here in her kitchen, she regretted nothing.

A box in the center of the table caught her attention. It was flat, black and tied with a silver ribbon. She saw a slip of paper beneath it.

Lifting the note first, she smoothed it flat across the table and found Remy's relaxed penmanship.

Hey boo,
Sorry I couldn't be with you this morning. I overheard you and your partner discussing Carnival Antiquities at the hospital last night. I've taken the information to my friend. You know the one. I'll see what we can turn up before the end of the day.

Don't be pissed at me for missing your birthday breakfast. I left you something lost. Check the microwave. Make a wish.
Remy

Sloane debated what to open first—the box or the microwave. Her stomach growled, so she crossed to the counter and yanked open the appliance door.

Inside, a plate was covered in a blue-and-white-checkered cloth. As she set it on the table, she took a peek underneath. With a gasp, she snatched it off. "Beignets." She grinned; a candle crowned the plump one in the middle.

He must have gone out early. She wondered how far he'd had to trek to find someone open at that hour. She pinched the corner of one pastry and licked the powdered sugar off her thumb and forefinger. Her waistline would suffer, but she was going to gorge herself.

The box caught her eye again. She pulled it closer and pried at the ribbon's knot. When it loosened, she freed the box and opened it slowly.

A pendant lay in a bed of white tissue paper. Rose gold flashed under the kitchen lights. In the center, the portrait of Our Lady of Charity was surrounded by ornamental diamonds at each point—north, south, east and west.

Her fingers fell away before they could touch it. Abuelo had given her a similar pendant at her quinceañera. Though she hadn't exactly modeled herself after the patron saint, Sloane had worn the necklace religiously.

She'd worn it to Mexico. A few weeks after her abduction, she escaped the house where the Solaros had held her in order to find Pia or Grace. She'd found Pia in Jaime Solaro's hacienda. Before they could escape together, Jaime had caught them.

The necklace had dug into Sloane's neck as he used it to force her, screaming, away from Pia, then into the garage where he beat her, breaking her leg. Afterward, he'd taken the necklace off her, kissed it and slipped it over his head.

She'd told Remy about the necklace once in a moment of weakness. As he sat by her bedside in the hospital the night her date slipped roofies into her drink, she broke down. She'd had to tell others how her leg had been broken and who had done it. But she hadn't had the heart to reveal what happened to the necklace.

Dampness touched the back of her hand. She pulled it away from her face, shocked to see the wetness on it. Swiping her cheeks, she felt hot tears there.

Damn it, Remy. He'd known what a gift like this meant. He knew exactly. Another reason he'd made himself scarce this morning. If he were here… If he had lifted the chain from the box, opened the clasp and hung it around her neck…she'd have done more than kiss him. He'd have wound up flat on his back on her breakfast table with her all over him.

After locating a lighter, she flicked its teeth against her thumb and touched the flame to the wick of the candle in the beignet.

Make a wish.

A smile stretched the bounds of her face. Hell, if she was going to wish for anything...

She blew out the candle. Then promptly disappeared in a cloud of powdered sugar.

The farmhouse sat on a rise. Remy had bought it after years of the nomadic lifestyle required by someone who had multiple lives.

Except for that job for the Escarras, he hadn't lived in Louisiana since shedding his identity as Baz LeBlanc. He'd gone east, bouncing from city to city, working several jobs before earning his GED and college credits. The past had felt like it was breathing down his neck...so he'd shaved his head and joined the navy. He'd needed to embody someone else. The military had handily made him someone else.

He did his first tour overseas. When he returned and was asked to re-up, he signed on for BUD/S, a grueling twenty-six-week program to prepare candidates for the SEALs. He hadn't expected to make it. Only twenty percent of BUD/S candidates completed Hell Week anyway. He just wanted to see if he had the mental toughness to survive.

He not only survived, he'd been chosen to join the SEAL teams. There, he found the family he'd sorely missed.

With his teammates, he'd been dropped into militarized zones. He'd executed amphibious landings, reconnaissance and demolition. He'd been shot at behind enemy lines and conducted shipboard assaults. He'd trained, raided, captured, killed.

There had been women, few and far between, to stave off the loneliness he felt when he wasn't training or overseas. And in his downtime, he went back to the thing he'd always been good at—the thing he'd thought Gretchen Guidry had hired him to do. He worked freelance as a hacker. It hadn't mattered who the job was for. He'd funneled the payments back to his mother and sister in Louisiana because they needed it more than he did.

He'd lost brothers-in-arms and brought their bodies home to their families. He'd mourned them as he still mourned his sister.

After losing his closest friend, Petty Officer Benjamin Zaccoe, in a mission gone wrong, he grappled with the same sense of blame and responsibility he had after Gabbie's death. He'd decided it was time to take an indefinite sabbatical from the SEALs until he could get his head and heart lined up again. To pay the bills, he accepted his first bodyguard job.

Apparently, he'd done well. Word of his services got around. He mostly turned high-profile clients down, not wanting to be seen in paparazzi photos, though he had guarded a CEO, a wealthy executive and an online influencer.

The jobs that mattered most to him, however, were those guarding domestic violence victims. Several of them went back to the partners they originally sought to keep at arm's length. When one of them died, he was ready to throw in the towel.

Then fate intervened and Sloane's mother contacted him. At long last, he'd returned home to New Orleans.

Remy parked the Jeep under the carport behind the farmhouse. He shut off the engine, then stepped out, absorbing the quiet.

When he wasn't on a mission or working a job, he used to migrate to cities. They'd felt safer. Even after so many years, he'd still been fighting to disappear. After losing Zaccoe and then the domestic violence victim on his watch, Remy had felt exhausted, body, mind and soul. When he met Sloane, he'd seen a kindred spirit. Saving her had felt like saving himself all over again.

After Senator Escarra dismissed him and Remy went to Mexico to convince himself that she could defend herself, he decided to disappear once more. Instead of a city, he chose the country. And for the first time, he'd been able to embrace the quiet and solitude.

The bulk of the time was spent with his thoughts. He felt something like peace here.

The farm sat on seventy-five acres. He hadn't done anything with them or the paddock and stables, but the possibilities were there when he was ready. He'd considered giving it all up—bodyguarding, hacking, those ever-present thoughts of going back into the military. For the first time, he'd felt the need to put down some roots. To build something of his own on his own land under the Louisiana sky.

But he'd kept tabs on his mother and sister and kept himself apprised of his father's doings, and Gretchen Guidry's until her death. He'd known Torben had become a member of the NOPD and was working Missing Persons. Remy had contacted him, and they'd become reacquainted.

Remy let himself into the farmhouse. The familiar smells of old pine floors and the herbs hanging in the kitchen windows struck him. He tossed his bag aside and took a moment to breathe it all in. The quiet wrapped around him, calming the noise in his head.

Brotherhood was born of more than blood and war. His and Torben's bond was forged long ago when they'd been Gretchen Guidry's playthings.

That bond was still unshakeable.

Torben had kept Remy in the loop about the human trafficking situation in and around New Orleans. Guidry's network may have dissolved after her death, breaking up into sectors, but signs had been there for some time that someone else was attempting to take her place. Someone making it damn near impossible for authorities to apprehend or even prosecute those under their employ.

Loup-Garou was born out of back-porch speculation. *What if*, Torben had suggested, *someone took matters into their own hands?*

Like Bruce Wayne? Remy had ventured, amused by the idea of a backwoods Dark Knight.

Why not? Torben had challenged. And Remy had known by looking at him it wasn't a joke. *They won't stop trafficking. Not without someone sending a message.*

Remy checked the doors and the cameras around the property. Nothing had been tampered with. There were no alerts of uninvited guests other than the doe who lived with her fawns in the spit of woods he could see from the den windows.

Spots are disappearing, he observed as he watched the fawns forage in the security footage.

Those disappearing spots made him think of the freckles once scattered across Sloane's cheekbones. His pulse picked up as he remembered the night before.

He hadn't pulled away when she kissed him. Not because he'd been frozen. Because he'd wanted it. He'd wanted her so badly it felt like an affliction. The effort not to move, not to touch her, had made him curl his hands into his knees.

I just wanted to do it once.

He groaned as the answering heat coiled around his navel. If they'd been anywhere else, he would have let her take more. He'd have taken her.

It was a five-hour drive to the farmhouse from New Orleans, but he could have told her about the trip face-to-face. He could've given her the beignets and the gift in person and wished her a happy birthday.

He was dodging her. It was dangerous being alone with Sloane.

He checked his office, where the blank-faced screens of the computer bay reflected back at him. Dropping his bag there, he moved to the bedroom and opened the closet. He shoved aside clothes on hangers and found the lead-lined door of the gun cabinet built into the wall. Pressing his thumb to the scanner, he waited for a series of beeps, then opened the heavy door.

The golden ears of the Loup-Garou mask flashed a greeting as light hit them.

He hadn't come for that. After making sure his stacks of cash had been left as they were, he palmed one of the portable hard drives he'd stashed there, shut the safe, shoved the clothes back into place and closed the door. Then he crossed into the office and settled into the ergonomic chair at his desk.

He'd learned to hack out of boredom. A junior high friend's nefarious big brother had shown him the basics, and he'd dedicated long hours to honing them. The first time he accessed his father's financial records, he'd nearly wet himself with excitement.

What he'd found had whetted his curiosity.

He got skilled enough, and knowledgeable enough, to trace the cyber breadcrumb trail of Sebastian LeBlanc's wrongdoings. Before long, Remy had known who his father was paying, when he paid them, how much and how often. *Blackmail*, he'd learned. *For what?*

A part of him wished he hadn't gone looking for answers. What would he have made of himself if he hadn't? Would he still be Baz LeBlanc, a disgraced politician's son? Would he be in contact with his mother and Emmanuelle? Would he have been able to help them navigate everything they'd had to endure?

He could have known his nephew and watched him grow up. He could've helped Emmie raise him.

If you don't leave, who's to say what happened to you won't happen to her? You're responsible for the death of one sister. You want both of them on your conscience?

Remy pushed the words away and booted the computers. He watched the clouds grow stern on the horizon as they hummed to life.

He'd seen his father only once in person over the past twenty years, while doing the job for the Escarras. The political arena in New Orleans was small. He'd known guarding the senator's daughter would put him in contact with the state's most notorious candidate for governor.

New Orleans society had welcomed Sebastian LeBlanc back from prison—the executives, party leaders, hoteliers and casinos. Where Sebastian LeBlanc went, crowds and television crews followed. The LeBlanc name still meant news and commerce. For many, it was entertainment.

While leaving a club one night on Sloane's heels, Remy had seen Othello, his father's longtime bodyguard, walking out of the topless bar across the street. It was impossible to miss the man as he was six-eight and two hundred and sixty pounds. Remy had once known him enough to testify that the guy was a teddy bear, one he'd admired and who had shown nothing but courtesy toward him, Emmie, Gabbie and their mother.

Remy's father had exited the bar behind Othello.

Remy had stood there, watching his father light his cigar, as fit and lean and striking a figure as ever. Prison had taken nothing from him but time and opportunity. Someone asked for his autograph. He'd smiled and obliged.

Sloane had started down Bourbon. Remy had kept her close at his side, even when he realized that Othello and his father were strolling along in the same direction.

Sloane had paused on the banquette after losing one of her high heels. Remy had stopped to pick it up. He'd glanced around to see if Othello and his father were still coming.

They were right in front of him.

He'd stood, unable to turn away. After all those years, he needed the bastard to face him.

Sebastian LeBlanc had looked right at him. He'd smiled, the polite affluent smile of someone for whom greeting the everyman on the street had brought him to the brink of governorship. And he passed by without a hint of recognition.

There had been a small space of a moment where Remy thought Othello had made him. The man's eyes narrowed on him before he followed LeBlanc through the crowd.

It wasn't just the high-and-tight haircut or the tattoos that made Remy unrecognizable to those he'd once called family. He was taller, harder, leaner, his experience stamped across his face. He'd never felt further away from who he'd been than he had on Bourbon that night.

Baz LeBlanc was really and truly dead.

It hadn't made him feel safe. It made him feel cold. The loneliness had come screaming back. Remy had felt invisible. He buried himself in the Escarra job, in protecting Sloane, to find himself again.

In his farmhouse office, Remy hard-lined the portable hard drive into the computer and brought up the data on-screen. Then he entered in a search for Carnival Antiquities.

When he first considered Torben's suggestion that someone take matters into their own hands where human trafficking in New Orleans was concerned, Remy had started digging. As he had with all his father's old offenses, he saved the information, filing it away for his own purposes.

He knew he'd seen the name Carnival Antiquities before. It didn't take him long to find out where—under the name Gretchen Guidry.

He leaned back in his chair as the name stared at him from the screen.

The shell company had been founded by Guidry Security. They'd laundered money through it—funds appropriated from their lucrative prostitution business under the guise of their aboveboard home security company. By the time Remy came into the organization, there had been a Guidry Security sign in every yard, from the Gulf Coast to Arkansas.

With a few keystrokes, Remy had Carnival Antiquities' history on-screen. It had been sold to the LLC in Delaware after Gretchen's death when her husband struggled to fill her shoes. The organization had tanked. The prostitution and trafficking cells each went their own way, leaving the husband to sell the family holdings to stay afloat.

Who bought someone else's defunct shell company? It didn't make sense. Unless, of course, that person wanted to reclaim Gretchen's status by spinning the same web of assets and resurrecting her underground syndicate.

The question was who?

Remy rolled up his sleeves, laid his fingers over the keys and dug in.

Chapter 15

"The mask's purchase was made via Cash App. I've got an account number, no name," Pelagie announced, holding up a folder as she breezed through the warehouse on Caronde-let. "May take some legwork, but we should have one soon."

"Did you get an address?" Sloane asked, motioning a crime-scene tech into the surveillance room.

"Mm-hmm. Jackson, Mississippi. The package was made out to Seb White."

"Who's that?" Sloane asked, knowing her partner had already done a search.

"No idea," Pelagie said, widening her eyes. "Guy doesn't exist. At least not off paper. The address is of an apartment. I called the Jackson police, who agreed to check the place out for us. Old building. No cameras. Very little security. They talked to the super, who informed them that the unit in question is leased but rarely visited. He's never gotten a good look at the tenant, but he gave a vague description."

"Read it to me," Sloane requested as Pelagie opened the Notes app on her phone.

Pelagie donned her reading glasses. They perched on the bridge of her aquiline nose. "White male, possibly Hispanic, over six feet tall. Somewhere around two hundred pounds. Maybe two-twenty. He gave better details on the tenants' ve-hicle."

Sloane perked up at the news. "Oh?"

"Yeah, the super's a car guy, so he noticed the Jeep. Newer model—probably a 2024 Rubicon. He said it was murdered out—all black. Lifted. Mud tires. I've already got tech culling a list of that make and model between here and Mississippi."

"Did the super get the plate?" Sloane asked.

"No. And there are no street cameras in that area, either."

"When was the last time the super saw him?"

"New Year's. Says he remembered because he wished the guy a happy one and got no reply."

"Huh," Sloane said thoughtfully. "I'd like to check the apartment out myself. For now, let's work the Cash App angle, see if something pops there."

"This is for you," Pelagie said, holding out the folder, "from your friend at Bonhomie Masks."

Célestine Clairmont. Sloane opened the file and found a copy of a missing persons report. The photocopied photo of Baz LeBlanc was grainy at best. She got a vague impression of a sharp-boned youth with defiant eyes and dark curls.

Skimming through the folder, she discovered a timetable of the cash envelopes delivered to Emmanuelle LeBlanc's son. A copy of the handwritten note was there, too, in tidy print.

For Azael.

Sloane noticed a tiny symbol underneath the lowercase *A*. It looked like a tree, a cypress by the shape of its base, with trunk and branch serving as a cross. "I've seen this symbol before," she mused.

Pelagie studied it through her specs. "It's Chitimacha. The cypress appears like this in their tribal logo. In the official version, this cross branch here is a pipe representing peace."

"Clairmont is Chitimacha," Sloane mused. "This gives weight to her theory that her son's behind the cash gifts."

"How's he coming up with all that cash? Money like that gets people's attention."

"Unless he's been earning it through back channels," Sloane considered.

Pelagie lifted her chin. "Maybe the apple didn't fall far from the tree."

Sloane thumbed through a private detective's dossier of findings. As she reached the back of the folder, something loosened from the pages and spilled to the floor.

She knelt and found more photographs—school pictures of Baz LeBlanc through the years, from gap-toothed kindergartner to a rogue-faced teen. A lopsided smile struck her. It had trouble written all over it. She saw more of his mother in Baz's face than his father.

She stuffed the photos back in the folder, alongside an obituary for Gabriella LeBlanc.

...survived by her father, Sebastian, mother, Célestine, and siblings, Sebastian LeBlanc II and Emmanuelle...

Newspaper clippings from the funeral service and the public procession that followed were also enclosed.

Sloane squinted at a procession photo of Célestine behind a black veil with her two surviving children on either side of her, their arms linked. Though Baz's face was downcast, he towered over his mother and sister. She got an impression of long limbs and a square jaw limned in barely harnessed tension.

That same odd sensation along her spine surfaced again.

"Find anything here?" Pelagie asked, surveying the warehouse.

"Maybe," Sloane said. "Computers need to be searched. There was surveillance throughout the building and the holding space where they locked the victims upstairs, even in the bathroom."

Pelagie's anger rarely rose to the forefront. Sloane saw it now. It stamped her cheeks pink. Her hands balled on her hips, and her lips pressed inward. "They watched them in the bathroom?"

"Yes," Sloane said tightly.

Pelagie let her breath eke out through flared nostrils. She shook her head. "Of all the crap we see on this job, Sloane, I shouldn't be shocked. Not by anything. But now and then something like this rolls around and…"

Sloane nodded. "I know."

Pelagie shoved her hands through the wild coils of her hair, staring hard at the closed blinds over the window as she collected herself. "It's your birthday. Let me take you to lunch at Arnaud's. We'll stuff our faces with shrimp and oysters, then go back to the office and start cracking on the Cash App account."

"Thanks," Sloane said with a smile. "I'm starving."

Pelagie's phone rang. She answered on the third ring. "This is Agent Landry. Yes, sir?" She sent Sloane a long, searching look. "Yeah, we can be there in under an hour. Thank you." As the call ended, she made a face. "Rain check. A suspect from the brothel in Abalone wants to talk."

"Which one?"

"McBride."

"First name Holler," Sloane recalled. "He and his counterparts have been buttoned up. What changed his mind about talking?"

"Looks like we're going to find out," Pelagie said as they moved out.

Special Agent in Charge Brick Houghton met them at the correctional facility where McBride and his men were being held without bond. A brick of a man with a perpetual sunburn, Houghton was a native Chicagoan who had yet to adjust to the

blistering summer sun on the Gulf Coast. Sloane knew him
to be a fair man but an unbendable one.

He greeted them with, "Ballistics report."

She took the document from him. "From Abalone?"

"Yes." He gave an almost imperceptible sigh. "It's not what
I anticipated."

Pelagie read over Sloane's shoulder. "Has anyone given
McBride this information?"

"No," Houghton said. "We held off so you two could do
your song and dance with him."

Sloane nodded, handing the paper back after another scan.
"Understood, sir."

"I'll be watching from here," he said, pointing to the door
to the observation room next to Interrogation. "If you need
me to step in, give me a signal."

"Will do," Pelagie agreed. When Houghton disappeared
behind the observation room door, she turned to Sloane. "You
want to take the lead on this?"

"I can," Sloane said. "Ready?"

Pelagie's grin was sour. "Let's crack this acorn."

Sloane moved through the door, Pelagie at her heels, and
found Holler McBride in a prison jumpsuit cuffed to the table.
His thinning streaks of hair lay flat against his head like fingers splayed too wide apart. His flat eyes watched them warily
as Sloane positioned herself at the table in front of him and
Pelagie leaned against the wall in a relaxed stance.

One of his eyes had been pressed shut by a large purple
bruise. Another bloomed, ugly and fresh, on his fleshy jaw.
These weren't injuries he sustained from Loup-Garou. The
vigilante didn't employ his fists to get the job done. McBride
had been beaten by fellow inmates. Child traffickers and pedophiles were often targeted on the prison block.

Sloane understood why he'd changed his mind about talking. "Mr. McBride. I'm Agent Escarra. This is Agent—"

"Don't care who you are," he drawled. "Let's just get on with it."

Sloane sat back. This acorn was surly. "You wanted to speak to the agents in charge," she indicated.

Holler squared his shoulders over the table's edge, scowling. "You confiscated the plane."

Sloane raised a brow. "You heard that, huh?"

"Word gets around, even in here."

"We took the plane," she confirmed.

"The heat's off us in Abalone, then."

"You're still facing charges, Mr. McBride," Pelagie pointed out. "You were holding children against their will. One of them was found dead at the scene."

"I didn't have nothing to do with that."

"Who did?" Sloane asked. "Who killed her?"

"One customer got a little overzealous, if you know what I'm sayin'. She got away from him, went out the window. Booker hunted her down. Took care of it."

"Terry Booker killed Esther Fournier?" Sloane asked.

"Didn't know her name. I never bother with any of their names. Sometimes the customer's got a name picked out for them anyway," McBride said with an indifferent shrug.

Sloane felt herself drifting off and away, back to Mexico. She'd been called other names, too. The Solaros had avoided calling her or the other girls by name at all. It was a dehumanizing tactic.

After the first two weeks, she'd longed for someone to speak her name. *Anyone.*

She blinked her way back to the present and found her arms locked across her chest, one hand around the pendant beneath the collar of her blouse. Clearing her throat, she shifted forward, placing both hands together on the table in front of her. "What can you tell me about the night of Loup-Garou's raid?"

McBride took a beat to think back. "The little guy came around about seven."

"What little guy?"

"The funny one with the feather on his hat."

"Ray de le Fe?" Pelagie supplied.

"That's the one," McBride said. He looked beadily from her back to Sloane. "We heard he got his throat cut. That true?"

"Back to the brothel," Sloane redirected. "Le Fe came in around seven. Then?"

"He dropped off the oxy. Last customer left about ten." He scratched his forehead, squinting into the past. "Yeah. 'Bout ten. It was a slow night. I told the kids to get to their quarters. Lights out at eleven unless we got customers. Then the power dropped. Pitch-black. We sent le Fe out to get the generator going, then Booker took out his gun. We knew about them other raids and had some idea what was coming. We heard something outside. Booker opened the door and got himself tackled before he could get a shot off. Couldn't see for nothing. Gun kept going off."

"Whose gun?" Sloane asked.

"Didn't know until I came out of it. Got hit by a Taser. When I came to, the police were there and Booker was dead. I figured the wolfman did it."

"You didn't have a weapon on you before you were disabled?" Sloane wanted to know.

"Nope."

"Do you have any other information about that night?"

He shook his head. "Don't think so."

"Okay," Sloane said. She spread her hands apart. "Now tell us the real story."

McBride's face fell. "I just did. I cooperated like I said I would."

"You lied," she pointed out.

"Who says?"

"Ballistics," she answered. "Gun residue was recovered from your hands and clothes. More, your fingerprints were found on the weapon that killed Booker."

"The hell they were. The wolfman killed him. He should be the one behind bars. Why would I shoot my partner?"

"It was dark," Sloane restated. "You could've gotten nervous, trigger-happy. The only gun that was discharged after Booker's misfire was yours."

The muscles of McBride's jaw jumped. His face darkened. "Son of a bitch," he hissed, rattling his cuffs against the tabletop with a frustrated clatter.

"It's my turn to talk," Sloane told him.

"I ain't got nothing else to say," he claimed.

"Good, then you can listen," she said. "You knew that girl was killed. That makes you eligible for conspiracy to murder."

"I didn't kill anybody!"

"Furthermore, I've got seven victims in the hospital who're all willing to talk if it means sentencing you and your men. If you're going to give us any more information, it'd better be before we take another run at your men and they roll on you first."

He dropped his face to his hands.

Sloane looked to Pelagie, who shrugged and nodded to the door. She counted to thirty before standing. "Very well, Mr. McBride."

She got halfway to the door before he let out a quiet, "Wait." It took him another minute before he lifted his head. "I can give you names."

"Names?"

"Customers. Suppliers. That sort of thing." He lifted his head finally. "But you got to understand. I need protection. They got reach in here, same as everywhere else, and I don't want to wind up like the little guy with the feather in his hat."

Sloane thought about it. "We can arrange for protection.

But you've got to give us everything, McBride. We want to know everyone involved in this, from the top."

"It's stacked. People at the top are insulated. I do know one name. It's a big one. He's been in on it from the beginning."

"As what?" Pelagie asked.

"Name it, he's done it. He handles the books, skims his cut off the top. He brings in kids, too. Part of the racket he's got going on."

"What racket?" Sloane pushed.

"Rallies. Political. They come in as volunteers. He gets to know them. He's got a way about him. Makes them let their guard down, trust him. From there, it's a cakewalk to the warehouse on Carondelet."

Volunteers. Corrine had mentioned volunteering when she had explained how she had wound up in the van at the airport. Sloane realized she was holding her breath. "Name," she demanded.

"You know him. Everybody knows him. It's that LeBlanc guy. 'Hands-on LeBlanc.'"

"Sebastian LeBlanc?" Pelagie asked.

"That's him."

Sloane exchanged a glance with Pelagie. "Are you certain?" she asked.

"Dead sure," McBride said with a bob of his head. "Seen him with my own eyes. He comes to visit them in Abalone. Likes to try out the merchandise."

"I'll be damned," Pelagie muttered under her breath.

It could be a spectacular lie. McBride had lied about Booker's slaying. He'd lied about the weapon in his possession. He could be lying about this—a last-ditch effort to save his own ass.

"I get my protection now?" he asked.

Sloane held up a finger. "A moment."

Pelagie opened the door, letting Sloane pass through, before closing it behind them. "Why does the LeBlanc family name keep coming up in connection with this case?" she hissed.

There was only one answer to that question. "Because whether or not McBride is telling the truth about how deeply Sebastian LeBlanc is involved, he's part of this."

The door to the observation room parted, and Houghton squeezed out. "Well, I'd say we're in a bind."

"Why's that, sir?" Pelagie asked.

"Because Sebastian LeBlanc's got all the right friends in all the right places," Houghton weighed. "We try to bring him in for questioning, they'll send their lawyers to tango with us first."

"What if we go to him?" Sloane blurted.

"You think he'll be amenable to that?" Houghton asked.

"If I can get through the door," she thought out loud, "he could be persuaded to talk."

"I don't have to tell you what happens if this goes south," Houghton told her. "LeBlanc's beloved. If word gets around, you'll be pressured out of the New Orleans field office. Is that a risk you're willing to take, Agent Escarra?"

She thought of Esther and Marlon. She thought of the girls recovered from the van last night and the countless others like Keesha who were still missing. She thought of Célestine Clairmont and her missing son.

"I am," she stated.

Remy wasn't going to dance. He'd debated whether to show up to Salón Tropicana. It would've been wiser to go straight to Sloane's place.

Then she arrived. Tan shapely legs capped by emerald heels, the rest of her draped in an unseasonable faux-fur coat.

Sloane came at him on a wave of heady perfume that nearly took him out at the knees. "I thought you left."

He leaned over her, turning his cheek against hers. It was

meant as a greeting, but he inevitably lingered. Her skin was petal soft. "You don't think much of me, do you?"

"I think of you," she returned, turning her lips to his cheek. They brushed across his stubble, inciting a thousand wayward shivers across his skin. "Too much and too often."

He wrestled with a groan, moving safely back. "I'll take your coat."

"There's a coatroom." She gestured to the door on the left. "In winter, there's usually an attendant."

He turned the handle to let her in. "Nobody anticipated you showing up as Koko the gorilla."

"Be a wise man and shut up," she advised, switching on the light.

He shut the door behind them, boxing them in. The room was long and narrow, a walk-in closet with hanging racks down the length of both walls. "I need to tell you something."

"Oh?" she asked, shrugging out of the coat.

"It's about Carnival Antiquities," he began. Then she turned to him, folding the coat over her arm.

He lost his senses.

The dress had splits in the skirt. It hung in near-sheer panels. There were cutouts above each hip. The neckline didn't leave much to the imagination. It was tied around her neck. The Our Lady of Charity pendant lay in the dip of her clavicle.

"Remy?"

"Mmm?"

"Are you okay?"

Okay? She might as well have doused him in lighter fluid. "Mmm," he managed again, fairly certain his tongue was glued to the roof of his mouth.

She sighed. "It's the dress, isn't it?"

"Mmm," he said, a little longer this time. He needed to stop staring at her décolletage before she gave him a firm round-house kick to the head. Then again, that might be precisely what he needed to snap him out of his stupor. Inside his pants, he felt hard and tight. Desire swept him, a head-to-toe assault.

"I knew I shouldn't have worn it," she said. "I can still go home and change before Abuela sees."

"Abuela." The name struck him. "What about her?"

"She wanted me to wear her dress," Sloane explained. "The one she had altered for me."

It was strange seeing Sloane so ill at ease. She had always been so confident, so comfortable in her own skin…a little too comfortable. "Sloane…"

Her eyes came to his. They fastened there. Her lips parted. "You've got the devil in your eyes, Remy Fontenot."

He had all the fires of hell inside him.

She licked her lower lip…then bit it.

He did the unthinkable. He took a step forward so the space between them shrank.

Her mouth curved into a slow, wicked smile, and she brushed the buttons of his shirt against the flat of her palm. "The devil looks good on you," she breathed, her mouth curling in a sensuous smile.

Spontaneous combustion. It was imminent.

She tipped her head back to better search his face. "Tell me how I look, Remy."

He shook his head. Stopped. No control. Damn it, he no longer had control over his body. The truth came out as a whisper. "Like gunpowder."

She hooked a finger through his collar, tugging him close. Closer. She shuffled backward, and she spilled the fur on the floor, guiding him deeper into the coat closet.

They veered left into an L-shaped turn. There, out of view of the door, she reached for his cheek with her right hand.

He deflected the touch. She couldn't touch him. That was a straight pathway to destruction.

She repeated the motion on the left side. He stopped that, too, holding both her hands between them.

She lifted herself onto her toes, smoothing her palms up his torso to his neck. Her eyelids lowered to half-mast, and her lips parted as she angled them up to his.

He must've lowered his head to her, because their mouths touched. A growl rumbled through his chest.

Her lips firmed against his, and her arms wound around him.

Suddenly possessive, his arms knotted around her waist, and he kissed her back with all the pent-up arousal he felt.

They stumbled over each other's feet. She lurched backward, toward the wall.

He cradled the back of her head, absorbing the impact from the wood panel. The kiss didn't break. Instead, they feasted on each other, bodies knit tight. His tongue tangled with hers, slipping, gliding. The heels of his hands rose steadily up the ladder of her ribs until they skimmed the swell of her breasts then back down to her waist, where he knotted the material of her dress in his fists, bringing her closer still. His erection reached diamond-hard proportions. As her hips rolled against his, he knew she could feel him, every inch of what he had going on.

A breath shuddered out of her. "Ay Dios mío, finally."

He halted all at once. Placing his hands beneath her shoulders, he picked her up, turned and placed her away from him so his back was to the wall. He stared at her—swollen mouth, soft eyes. Gorgeous and mussed and his.

No, he thought firmly. Not his. Very much not his, for so many reasons—all of which he'd remember once the blood rose back to his brain. "We aren't doing this," he grated from his throat.

She arced a single brow. "You could've fooled me, cher."

"Sloane."

"I know what it is now," she told him, "to have your hands on me. There's no coming back from that."

"Goddammit," was all he could manage.

Her panting was starting to shallow up. "Remy...what is it that you want?"

He wanted to answer truthfully. He felt the reply rising up his throat before he choked it back down. "This was never going to be us," he said. "We've always known that."

"Have we?" she asked.

He made himself continue. Made himself say it. "I have."

Pain flashed across her face. "I guess I still learn things the hard way." She squared her jaw. "You're going to have to hurt me."

He shook his head. "Don't make me do that. Sloane, please."

"Go on," she challenged. "You want this torch I can't stop carrying to burn out? You're going to have to put me down hard. Do it now, so I can quit dreaming that this could be real."

She was killing him. Death by a thousand cuts. "I don't want to hurt you."

"You've already made a fine start," she rebutted. "Come on, Fontenot. Be a man and finish it."

He lowered his face into hers and growled through his teeth, "That's not what a man is."

A knock came at the door.

She brushed by him, full-body contact.

He closed his eyes, drowning in her scent. "Sloane."

She turned at the door. "You're going to have to finish what you start. I'm done settling for anything less."

Chapter 16

Salón Tropicana was filled with all the usual suspects. Tías, tíos and primos gathered with Sloane's father and Abuela to usher in her thirtieth birthday with music, drinks and dancing.

Abuela pursed her lips at the sight of Sloane's salsa dress. Folding her shawl around her discerningly, she said little. Sloane danced with Miguel several times to please her.

"I'll get you a drink," Miguel said after the third round.

"Thanks," she said and searched for her table. Perspiration was a fine mist on her skin. She'd forgotten about what had happened in the coatroom and Remy's subsequent disappearance. Or so she told herself.

"Something's troubling you," her father said knowingly as he settled into the chair next to hers. "Are you not pleased with your party?"

"I'm having a great time," she argued. "Why aren't *you* on the dance floor?"

His expression folded. "Judith and I… We ended things."

She balked. "Papá. I'm so sorry."

"It's for the best," he said.

He didn't mean that. "You really liked her."

"I did."

"What happened?"

"Some forces are beyond our control."

Sloane darted a look in Abuela's direction. "Did she pressure you to break it off?"

"I didn't end things," Horatio told her. "Judith left."

"Why?" Sloane asked, wondering how anyone, her own mother included, could leave this man.

"She knows what family is to me," he said, turning his palm up to meet hers. Their fingers laced. "She didn't feel as if she belonged."

Sloane shook her head. "If you make each other happy, it shouldn't matter what the family thinks."

"Sometimes, a person looks for belonging their whole life. Some people never find it. But it doesn't mean that they stop looking or should. We are lucky, niña, to have been born into this family."

Why did he sound so forlorn? Regret hung about his eyes like shadows. She tipped her head to his shoulder. "I liked Judith, too. I liked how you were yourself around her." Not the former senator—or the family patron, who bore so much responsibility. Just him.

"Is that how it is with you and Remy?"

"I don't want to talk about Remy," she told him.

"All right," he agreed. He pressed her hand to the center of his chest. "Corazón. I'm always here for you."

"I know you are," she told him. He'd always been that place of belonging for her, even when she hadn't wanted it or she'd resented it. She'd been a troublesome child, and he'd loved her all the same.

Enrique took her out onto the dance floor. After that, Sloane excused herself to freshen up in the ladies' room. She took a moment at the mirror to run her finger over the ugly red graze on the back of her arm. Despite the questions she knew she would face for it, she'd left the bandage off. It felt good to let the wound breathe. The pain wasn't bad anymore unless she tweaked it like she had detaining the suspect at the airport.

When she stepped out of the bathroom into a long corridor, she froze.

Her tío Nestor stood nearby, speaking in low tones to a man in an impeccable blue suit.

The man was Sebastian LeBlanc.

Arrows of alarm raced through her, even as he nodded politely to her. LeBlanc patted Nestor on the shoulder and walked away.

She gripped her tío's elbow.

He jerked in surprise. "Santana. Where'd you come from?"

"The ladies' room," she told him. "You know Sebastian LeBlanc?"

He grimaced. "He's an old family friend."

"That's news to me," she said incisively.

His eyes lowered.

She followed LeBlanc down the corridor.

"Santana," Nestor called in warning.

Before LeBlanc could reach the side door of the club, she planted herself in his path. "Mr. LeBlanc."

He blinked at her, a slow, lazy movement of the lids. He'd taken out a cigar and held it between his thumb and first finger. "I'm not sure I've had the pleasure, Miss…"

"Escarra," she asserted. "Agent Escarra. FBI."

"Escarra," he said with some surprise. He glanced back down the corridor, where Nestor watched them at a distance. "I didn't know the Escarras were associated with the government."

"Just me," she pointed out. "I met your ex-wife recently."

"Which ex?" he asked, not perturbed in the slightest. If anything, he seemed relaxed, like a man not shaken by anything. "I currently have three."

"Célestine Clairmont," she stated.

"Célestine. How is she? Still making masks?"

"She's still looking for your son," Sloane informed him. "She's asked me to look into his missing persons case."

His shoulders lifted, then fell on a sigh as he took a gold lighter from his suit pocket. "Who hasn't, at this point?"

"You don't want your son to be found?"

"He's my son." He flashed a winning smile. "What kind of father would I be if I didn't want him home?"

Célestine Clairmont had asked something similar. Sloane had believed her question to be sincere. Something about LeBlanc's was off, charming smile or no. "If you're open to it, I'd like to ask you a few questions about his case."

"It's been twenty years, Agent Escarra," he pointed out. "It's my understanding that a quarter of missing persons cases remain unsolved, despite the police's best efforts. The colder they get, the harder they are to bring closure to."

"From the information I've gathered, I don't believe the police did give your son's case their best efforts."

His brows winged up. Despite his age, no lines appeared on his brow. Rubbing his thumb over the skin of the cigar, LeBlanc measured her. Then he glanced at her tío, who hovered within earshot.

"Would you be available for an interview?" she asked. "I'd like to hear the timeline of Baz's disappearance and the days that followed. It shouldn't take up too much of your time."

LeBlanc let the request simmer. "Very well, Agent Escarra. How about tomorrow? I'm at The Roosevelt."

"Tomorrow," she repeated, surprised he wasn't putting her off. "Does noon work for you?"

"Lunch à deux," he drawled. The smile returned. "I look forward to it, chère."

When he offered a manicured hand, she placed hers in it to seal the deal. His palm felt baby smooth. No callouses. The signet ring on his pinky pressed cold against her fingers as he closed around them and lifted her knuckles to his mouth.

"I do apologize," he said, his breath warm against her skin. "I didn't catch your first name." The corner of his mouth curled. "I assume you don't go by 'Agent.'"

Something more than unease siphoned through her. She fought the urge to back out of his sphere. There was danger there. It skittered down her arm.

She could walk away, return to her party, leave it at that. But if she had any chance of tying him to the trafficking ring—she needed him to keep his guard down. His son's missing persons case was her in. She needed LeBlanc to keep the door open, no matter his vibe. "It's Sloane," she answered.

"Unusual," he murmured. "Am I right to assume that isn't your given name?"

Her frown deepened. "No." While her mother had wanted to name her Sloane, Abuela had insisted she be given a family name like Santana. Her father had caved to pressure. However, her mother had referred to her as Sloane from birth to spite them both. Sloane came by her rebellious streak honestly.

"And to which of Ezmeralda's sons do you belong?"

"The eldest," she told him.

"The noble Horatio," he said knowingly.

He still had a hold of her hand. She gave it a small tug and was relieved when he finally relinquished it. She could still feel his words whispering across her knuckles and ignored the urge to wipe them on her skirt. "You know my grandmother?"

Again with the enigmatic smile. "As well as one can."

What the hell does that mean? Sloane thought wildly.

"I knew your grandfather, Arturo, as well. He parted this world too soon."

"He did," she agreed.

"He was well acquainted with public disgrace just as I've been," LeBlanc considered. "I'm sorry he didn't live to see his family and name vindicated. I hold a firm belief in vindication."

"Do you?"

He emitted an assenting noise, then tipped the cigar to his brow in a casual salute. "Until lunch tomorrow."

She waited until he'd gone through the door, pondering the exchange. Not once in the entire conversation had he uttered his son's name.

Nestor was still several paces away. She crossed to him. "How does Sebastian LeBlanc know Abuela by name?"

He shifted his feet. "They're old friends."

"And how am I just now learning this?" she demanded.

"LeBlanc makes it his business to insert himself in the paths of those who are wealthy and well-connected," he said. "Our family was once all of those things."

He said it with such vehemence and resentment, it would have set her back a step if she didn't know him. "You're afraid of him," she realized.

Nestor made a dismissive noise. "You're mistaken, Santana."

Before he could brush by her, she gripped his arm, bringing him to a halt. "Then why're you carrying?" She held up the Glock she'd swiped from underneath his jacket.

He frowned even as pride shimmered in his gaze. He'd taught her many things, growing up—how to fight, how to shoot, how to lift a bracelet from a woman's wrist in one imperceptible swipe. "You did that well."

Her smile wasn't meant to be friendly. "Learned from the best, didn't I?"

He gathered a breath, fighting for patience. "That shifty *cabrón* doesn't scare me."

She tapped the side of the barrel against his chest. The grip was smooth from his handling, and the gun was heavy. Fully loaded. "Then make *this* disappear."

He took the Glock, holding it like a man who knew how. "Stay away from LeBlanc. Lo entiendes?"

"Get rid of the gun," she said again, watching him closely.

He stared back for several moments before exiting the same way LeBlanc had.

Sloane watched him go, wondering what to make of him and LeBlanc and everything else.

Chapter 17

Sloane walked home, getting good and drenched in the down-pour that cooled the streets. Her dress was ruined, but the rain helped pull the cobwebs away from her mind.

It was well after 2:00 a.m. when she unlocked the door and found her house empty yet again.

She tossed her purse and keys onto the table. The empty plate of beignets was still there, along with the single birth-day candle and the empty gift box.

She opened the old pie chest by the door and pulled out one of her scrap towels. She ran it over her face and hair, then started on her arms.

The door opened behind her.

She whirled as Remy entered. He froze, rain dripping down his face.

Her heart raced at the sight of him. She swallowed. "Where have you been?" she asked, trying not to notice how his shirt clung to him.

"Out," he said simply and shut the door.

She rolled her eyes at the one-word answer. "Avoiding me much?"

"I was visiting a friend."

"The hacker?"

"Someone else."

She pointed to the pie chest. "Towels are in there."

He took one, draped it over his head and rubbed it roughly over his hair.

She pried off one heel, then the other. Her toes wept gratitude, and her arches sang as she lowered them flat against the floor. Raising one foot to a seat, she pulled back her skirt to remove her thigh holster with her off-duty weapon.

Remy watched, dripping on the welcome mat.

She set the holster on the table next to her purse and ignored him.

"You walked home," he observed.

She lifted a shoulder. "Felt nice." She turned away to remove her earrings. Depositing them in the spoon rest next to the stove, she debated taking off the necklace but found she didn't want to part with it. Not yet. "You're still dripping," she pointed out. "In or out, cher?"

When he didn't answer, she moved toward the stairs.

Like a shadow, he was there in her path.

Her breath hitched. Her pulse ran away at a fast clip.

He caught her, his hand firmly on the nape of her neck, tugging her to him. His mouth lowered to hers and claimed it.

Surprise and relief blinded her to everything else. She threw her arms around him.

He angled his head, taking the kiss deeper, darker.

She felt the heat of him through the wet material of her dress. She felt his need, hard and long, against her navel. He'd chosen to come back. He'd chosen her. There was no going back now.

"Take me upstairs," she said. "Be bad with me. Once."

A guttural sound ripped from his throat. He crouched and slung her headlong over his shoulder.

She let out a startled laugh. As he headed for the stairs, his arm secure across the back of her knees, she found a place along his ribs to nibble.

"No biting," he chastised and turned his stubbled jaw

against the place where her skirt fell high against the back of her thigh, where her skin was bare. He grazed kisses across it, and goose bumps climbed down her legs and arms, drawing her skin up tight. She burned.

She was finally going to know what happened with Remy after dark. She was going to find out who he was when the lights went out.

Yes.

He reached her room.

She tilted her face up to his. "I've thought about this," she whispered. "Dreamed about this. A thousand times. A thousand different ways."

His eyes, dark as pitch, glittered. "Me, too," he revealed, and he kissed her as he had at the club—urgently. As if his need had built like a geyser. "You taste like witchcraft," he groaned, nibbling her lower lip from corner to corner.

He tasted just as he looked—like decadent sin. She was already wet for him. "I need to get out of this dress. Will you help me?"

He gripped either side of her waist and turned her. Brushing the wet reams of her hair out of his way, he went to work on the tie of her halter.

She let him tug it down her body. It landed with a wet plop on the floor. She toed it off.

He turned her back to face him, looking his fill of curves and flesh. His tongue wet his lips.

Indulgently, she reached back, unhooking her bra. She discarded it, the rain on her skin making her shiver at the promise of his heat. She reached up to toy with her nipple for him. "Take off your shirt."

He obeyed, undoing the buttons one after the other. He rolled his shoulders, shrugging it away.

He was big, his chest one large rock-hard slab—like the hot-guy sculptures of ancient Greece. The illusion was broken only by the art he'd taken upon his body. She traced lines and shapes she couldn't quite make out in the dark. Keeping her touch light, she followed them over his rib cage. She felt scars in the space above his left hip, shiny healed skin, indented slightly. Something had taken a chunk out of him. Then she found the thick line of hair over his taut abdomen and followed the happy trail with interest.

He shivered as her fingertips followed the path beneath his beltline. Because she liked him open and sensitive this way, she went to her knees.

She worked his belt loose, then the clasp of his pants. She was thrilled to see he'd gone commando.

He *was* a work of art. The intersection of obliques and abs were cut deep, arrowing down to his sex. It loomed high and was thick and hot to her touch. She wrapped her hand around it and stroked, catching the glistening bead at the tip with her thumb.

He drew in a sharp breath. His hands twisted in her hair, tugging to bring her to her feet. His kiss swept her away as he flattened his palms and spread his fingers underneath the waist of her panties, enjoying the shape of her bottom.

She tugged her panties down, wanting to be bare with him.

He banded both hands beneath her ass and lifted her against him.

She crossed her ankles at the small of his back and held on as he drew his mouth back to hers. She found all the warmth she'd wished for.

He tipped his head back. "Wait," he said.

"I can't."

He reached up with one hand to stroke her cheek, the movement impossibly tender. He made a soothing sound and placated her with a chaste kiss to the lips. "I need to know. Is there anything that sets you off?"

"God alive," she laughed. "You. Always."

"No, boo," he said, serious. "You misunderstand."

"Make me understand, mi amor."

She saw the nickname hit home. His arms tightened around her, and his eyes went deep. His voice followed, guttural. "Is there anything you don't want? Is there anything that triggers you?"

Touched that he would ask, she felt the cool press of the pendant at her clavicle and confronted his worry with an open-mouthed kiss. "Not with you."

His breath shallowed. "I need a condom."

She nodded toward the dresser. When he stepped closer, not letting her down, she pried open the topmost drawer and fumbled for the pack. It fell to the fluffy rug.

"Leave it," he told her, then knelt at the foot of her bed with her astride.

What was between them took on a different tone. Time slowed, honeyed, sweet and thick. His hands slowed, and even though need was a pulsing ball of light inside her, she didn't mind. In fact, she lost herself to him. The backs of his hands over the sides of her breasts. More, as he drew the peaks inside his mouth and suckled. She leaned back as he took his kisses lower, over her sternum, lips tracing a circle around her belly button.

He found every sensitive place, escalating her excitement so that when his touch reached the juncture of her thighs, she was ready. His thumb flicked across her, and she gasped. He hummed in answer and repeated the motion, satisfied when her whole body jerked in reaction.

"You want me?" he asked experimentally.

She bobbed her head in a nod, then stopped—everything stopped—as he hit that spot again. Just there. She moaned.

"Then come for me," he directed.

Something caught at her throat. A low, plaintive sound she

didn't recognize. She circled her hips, circled his fingers. One slipped inside her.

She threw her head back and circled again, bringing him up against the place where she needed him most. He stroked her there, too, settling into a rhythm.

"Don't stop, boo," he groaned as she continued to glide against his touch. He worked her into a fine frenzy. "Not 'til you get exactly what you want."

He was what she'd wanted, what she'd always wanted, so she called out for him as the climax took her.

He palmed the package that had fallen to the floor and opened it. He ripped off a square and smiled at the label. "Ribbed?"

She gave a vacant nod, shattered by ecstasy.

Then he hitched her onto his lap again, one hand banding her hair at the base of her neck. The other guided her hip.

He watched her face as she opened and took him, all of him. He cursed. "You're so tight."

"Been a minute."

"Does it hurt?"

Should she tell him—that no man had ever stopped to ask her that before? Should she tell him what it meant to her? "You're right where you should be."

Muscles knotted under his skin. "I'll make it last as long as I can. Promise."

She went back to his mouth, dappling her lips across his as he remained still, letting her stretch. When she circled her hips against his, he slammed his eyes shut. "It's your turn," she claimed, letting him slide out and back in.

He shook his head, tightening his hold on her hair. "Only if you come with me."

"Okay," she agreed. Then, because it felt so good to do so, she hooked one arm around his neck and leaned back again, absorbing every flicker of sensation. Reveling in it.

He found that spot again where their bodies joined and teased her up to the brink of release. She nodded rapidly for him to continue.

He hit the spot. Heat and sensation reached its zenith, and she flew over the edge once more.

He drew her against him so they were pressed together from collar to thigh, slick from rain and perspiration. Brows gathered, he quickened inside her.

Her hands spread through his hair. She kept pace and moaned when his stubble skimmed her neck.

His body seized, and he slowed to a grind, the breath backing up in his lungs before releasing in one long tremulous tumble.

Even as he wound down, his lips sought hers.

The kiss was tender. It fed her and all the lights inside her. She released his hair from her hands to frame his face between them. "Be here in the morning."

He absorbed the kiss, then pressed his brow to hers. "I'll be here."

They made it onto the bed. He put them there after disposing of the condom and bringing her a warm, wet cloth.

Before the light hit the windows, he woke, found his face buried in her hair, their hips cradled together and the smell of her on his skin. She stirred. Her arm rose around the back of his neck, and her hips ground against his.

He was hard again. Smoothing his hand over her bare shoulder, he lowered his head and nibbled.

"I thought you said no biting," she said dreamily and circled her hips back against him again.

He touched his lips to her ear. "I lied," he whispered and nipped her lobe.

She gasped. "You're fast on your way to becoming my favorite way to lose sleep."

"How many ways are there?"

She snuggled into her pillow. "Too many."

Smoothing his hand over her hip and down her thigh, he found the back of her knee.

"Mmm. Your hands are nice."

"My hands are hard."

"I like them hard," she murmured. "I like how you use them."

He wedged his hand between her knees, spreading her. Following the seam of her legs, he traced it to the nest of her thighs and cupped her. "Like this?"

She took his wrist, held him there. "Yes."

"Not this?" He let the rough pad of his thumb whisper across her.

She hissed. "Maybe I like that, too."

She was already quaking, so he went a step further, guided by the wet path to her opening. "This?"

"Huh," she expelled in a rush. Her hand clamped down on the back of his, guiding.

Her hair had dried. It drew his nose because it still smelled like rain. "Fast or slow?" he asked, eager to learn her.

"Just like that," she bade, her neck arching back as it had before. Her breaths came quick. "God. *Yes*, Remy."

She'd asked him to be bad with her. Nothing they'd done had felt bad. It had felt right.

He chased her up to completion, touching her in all the places he knew from the first round that she responded to most. She was coiled so tight with tension, he felt her toes curl under as she pressed her foot into his calf.

She shuddered over the peak, her face pressed to the pillow.

"My legs may not work tomorrow," she mumbled when she'd gathered her wits. "I'll need to call in sick. We'll have to spend the whole day in bed."

"Bummer," he mused, skimming his knuckles up and down

her arm. He found the telltale flush on her neck that told him she was well satisfied. Laying kisses up the trail, he found her mouth as she turned it to meet his. "I'm not finished."

She sighed. "Thank goodness." Turning onto her stomach, she stretched.

He clasped her hand, raised it over her head, intertwined their fingers. Smoothing his other palm down her spine, he followed it to the curve of her bottom. Sweeping her hair from the column of her neck, he found the Our Lady of Charity pendant facing backward. It'd gotten turned around. He took a moment to fix it. "I found this in the French Market. I wasn't there to buy anything. But then there she was. I swear she said your name."

"Why have we never done this before?"

"You needed someone whole when we met. I wasn't."

"You pulled me out of hell."

"I was treading water," he admitted. "Same as you. If I saved you, it was because you did the same for me."

She drew in a long breath. "I'm going to say something. Something neither of us may be ready for."

"Go ahead, boo."

Her throat moved around a swallow, and her eyes closed. "I love you. From day one, I've loved you. I've never been able to make myself stop."

The confession came at him like a bullet train. He didn't know how to step out of the way.

"It's always been you," she added.

Later, he'd think about all the things she didn't know…how he wanted to tell her the truth of who and what he was without losing her…and the impossibility of that. Now he let her words wrap around him. And he held on to them.

"I know it's a lot," she continued. "But don't walk away."

He shook his head. "I'm not going anywhere."

She arched beneath him. "Take what you want."

Like a good soldier, he did as he was told. After fixing another condom in place, he joined with her, then followed the rolling motion of her hips. She gripped the sheets and clamped down on his thumb when he brought it to her mouth.

When he reached underneath her belly to stroke her, her hand was already there. With a groan, he spanned his arm across her low belly, knowing where the pleasure built inside her. He angled her hips up to meet him.

She keened into her pillow. He kept going, just like that, pulling moans out of her until his undercarriage drew up so tight to where they joined that he had to bury a groan in her neck to stop himself from climaxing.

A head-to-toe shudder racked her, and she quickened around him, releasing.

He broke. Not little by little. He shattered fully and knew if life gave him a choice, he'd give it all to her—past, present and future.

He'd choose her, whether it damned him or not.

Chapter 18

Sloane woke to find her face stuck to the pillow. She'd slept so hard, the bed had accepted her as its own.

Flipping slowly, she took stock of how she felt. Tender, she found, but in all the right places. Everywhere else, she felt warm and lax and sated.

She reached for the space beside her.

It was cold.

A frown set upon her lips as she turned and found Remy's side of the bed empty. She sat up and faced the sunshine and birds' chatter through the window. Checking her watch, she saw she'd slept past seven. She untangled her legs from the covers and rose.

She showered, brushed her teeth and went through her hair-and-makeup routine. When she went to the closet to pick her work wear for the day, the garment bag that held Abuela's dress reached for her.

Abuela had left the party early last night. She also had kept her distance, choosing silence over confrontation.

Sloane had always found silence sharper than words. She'd need to stop by Abuela's house today to explain.

The conversation with Sebastian LeBlanc lingered, as did the one with Nestor. She had questions, ones she sensed only Abuela could answer.

She dressed and descended the stairs to the kitchen.

Her relief upon seeing Remy shirtless at her stove nearly blinded her. Unlike all the mornings before, she went to him.

"Hmm," he uttered, and she heard the smile in his voice as her nails trailed lightly up his ribs. He tipped his head back so that it reclined against hers.

"Buenos días," she said low, drawing the words out.

"You slept well."

"I slept deep." She viewed the grits in the pot on the stove and smelled shrimp. "You realize for someone who's not a morning person, you do more before business hours than the average citizen."

"After last night, I figure we both need carbs."

"I like a wise man under my roof." She kissed his shoulder blade and smoothed her hand over the name etched across his upper back in block letters: GABBIE. The desire to keep the morning-after glow trucking on won out over her curiosity. Patting his jean-clad buns, she made herself step away. "Coffee?" she asked, taking mugs off the rack.

"Absolutely."

She served it black. He took the shrimp out of the oven and plated them on top of the grits, adding cheese and herbs, before bringing the dish to her at the table. She peeled an orange, split it with him, and they both dug in.

"I could get used to this," she said several bites in.

"Perhaps you should," he suggested as he offered her a bite from his fork.

She held his gaze as she took the shrimp into her mouth, feeling a strong buzz. It joined the hopeful bleating of her heart. She could see him here with her every morning.

She'd told him she loved him. He hadn't said it back. She was okay with that. But there was so much about Remy she didn't know.

Before this was over, she would know him.

The light from the windows kissed his skin, making it look

golden. The tattoo on his left pec had faded to blue with time. The ink had bled, making it hard to identify. She tapped it. "What's this?"

He glanced down. "My first tattoo."

She tipped her chin, trying to discern the shape. "An old man with a beard?"

He barked a laugh. It looked good on him, engraving itself into the crow's feet at the creases of his eyes. "A tree," he corrected.

"Oh," she said, tilting her head now. She squinted. "I guess I can see that."

"I didn't have money to pay for a better artist. But I felt rootless, and I wanted roots more than I wanted to wait."

She savored this glimpse into his past. He gave so few of them. "Do you still need those roots?" she asked.

His brow furrowed as he searched her face. He stroked her cheek, eyes clouded. "Ask me a less complicated question."

"Okay," she said, seeing a chord of pain she'd never seen in him before. She rubbed a hand over the flat line of his stomach. "Can you tell me who Gabbie is?" she asked carefully.

He looked away and picked up his fork. He let the silence simmer for so long, she thought he wouldn't answer at all. Then finally, he said, "Ask me again. In the future."

The future. Her heart flipped.

"Will you?" he asked, bringing his eyes up to hers again.

She nodded and let a smile play at her lips. "I will."

He caressed the wound on the back of her arm. Raising her wrist, he kissed the spot just above the broken skin.

With one hand on his chin, she brought his lips up to hers. The kiss was whisper-soft at first. Then he angled his head. She absorbed him, straight to the bone.

She remembered the night before—all he'd taken and given. All she'd gleaned from him, the shiny glimpses of his soul. It had only made her want him more.

The table legs shrieked as he bumped it back and hoisted her into his lap.

She settled there, bending her mouth to his and taking what she wanted. The kiss turned heady. Need pulsed between her legs, and she felt his tandem response beneath his jeans.

His hands cupped her face as he broke the kiss. His chest rose and fell beneath her palms. His dark eyes reached for hers. The hankering behind them made the ache in her so keen.

He traced the line of her chin with his thumb. "There're things you and I need to talk about."

"About?"

He hesitated. "Me."

She licked her lips. "Tell me."

He shook his head. "I'm not a saint, boo."

She smiled. "I'm hardly a good girl."

"Sloane."

There was something grim about him. Something raw, honest and real. Her mouth parted. "What is it you're trying to say, Remy?" she asked.

"I'm saying there are things about me…who I am, what I've done…that you may not like."

"Is this about what you did in special ops?" she asked. "If it is, that's not—"

"It's not that," he said. "I have secrets. Things I haven't shared with anyone in a really long time."

She scrubbed her hands through his stubble. "Sounds like you need to unburden yourself, cher."

"I want to," he said. "I would if I knew you were ready."

"There's nothing you can say that—"

He cut across her. "Don't say that, Sloane. You have no idea who I am."

"I've known you for eleven years," she tossed back. "I'd say I know you a sight better than the majority of people."

He circled her wrists with his hands and lowered them. "Not everything."

"Dammit, Remy. If there are things I don't know about you, it's because you've never let me in. You know *everything* about me, who I am and what I've come through. You want me to know who you are? Tell me!"

A muscle in his jaw jumped as they stared each other down.

Just when she thought he would speak again, her phone rang.

She scowled, snatching the device up and answering, "Escarra."

Pelagie's voice filled her ear. "I just had a call from Tech. They've got account information from the Cash App purchase."

Sloane slid off Remy's lap. His hands fell away from her as she rose to walk around the table. "Do they have a name?"

"Yes. You better get down here because this is big."

"I'll be right there," Sloane agreed.

Remy remained at the table. "You're going?"

"There may be a break in a case."

"Which case?"

"You've got secrets," she pointed out. "Let me keep mine."

His gaze slid away from hers. "Fine."

"I need to discuss things with Pelagie, possibly our tech team. Then I need to prep for my lunch with Sebastian LeBlanc at The Roosevelt."

His fork clattered loudly to his plate. *"What?"*

The exclamation stopped her in her tracks. "What do you mean 'what'?"

Picking up his napkin from his lap, he tossed it on the table and stood. "You're meeting Sebastian LeBlanc? *Why?*"

"That's none of your business."

His eyes fired. His anger was normally tightly wound. It

was nothing short of shocking to see it break the surface. "Do you have any idea what you're dealing with?"

"A former candidate for governor who sadly lives in a hotel?" she asked.

"Do not underestimate him."

"What do you know about him, exactly?" she asked, sensing something here. That strange frisson along her spine set her ill at ease once again.

"I know he likes to hurt people," Remy told her. "I know he enjoys it."

"Underage girls, you mean."

"Doesn't matter your age, sex or rank. If he thinks he can use you, he will."

"How do you know this?" she challenged.

"You can't go to The Roosevelt."

"Are you forbidding me from doing my job?"

"I'm asking you not to meet with him," he said through his teeth.

"It's not your job anymore to tell me where to go or what to do," she informed him, her own fury bubbling beneath the surface. "I'm meeting Sebastian LeBlanc at noon, and there's nothing you can do about it."

As she stalked to the sideboard where she kept her purse, he walked around the table. "Sloane—"

"Don't follow me," she warned, swinging the door open. "I need to cool off."

Pelagie's eyes practically danced as she presented Sloane with the latest. "The Cash App account traces back to Seb White. Same individual who owns the apartment in Jackson and drives a black Jeep."

"You act like this is good news," Sloane observed. "Seb White only exists on paper."

"He does," Pelagie granted. "But we were able to access

credit card information on the account, too. He used a Chase Visa under his real name to complete the purchase."

"How do you know it's his real name?" Sloane asked.

Pelagie handed her the report from the tech team. "Take a look."

Sloane scanned the printout. Her attention seized on three words.

Sebastian LeBlanc II

The world slowed. "Baz LeBlanc?"

Pelagie nodded as Sloane handed the report back to her. "We have witnesses who claim his father is involved in trafficking. His mother believes strongly that Sebastian LeBlanc made his son disappear because he knew too much about what he was involved in. I also did some research on LeBlanc the Second. Four point oh student, whip-smart, top three percent of his class, but he had a predilection for trouble. When he was fourteen, he lost a private school scholarship for hacking into the administrative database."

"A hacker?"

"That gives him means and motive," Pelagie said. "And there's something else you need to see."

Sloane followed her to her desk.

Pelagie shook the mouse, and the computer screen lit with an image. "Once I got word that the credit card was still active, I asked for its recent transaction history. Two weeks ago, LeBlanc the Second stopped for fuel at a Shell station in Saint Francisville." She pointed to the vehicle in the image. "That's the black Jeep the super of the apartment in Jackson saw Seb White driving. And this…" using the mouse, she zoomed in and enhanced the image "…is our suspect."

That feeling again. Sloane felt it prickling along her spine as she studied the profile of Baz LeBlanc.

Taller, she discerned. Much taller. Broader. He wore a black baseball cap, but she could see enough of his face to distinguish his square jaw.

More unease winged through her. "Did the cameras pick up a plate number?"

"No dice," Pelagie says regretfully. "But this is our guy. Baz LeBlanc is our vigilante. He's Loup-Garou."

Sloane stepped closer to the screen. She planted her hands on the desk, leaning in to get a better look. "I've seen him before."

"In the photos Clairmont sent?"

"Yes," she said. "And somewhere else…" Her stomach lurched, a sensation like falling. "Pelagie?"

"Yeah?"

"Baz LeBlanc's case file. Can you grab it off my desk?"

Pelagie retrieved it. Sloane opened the file, riffling through the pages fast until she found the note that Emmanuelle LeBlanc had found inside the first cash envelope for her son.

There were the words—*For Azael*—printed carefully in blue pen. And there was the small symbol underneath with the cypress and pipe from the Chitimacha tribal logo.

Even as her mind turned away from the possibility, she traced the cypress boughs as she'd traced Remy's tree tattoo this morning.

The images weren't identical. But they were similar enough. She glanced back at the man on Pelagie's desktop and felt cold.

"Hey," Pelagie said as Sloane stalked back to her desk and snatched up her purse. "Where are you going?"

Sloane didn't bother answering. She didn't know how to answer.

…I'm not a saint… I have secrets…

The tattoo on Remy's back. GABBIE… His youngest sister, Gabriella, had died in a hit-and-run accident one year before Baz's disappearance.

He'd been carrying her with him since.

The signs had been right in front of her all this time. She'd just been too stupid, too wrapped up in him to look.

"Son of a bitch," she bit out as she followed the path to the French Quarter. "You son of a bitch."

Chapter 19

Remy waited outside The Roosevelt, ball cap pulled low over his brow. The asphalt steamed, the sun burning off the night's dampness. The thick, sticky air tasted of brine and tarmac.

From his position, he could see the entrance to the hotel, designated by red-carpeted steps under an awning whose flags lay limp at their poles. Doormen hovered, trying not to wilt in their uniforms. Tourists looked worse for wear as they weaved around Remy.

He knew the moment Sloane arrived, jewel bright in green wide-leg slacks and matching vest. Her hair was piled atop her head, dark sunglasses in place. A ready scowl hardened the lower half of her face.

Before she could make for the entry doors, he hooked a hand around her elbow.

She stiffened, her hand diving to the bag at her hip. When she realized it was him, she didn't relax.

"Been a while since I got the jump on you," he noted.

She shrugged off his grip. "What are you doing here?"

"I told you," he returned. "I can't let you go in there."

The skin around her mouth tightened. "And I thought I made myself clear. You don't own me, nor do you give me orders. Now get out of my way." She ducked around him.

"Sloane…" he cautioned, following. "I'm asking you not to do this."

"Why not?" she asked, whirling on him. "Because you don't want me sniffing around Loup-Garou's real identity anymore?"

His heart plummeted.

She lifted her chin when he remained silent. "You weren't lying this morning when you told me you had secrets."

A ready apology sprang to his lips. But the long-ingrained response of self-preservation beat it. "What gave me away?"

She shook her head. "Does it matter?"

He closed the distance between them.

She hissed, separating them again in marked increments. "You lied about your real reasons for coming here."

He felt covered up in lies. The coating felt as viscous as pine sap. The taste of turpentine and duplicity settled on his tongue. "Yes," he admitted.

"You used me to get to le Fe," she added.

She was slipping away from him. There was nothing he could say to bring her back, to make her understand. "Yes."

"Do you know what this means?" she asked in a near whisper. "Once they find out I know you, that I let you sleep in my house, they'll put me on administrative leave. I'll be thoroughly investigated, just as you will be."

"You didn't know anything," he said. "I made sure you knew nothing of the truth. You're covered, Sloane."

Her lips parted and her voice rose. "I'm covered?" Several people turned to look as they passed them by, but Sloane neither noticed nor cared. "I'm standing here with my heart broken, and you're saying *I'm covered*?"

Again, he moved toward her.

She slapped at his hands. "Don't touch me. Don't you *dare* touch me. Who are you? Who did I let into my life? *My bed*?" Before he could open his mouth, she cut him off. "Don't answer that. I'm late for my meeting."

Panic seized him. "Cancel it."

"Why?" she asked. "Why are you so afraid of your father?"

Remy flinched. "That monster is not my father."

"He is," Sloane replied, grim and knowing. "You're Sebastian LeBlanc II. People called you Baz. You ran away from home at sixteen."

"I didn't have a choice," he barked.

"But you did," she argued. "You could have told me."

"You don't know who you're dealing with."

"So tell me, junior," she said. "What is it that I need to know about Papá LeBlanc that makes him so dangerous?"

"He'll use you."

"How did he use you?" she wanted to know.

"He sold me." It shocked him to hear the truth spring from his own lips. He'd spoken it out loud for the first time. There was no going back.

"He what?"

"He sold me," he said, slowing it down.

"His own son?"

"Yes."

"Why would he do that?" she asked.

"He needed the money," he said. "Blackmail's expensive. I was bankable, apparently. I tried to tell you, Sloane. There's no line he would not and has not crossed to achieve his own ends."

"How long?"

"How long what?"

"How long did it last?" she asked.

He tried to pull in a breath, but his lungs wouldn't expand. "I was fifteen when I went in and almost seventeen when I got out."

She cursed fluently.

"I'd gotten into trouble, got kicked out of school and then Gabbie…"

"He didn't blame you for her hit-and-run?"

"I was supposed to meet her," he said. "I messed up. She

had to come to me instead. She was killed on my watch. He never let me forget that. There wasn't a school within fifty miles that would take me—not the right kind of school, in his eyes. Homeschool didn't last long before I blew that off, too, so he sent me 'to work,' as he called it, with the Guidrys."

"Guidry. As in…"

"Guidry Security." He nodded. "On paper, a security firm. On the backboard, they were—"

"The figurehead of trafficking in New Orleans for over a dozen years." Sloane released a sigh. "*She* was the one your father sold you to?"

"Gretchen." He could say her name. For years, he hadn't been able to without choking on his own bile. "At first, she treated me like a security hire. She asked me to show her cyber team how to hack a system, how to create firewalls and protect their own. I worked overtime, thought I was making bank. I spent long nights at the office with her."

"She groomed you."

"Skillfully. I wasn't the first nor was I the only underage hire she was working over. When I called LeBlanc to come and get us out of there, he made it clear I was to stay. He said it was penance."

"That's bull," she snapped.

"I knew it," he said. "And I was desperate. I threatened Gretchen, told her I'd go to the cops, the press… She made it clear she owned both. There was nowhere I could go, no one I could talk to who wasn't profiting off her organization or beholden to her."

"And you believed her because you were just a kid," she said sympathetically. "So you disappeared instead?"

"I ran," he acknowledged. "I went back home. When LeBlanc found out I'd left the Guidrys, he tried to take me back. I'd never seen him that afraid. He was so deep in Gretchen's pocket. She knew things about him. She had footage of him with girls, hours of it. The idiot would meet with them at the Guidrys' own private residence. There wasn't anywhere she didn't have cameras. He said if I didn't go back, he'd send my sister, Emmie, in my place."

"Oh, God, Remy," Sloane said. She milled away, paced in jerky footfalls before returning to him, hands braced on her hips. "Gretchen Guidry's dead. She was murdered two years after you disappeared."

"That's right," he muttered.

"Did you kill her?"

"I thought about it," he revealed. "I wish it had been me. Would you blame me if I had?"

"You really need to ask me that question?" she retorted. "You really believed you couldn't share all this with me before? Of all people, Remy—or Baz. Whatever the hell your name is."

"I wasn't free to tell you," he explained.

"What was stopping you?" she demanded. When he kept his mouth closed, she wavered. "Or who's stopping you?"

Torben's face came to mind. The friend who'd walked through hell alongside him.

"You say your father used you," she said after a long simmering silence.

"Yes."

"You used me, too," she accused.

Their separation yawned before him. "I did," he admitted.

She reached up around her neck.

He saw the chain of the pendant he'd given her. "Don't," he warned.

She took off the necklace. Then she lifted his hand, palm up, and placed it there. "You will not follow me," she ordered. "And you'll be at my place in an hour with a full explanation."

"Or what?" he asked. "You'll take me in? You're going to have to do that anyway."

"That's right," she said with a nod. "Because if I don't, you know what's going to happen to me. This job… It's all I am anymore. If they let me keep my badge, I'll be lucky."

He memorized her face, the angles of it.

"Will you be there?" she asked.

His heart beat in his ears. "Come with me," he whispered.

"What?"

"Come with me, Sloane," he murmured. "I need…" Everything inside him was building up to the surface. "I need you. We can go anywhere. Anywhere you want to go, boo. Just… come with me."

For a moment, he thought he saw her lips tremble with emotion. Before he could say anything further, however, she turned away. In a determined stride, she reached the entrance to The Roosevelt.

He didn't see her look back.

Come with me.

Sloane knew what the words meant. Remy was going to run. The chances of him leaving behind a paper trail again for her to follow were slim.

What gave me away?

She needed a corner where she could collect herself. The betrayal bit. It had fangs. But the overreaching heartbreak was worse. Her ribs strained, as if it were tearing its way through her.

She hissed at the tears behind her eyes. She'd sworn after Mexico that a man would never make her cry again, that she'd never be hurt by one in any way, shape or form.

How could it be that the one man she'd chosen to put all her faith and trust in was the one man with more secrets and lies than she could contemplate?

She wasn't in the right frame of mind for her interchange with Sebastian LeBlanc, but this meeting was vital to the investigation. If the FBI was going to lock Remy up for his vigilante activities, they could lock her up, too. But not before she yanked the entire New Orleans trafficking industry up by its roots.

If LeBlanc had been embroiled with the Guidrys, entanglement with the new trafficking web wouldn't be that big of a stretch.

In the hotel lobby, she stopped to gather herself. The Roosevelt had opened in 1893 under the banner Hotel Grunewald. Through the years, it had hosted stars the likes of Elvis, Ray Charles, Jack Benny, Frank Sinatra and beloved hometown hero Louis Armstrong, among others. The surrounding opulence warred with her turmoil. She did her best to focus on the bronze statue of a woman in front of her who balanced a rotating nineteenth century clock ten feet above the floor.

"May I help you?"

Sloane glanced at the concierge. She cleared her throat. "I'm looking for Sebastian LeBlanc."

"Are you expected?" the clerk asked.

"Yes, we have a meeting," Sloane acknowledged, turning now that she was sure she had a handle on herself.

"One moment please," the clerk said before walking back to the check-in desk.

Sloane felt chilled. Rubbing her hands over her arms, she watched the concierge pick up the phone and place a call. She chatted for several seconds before hanging up and gesturing Sloane over. "They're sending a man down to collect you. They asked you to wait by the elevators."

"Thanks," she said and dug her badge out of her bag as she crossed to the closed lifts.

To her surprise, the doors whispered open almost immediately. She stared at LeBlanc's man.

He seemed to take up most of the car. A meaty hand gripped

the door before it could close on her. "Agent Escarra?" he asked in a baritone.

She held up her badge in response. "Who're you?"

"Othello."

"Seriously?" She noted the telltale bulge of a weapon under his sports coat.

"Mama liked her Bard," Othello grunted, a heavy dose of Louisiana brogue on his tongue. "'Nuff to name me after a tragedy."

"Hmm," she mused as she ventured onto the lift. "Teacher?"

"Lit major," he said, that deadpan voice unchanged as the door whished shut. "She had me before she could graduate. Willy don't pay no bills in Lafourche Parish. She went out on the shrimp boats with my uncle. Family business."

Othello didn't look like any shrimper she'd ever seen. "'Bait the hook well, the fish will bite.'"

He raised a brow. A ghost of a smile floated around his stern mouth. "Mama woulda liked you, chère."

"How long have you been working for LeBlanc?" she wondered.

The mirth dissipated. "Long time."

She watched the floors pass them by on the gauge. "Long enough to know his son?"

Othello gave a nearly imperceptible jerk. "Baz?"

That was an affirmative. "Does he have another son?"

"Just the one," Othello said. "Boss says you're lookin' for him."

"Did you help the boss look for him when he disappeared?"

Othello grew quiet. "What makes you think that kid wanted to be found?"

The lift chimed. The door opened onto a private corridor. Othello stepped out first, then lifted a hand for her to walk ahead.

The door they came to read PRESIDENTIAL SUITE. "Who pays for this?" she asked.

"Boss pays his own way," Othello told her. "I can't let you in. Not till you hand me your piece."

"We both know I'm not going to do that."

"Rules is rules."

"My badge says I keep my weapon," she pointed out. "It stays where it is unless you draw on me first."

The bones of his face jutted outward as he tensed. "Ain't got no reason to draw on an officer."

"Then we understand each other, Othello," she concluded.

Othello waited a beat before opening the door and admitting her into the suite.

It was luxury at its finest, a classically appointed twelve-hundred-square-foot home away from home for the elite, complete with piano, bar and a fifty-five inch TV.

LeBlanc stood from his seat at the head of the dining table. He set down a newspaper and buttoned the jacket of his three-piece designer suit. "Agent Escarra," he drawled. "Lovely to see you again."

When he rose and lifted her hand to his lips, she took it away. This was the man who'd sold his own son to save himself? Anger boiled beneath the surface, writhing hot. She pressed her lips together to contain it before she said, shortly, "Mr. LeBlanc."

"Have a seat," he invited, gesturing to the table where silver platters remained covered. "I had something sent from Restaurant August. You like red snapper?"

"I do," she said, settling into a seat when he pulled out a chair for her next to his. She set her bag on the table next to her and noted that Othello had positioned himself by the door, hands folded in front of him.

"Excellent," LeBlanc replied, moving back to his seat. He shook out his napkin and patted it against his lap.

She rolled out her silverware and covered her green slacks with white linen. "I will remind you I'm not here for small talk, Mr. LeBlanc."

"Of course not," he mused, something of a teasing grin transforming his face. Taking the lid off his plate, he added, "Fire away."

"Were you aware your son was working for Guidry Security at the time of his disappearance?"

LeBlanc paused in the process of lifting his fork. He smoothed over the hitch with a nod. "I was."

"And were you aware of the Guidrys' ties to sex trafficking?"

"Not at the time, no," he answered. "You shoot from the hip, Agent Escarra."

"So you were a stranger to Gretchen Guidry's tendencies?"

"What tendencies are those? Gretchen had a fair few."

"Her tendencies toward minors," she supplied. "Thirteen to seventeen-year-old boys like your son, for instance."

"If I had known about that, do you think I would have allowed him anywhere near her?" LeBlanc asked.

"Would you?"

"I wouldn't have dreamed of it."

Liar. Fighting the urge to stab him with her fork, she used it to cut her fish. "When Baz disappeared, how long did you help search for him?"

"Until I was informed he most likely ran away of his own volition," LeBlanc pointed out.

"His mother never stopped looking for him, regardless."

"Yes, well," LeBlanc said, lifting his brows, "Célestine never gives things up easily. It's my understanding she still carries a lock of our daughter Gabriella's hair in a locket around her neck. You know about Gabriella, I assume?"

"I do."

"Tragic," he murmured. "She was so very little at the time of her accident."

For the first time, Sloane thought she saw a glimmer of genuine emotion behind his facade. Wavers of genuine grief broke his trained edifice. "My condolences," she offered. She thought of Esther, and her tone sharpened. "No parent should have to bury their child."

"Indeed," he said and forked a large bite up to his mouth.

"There are some who suggest that you pressured the police to wrap up Baz's missing persons case despite the alleged contact he'd made with your daughter Emmanuelle," she continued.

"People make many suggestions about me," he said. "I simply choose to ignore them."

"So you didn't pressure the NOPD to close the investigation?" she pressed.

His snort paired good-naturedness with subtle derision. "I assure you, no."

She moved in for the kill. "Do you know a man by the name of Holler McBride?"

His fork clattered to his plate. He lifted the napkin from his lap to his mouth. Clearing his throat, he said, "I don't believe I do."

"He's currently serving time in Orleans Parish Prison."

"For?"

"Trafficking minors and accessory to murder, among other charges."

"I have never willingly associated with people who are prone to murder."

"But you have willingly associated with people who traffic minors."

His good-naturedness vanished. "You seem to think very little of me, chère."

"Answer the question," she pressed, fine food forgotten.

His eyes narrowed as he leaned against the chair rest. "This isn't really about my son's missing persons case. Is it, Agent Escarra?"

"Say his name."

"What?"

"Your son's," she snapped, losing her already tenuous grip on control. "Not once in any words you and I have exchanged have you spoken his name out loud."

She saw the sweat beading on his upper lip before he patted it with the linen. "Perhaps because it causes me a great deal of pain."

"You said Gabriella's name," she said. "And I sense you feel a great deal more pain about what happened to her. Why is that?"

"As I said, she was so young when—"

"You still haven't said his name," Sloane tossed out.

He threw his napkin onto the table. "I will not be badgered. And I'd be careful, considering what I know of your family."

"My family?"

He gleaned something from her blank expression, something that made his swagger reappear like magic. "I know things about your dear abuelo that would curl your beautiful toes."

She shook her head, then quickly made herself stop. There was no way she was playing his game. "You know he's alive."

"Who?"

"Your son. Baz LeBlanc." She drew the name out, needing him to hear it. Wishing she could weaponize it.

"If I knew where my son was, I'd have reunited with him long ago."

"He knew things, didn't he?" she asked. "About you and the Guidrys. He knew things that could make you all suffer if it came to light."

"I think I'm finished with this interrogation."

Not a chance. "Is that why you had Gretchen Guidry killed?" she asked. "Like you had Ray de le Fe killed? The MO in both cases is almost identical."

LeBlanc lifted a hand for Othello.

The bodyguard's hand closed over her upper arm and pulled her up from her chair. She glanced into his wide face. "Take your hand off me," she told him, calm.

"It's time for you to go," Othello returned.

"Fine," she batted back, clutching her bag. She spoke slowly. "Take your hand off me."

It took a moment, but he released her, even if he didn't step out of her personal space.

"It's been fun, Agent Escarra," Sebastian said. "I hope you've enjoyed your visit."

"It was the Guidrys, wasn't it? They were behind the 'accident' that killed Gabriella. That's why you sent Baz to work for them. Because you could no more afford the Guidrys' blackmail than you could afford to lose another daughter. Baz was the troubled child you blamed for Gabriella's death. In your eyes, he was the pawn to your king, easily replaced in your and Gretchen's game of risk."

That flash of feeling returned, but it was gone again in a blink. "You know where the door is," he said.

The former candidate for governor looked more than a little rattled as Othello led her out.

Chapter 20

She rode the elevator down, dreading going home and finding the guest room empty, just as she dreaded going to the office and reporting everything to Houghton—the identity of Loup-Garou, the inevitable manhunt that would follow and the investigation into her involvement with Remy. The possibility of wrapping up the case against LeBlanc or the probe into le Fe's death was small. Not to mention the messy splash the media would make of Loup-Garou and Baz LeBlanc's connection.

Remy's secret would break. While the betrayal and the heartbreak of his lies hurt so bad that she struggled to take in a breath, she had no desire to bring his identity to light.

When she hit the street, her phone rang. She scrambled to pull it from her bag, her heart rapping her sternum hard on the downbeat. It wasn't Remy calling. It was Grace.

She answered as she rounded the corner of Roosevelt Way onto Canal Street. "Where y'at, chère?"

"I just checked on Pia. She's in the city for an ob-gyn appointment. I had a few minutes before I have to scrub up. What's wrong? You sound down."

"I'm fine," Sloane snapped. Then she gritted her teeth and released a breath. "Sorry. It's been a morning."

"Come by and see her. She's not driving back home to Flamingo Bay for another hour. It'll cheer you up."

It was tempting. Seeing Pia always lifted her spirits. "Can't.

I'm headed back to the field office. Tell Pia I'll call her to-night. Is she okay? How's the baby?"

"She's craving the crawfish étouffé and bananas foster cheesecake from Coterie."

"Noted." Sloane squinted at a figure walking in her direc-tion. When she recognized her tío, she lifted her hand in a wave. "Hang on, Grace. It's Nestor." She lowered the phone slightly. "What're you doing here?"

He peered around them. "You met with him. Didn't you?"

She frowned. Disappointment and irritation made a corro-sive brew. "You're going to give me a hard time, too?"

"I told you to stay out of it," he reminded her. "Why couldn't you listen for once, Santana, and stop meddling in things you shouldn't?"

"It's not meddling. It's my job!"

"Your job's becoming a liability," he warned.

"What's that supposed to mean?" she asked, the low sim-mer of impatience rising.

"Either heed what I say and keep away from LeBlanc," he told her, venturing close so they were nearly nose to nose, "or I can no longer protect you."

Sloane heard Grace's urgent tone on the other end of the phone. She felt prickles of alarm surface on the backs of her arm. They rose up her neck and scalp as the stare-down con-tinued.

"What's it going to be, Santana?" he asked with a dark un-dertone, his thick black brow lifting expectantly.

"Sloane?" Grace called, her voice tinny. "Is everything okay?"

Nestor's gaze roved over her phone. "Hang up."

"Why are you being like this?" Sloane demanded.

"Give me the phone," he said, reaching for it.

She held it out of his grasp. "No."

He took her arm in a bruising hold. "Hang up, Santana!"

"Let go!"

A black van skirted into the parallel parking spot next to them, blocking the view of Canal Street. The front passenger tire bumped over the curb. The side door rolled open.

Sloane took one look at the masked men inside, and her fighting instincts kicked in. Her elbow whistled up, catching Nestor in the nose. He grunted, tumbling back, losing his grip on her.

She spun, taking the first lunging step in a run.

Someone grabbed her from behind. Before she could call out for help, a gloved hand cupped her mouth. Her captor dragged her backward into the confines of the van.

She bit down, clawing at the restraint. She kicked out to stop the door from rolling closed.

A small, familiar pain went in above her left hip. She flinched, shocked, and glanced down. When she saw the needle, panic struck her.

The last thing she saw before the door closed was Nestor on the banquette, nose bleeding, eyes twin jets fueled by pain and remorse.

Remy gripped the Jeep's wheel at ten and two. It wasn't moving. In fact, it hadn't moved since he'd ducked inside and started it up.

He stared through the tinted windshield at nothing and no one, every voice in his head telling him to put the car in Drive and go.

He couldn't make himself move.

Everything Sloane had said was true. He had used her. Her ties to him would mean trouble for her. He should have never involved her, should've stayed the hell away.

The thing that haunted him most was what he'd seen when he followed his impulse and asked her to come with him. There had been sadness there more than accusation, and a glimmer of understanding. She knew he planned to run again and could have detained him there on the spot.

Instead, she'd walked away.

Was she willing to risk her job to let him run?

His phone rang. He reached for it blindly. "Yeah?" he answered.

"Remy? It's Grace. I was just on the phone with Sloane, and we got cut off…"

Remy squinted against the sunlight bouncing off the Jeep's hood. "What do you mean, you got cut off?"

"She was headed back to the field office and saw her tío Nestor on the street. I only picked up pieces of their conversation before things turned. I heard her telling him to let go of her. Then I thought she screamed, and the line went dead."

Remy straightened in the driver seat. "Do you know where she was?"

"When no one could locate Pia after Jaime Solaro's jailbreak, the three of us agreed to put a locator app on our personal cell phones. I looked up Sloane's location after the call ended. She was on Canal Street, between Roosevelt and Baronne."

That was only a few blocks from Remy's location. "I'm on my way to check it out. Did you hear anything else?"

"Yes," Grace said breathlessly. "I'm pretty sure I heard Nestor tell her to stay away from LeBlanc or he couldn't protect her."

Remy fought back a curse as he backed out of the public parking space. "Stay on the line with me unless she calls back."

"Okay," Grace said.

"Has her phone moved since you lost her?" he asked, swerving out of the parking lot onto Decatur, using the heel of his free hand to steer. He all but stood on the accelerator and sped toward Canal Street.

"No," Grace said apprehensively.

"Keep checking." He braked, and his tires skidded at a red light. Spinning the wheel, he took a sharp right onto Bienville, mapping the route.

"She's still not moving," said Grace in a reed-thin voice when he hooked a left on Royal.

"Damn it," he muttered, his pulse jacking up. He reached Canal finally and crossed the streetcar lane. "Nearly there," he promised.

There was a pharmacy on the corner of Baronne with a restaurant beside it. He pulled a U-ie at the next light, then bumped the Jeep's tires over the curb of the banquette. People jumped out of the way. Someone cursed a blue streak at him when he left the driver door open to search. "I don't see her," he said after a moment. "Where was she?"

"In front of the men's clothing store," Grace said.

He found windows with faceless mannequins but no Sloane. "She's not here."

"Mon Dieu, Remy. Where is she?"

Then he spotted it. The phone lay in the middle of the banquette. He bent down. Cracks wove every which way across the screen, but when he toggled the power button, it responded. The lock screen was a still photo of Sloane, Pia and Grace together at Casaluna.

"She's not here," he said again, unable to summon anything more.

Someone tapped him on the shoulder. A man with dreads and a Bob Marley T-shirt must've seen the look on his face because he dove back a pace. "Easy, homie. You looking for the woman in the green suit?"

"You saw her?" Remy asked.

"Got herself picked up by some guys in a black van. She struggled, but they drove off with her."

The muscles in Remy's jaw were wrapped up so tight he

had to form the words through gritted teeth. "What did they look like?"

"Not much I could see. They had masks on, full-face balaclava types."

"And the van?" Remy asked. "Did you see the plate?"

He shook his head. "It was a black BMW. Not the type you'd expect someone to get snatched in."

"Which direction?"

The man pointed. "Away from the river."

Toward Interstate 10, Remy thought, uneasy. "Grace," he said, "I need to make another call."

"She's gone," Grace said, sounding far away. "Isn't she?"

"I'll find her," he swore. "I promise you."

"Street-cam footage confirms what Grace heard and what the witness saw," Torben said as he bent over the screen of his computer, running the footage for Remy. "It shows Escarra, her uncle and the black BMW."

"Have you pulled the plate number yet?" Remy asked. His insides roiled as he watched Sloane struggle to get away from her attackers. Her phone was still clutched in his fist. He couldn't seem to let it go.

"It came up under another LLC."

Remy watched the screen after the van sped away from the site of the abduction. He pointed to Nestor Escarra, who stood alone on the curb. "Someone needs to pick him up."

"I've got an APB out," Torben assured him, "and we sent officers to his residence. We'll find him and question him if the FBI doesn't get to him first. Nestor Escarra has an interesting rap sheet. In his twenties, he did a nickel for drug possession. He was also found with an unregistered firearm on his person. Since he got out, he's kept his nose clean. But word is he was the one cooking the books in the family rum business before it went under."

How many times had Remy ignored the frisson of suspicion Nestor had given him while he was living under the senator's roof? Then it hadn't been his job to look deeper. Nor had he thought it was his business. Now it looked like Nestor was embroiled in Sloane's kidnapping. The footage showed him doing nothing to stop the men from pulling her into the van.

He remembered what Grace had heard on Sloane's last call. *...stay away from LeBlanc...*

The Roosevelt was less than a block from Sloane's last sighting. Moreover, the estimated time of her abduction had taken place under an hour after her meeting with LeBlanc.

"Call me if you learn anything more," Remy said.

"Where're you going?"

"To retrace her steps."

The elevator door opened. At the sight of Othello, Remy's lungs burned.

The man who'd known him since he was a boy didn't recognize him. He regarded Remy expectantly, his brick hands linked in front of him. Remy noticed the Rolex on his wrist and his custom *Men in Black* suit.

Othello refused to move out of the lift or extend the first greeting. Remy assumed he had the time it took the elevator door to close again to explain why he insisted on seeing the big man upstairs without an appointment. "Been a long time, O," he said.

Othello's high brow furrowed into neat rows. His eyes slowly cleared as he searched Remy's face. Recognition struck a heavy blow because his shoulders lowered and his hands fell limp at his sides. "Baz?"

"You're still working for the man," Remy observed, letting muted distaste cut through.

When the elevator door began to close, Othello blocked it

with his arm. "Baz," he said again. He shook his head. "What are you doing here?"

"I'm here to see LeBlanc," Remy told him. "Take me to him."

Othello's small eyes widened slightly. He glanced around the lobby. Then he shook his head again. "That's not possible."

"The hell it isn't," Remy said, crowding his way into the elevator.

Othello's arm blocked him. "Baz. You don't wanna do this."

It wasn't a warning. Remy recognized a plea when he heard one. "Move out of my way, O, or I'm taking the stairs."

"He's in a meeting," Othello said apologetically. "You know how it goes."

"You mistake me for the kid he dismissed on a dime at every opportunity." Remy felt his voice clawing at his throat. Every minute Othello stood in his way was another mile Sloane's kidnappers could be putting between him and her. "You don't know me anymore. You don't know who I am or what I've done, and you will *get out of my way.*"

Othello, no stranger to warnings, threats and worse, blinked. Whatever he saw in Remy's face made him back up a step.

Remy followed him into the car and punched the button for the top floor. The elevator doors closed.

He tried taking a steadying breath as they began to ascend. He was too worked up. Irrationality was riddling his logic with holes. Sloane was missing, and he was walking into the monster's den for answers. His heart pumped, rapid-fire brisk. He felt his focus slipping, his hold tenuous. A light slick of perspiration adhered his clothes to his skin just enough for discomfort. The bones of his hands itched. He curled them into fists until they ached, reaching for something other than the violence he felt there and finding nothing else.

The elevator dinged. The doors opened. Before Othello

could escort him out, Remy crossed the distance to the entrance to the presidential suite.

"Baz…" he heard Othello call.

Remy lifted his foot and kicked the door in. It swung open with a resonant crash, leaving the locking mechanism in place.

Someone screamed as Remy stalked in. A woman…no, a girl, bare from the waist up, ran from the room, braids streaming behind her.

LeBlanc stared warily at him from the cushions of the couch, belting his robe. "Othello?"

"Here, boss," Othello said at Remy's back.

"You let this man past you?" LeBlanc asked, arranging the robe over his waist carefully before he climbed to his feet.

Othello struggled for an explanation. "I tried, sir."

LeBlanc raised one wide eyebrow. "You must be something special to get past Othello," he told Remy. With an unbothered air, he went to the door the girl had disappeared behind and closed it.

The air had gone to ice. Remy's lungs rose and fell in quiet pants. The violence spread from his hands to his arms in ready vibrations. "Who is she?" he growled.

"My companion," LeBlanc said easily enough. He faced Remy fully. His back remained to the bedroom door. His legs were coated in dark hair beneath the folds of the robe. The sight of his bare feet gave the scene a tinge of unreality.

"How old is she?" Remy demanded.

LeBlanc considered the question, then started to slide his hands into his pockets.

"Keep your hands where I can see them," Remy stated clearly.

LeBlanc paused. He looked to Othello, who was still in the entryway and hadn't made a move to stabilize the situation. Eyes narrowing, he zeroed in again on Remy's face. "Who are you?"

Remy stood very still. If he moved, he'd lunge and the results wouldn't be pretty. "I'm the Ghost of Christmas Past, asshole."

He had the pleasure of seeing LeBlanc's expression slacken. Though it was difficult to enjoy it when urgency was a beehive in his ears. Pushing himself forward, he asked, "Where is Sloane Escarra?"

LeBlanc shook his head slightly. "Baz."

"I won't ask again." Remy reached around his back, palming his weapon.

Othello moved forward. "You don't want to do that, Baz."

Remy turned his head slowly and met Othello's stare. "Don't I?"

Othello raised his hands, cautious. "Hand over the gun."

"You'll have to fight me for it," Remy warned. "You don't want to do that, O. Trust me."

Othello wavered for a split second.

LeBlanc cleared his throat, drawing Remy's attention back to him. "What business do you have with Agent Escarra?" Suspicion came with the slight narrowing of his eyes. "Have you been working with her?"

"I'm not the only one in this town who knows exactly what kind of man you are."

"You've been playing the long game."

Remy ignored the note of pride in his father's voice. "Where is she?" he said again.

"She was here," LeBlanc noted. He lifted his hands. "Now she's gone."

"Don't try to con me," Remy said, taking his gun off his belt.

Othello stiffened, reaching for his own. Remy kept one eye on him and the other on LeBlanc.

By all appearances, LeBlanc looked unaffected by the ordeal. However, Remy saw the sweat on his upper lip. "I don't know where your woman is, son."

Remy's hand tightened on the gunstock. "Don't call me that. You lost the right to call me that from the moment you handed me over to the Guidrys."

"Gretchen's dead, Baz," LeBlanc said evenly. He tilted his head, vying for compassion. "All that's over now."

Remy's jaw hurt. The muscles flared underneath as he took a step forward, one that had Othello hissing. "You son of a bitch."

"Baz," Othello said at his shoulder. His voice was soothing. "It's all right. You don't have to do this."

"The hell I don't." Remy ignored the vibrations that had turned to shaking in his limbs. He felt so bitterly cold. The buzzing in his ears had climbed to a scream.

Othello's hand touched the wrist of his gun hand. Remy flinched away, but Othello persisted. "Baz. Give me the gun. Nobody has to get hurt."

The plea in Othello's eyes nearly broke him. "You can walk away," Remy told him. "You owe him nothing if he's gone."

Othello blinked again.

"Othello," LeBlanc said. He moved forward.

Remy snapped his eyes back to LeBlanc, making the man still instantly.

"Othello," LeBlanc said again, softly now. "Don't."

"He's paid his debt to you a dozen times over," Remy pointed out. "He's free to walk. Now let him go, so you and I can finish this, man to man."

Othello's grip was no longer restraining. His hard features were transfixed by something like hope.

LeBlanc shook his head. "You don't give me orders, son."

"Call me that again," Remy said.

"You can't just walk in here," LeBlanc added, holding out

his arms to encompass his spacious surroundings, "and pretend you're in charge."

"If I say I'm in charge," Remy drawled, "then I'm in charge. And you'd be wise not to question me about that fact. Let Othello go and let him take the girl with him."

"Keesha." It wavered out of Othello in a whisper.

Remy saw that he looked sick, and his stomach clenched.

"Her name's Keesha. He's been drugging her. Kept her locked in the bedroom, even when Agent Escarra was here."

"There's a surgeon at the hospital uptown," Remy explained. "Dr. Grace Rivera. You'll take Keesha to her. She'll get the attention she needs."

Othello gave a nod. He moved forward.

LeBlanc gripped the knob of the bedroom door. "Othello. Think about what you're doing. Think long and hard."

"I've had a lot of time to think," Othello said heavily before he pushed LeBlanc neatly out of his way. He went through the door.

LeBlanc glared at Remy. "If I go down, you know I'm taking him with me."

"You can try," Remy acknowledged, nonplussed.

"No one knows more about what Othello's done for the last thirty years than I do," LeBlanc pointed out.

"It's the same the other way around, and you're a bigger fish for the Feds to fry once Othello rolls on you," Remy explained. "You're going to learn that extortion doesn't buy you loyalty. Not in the long run."

The door opened again. LeBlanc moved back as Othello carried Keesha out. He'd helped her into a baggy T-shirt.

Her glazed eyes wheeled around the room. "Where are we going?" she asked.

"Somewhere better than this," Othello promised. He went to the door and paused only briefly with a nod to Remy.

Remy returned it, a knot forming in his throat.

"You'll pay for this, Baz," LeBlanc said. His glossy demeanor had vanished. Without Othello, he'd been stripped. "I'll make you pay, just like you did for Gabbie."

Remy remained still, ignoring every voice inside him that told him to wrap his hands around LeBlanc's throat. He closed the distance between them. LeBlanc stood over six feet tall, but his shoulders bowed at Remy's height.

Remy inserted himself in LeBlanc's space and saw the impulse to squirm swim behind the man's eyes. He allowed his lips to curve into a cold, false smile. "You want to know something?"

LeBlanc eyes pinged back and forth between Remy's. "What's that?"

"I'm not afraid of you," Remy told him. "I've never been afraid of you. The world may see a cultivated political player with spit and polish, but all I see is a pedophile sitting in somebody else's suite. The best part is that the world is going to know it. Your friends are going to know it. The media's going to know it. And all the people you've wronged, all the people you owe, will come after you like wolves. I'm just the beginning. Now tell me where Sloane Escarra is."

"I don't know what you're talking about," LeBlanc fired back.

Remy's hands flashed. Before he knew what he was doing, he'd pinned LeBlanc against the wall, one hand wrapped around his chin. Remy bent down, a breath away. Bourbon was strong on LeBlanc's breath. He'd drunk it with the Guidrys, too. He'd probably raised it in toast after selling Remy to Gretchen. "Talk," Remy instructed.

LeBlanc struggled. He thrashed once against Remy's hold. His robe slipped over one shoulder. Then he stilled, knowing he was the weaker adversary. "She left here of her own accord."

"Who'd you send to snatch her?" Remy demanded. "Someone you hired? Someone else you've bribed? Nestor Escarra, for instance?"

LeBlanc attempted to shake his head, failed. "Nestor's not my dog. His leash is controlled by someone else."

"Who?" Remy asked. When LeBlanc didn't answer, he raised his gun into his line of sight. LeBlanc visibly paled. *"Who?"*

LeBlanc bore air in and out of his nose like a wounded animal, wheezing slightly. "If you're looking for answers, I suggest you go to the Escarras."

"Why?"

"They wouldn't want her sniffing too close," LeBlanc explained. "Not if she values her oath more than her family."

"What's Nestor up to?" Remy asked. "Who's pulling his strings?"

"Blood," LeBlanc answered simply.

"Tell the truth," Remy warned.

"I am telling the truth," LeBlanc snapped. "Now let go of me, you bastard—"

Remy tossed him onto the floor in a heap. "I don't believe you."

LeBlanc steadied himself on his hands and knees. It took some effort. Remy saw the tremors tuning his limbs like a fork. "Sometimes the truth is closer to home than you realize," he said resentfully.

Denial flitted across Remy's mind. He pushed it aside, making himself think through the possibilities. "Are you saying the Escarras are involved in this?"

"Remy."

The voice behind him made Remy revolve on the spot. He watched Sloane's father cross the threshold.

LeBlanc gave a breathless laugh, gesturing from one man

to another. "Tell him, Senator. Tell my boy here that your family's responsible for your own daughter's kidnapping."

Horatio had the grace to look ashamed.

Remy struggled for a moment to speak. "You know what she went through. You watched what came after. All this time, you were involved in trafficking?"

"I wasn't," Horatio said. "I wasn't even aware of my family's illegalities. Not until it was brought to my attention during my campaign for reelection." He looked to LeBlanc.

Remy, too, looked at his father, still on his hands and knees on the floor. More blackmail. More extortion.

"I confronted them," Horatio went on. "I was angry. If their activities came to light, it would ruin my chances politically. It would ruin the family. My pleas fell on deaf ears until Sloane returned from Mexico. Seeing the toll her captivity and trauma took on her, my father saw fit to give control of the trafficking network back to the sectors."

"Sloane's abuelo was involved?" Remy asked.

"Not just him," Horatio said grievously.

"If he gave up control," Remy said carefully, "how're you involved in this?"

"Recently, it came to my attention that after my father's death, the role of the Escarras resumed."

"Picked up where they left off," LeBlanc muttered. "But it wasn't the patriarch running things this time. Makes sense. It's the female spiders that dominate the males." He gave a nasty chortle. "Cuban boys, following mami's orders."

Remy's features hardened. He shook his head at Horatio. "Why haven't you told Sloane?"

Horatio's throat moved in a swallow. "As long as she sought other leads, she was safe."

"You mean to tell me she isn't safe now?"

"I've come to you for help."

"You know where she is," Remy realized.

Horatio nodded, grim. "I know where my daughter is. And you're the only one I trust to get her out."

Chapter 21

Sloane's eyelids felt cumbersome. It took time and effort to lift them. She peered through a muzzy film. Her surroundings made little sense even as her eyes cleared. She stared at the ceiling...or what was left of it. Parts of it had fallen in, complete sections of insulation exposed. She smelled rotted wood, dirty laundry water and mold.

She tried lifting her head, but her neck protested. The surface underneath her felt hard. As she moved her arm, she heard metal sliding against metal. Turning her cheek to her shoulder, she peered down.

A cuff latched her wrist to the rail of a table with a three-inch railing.

"Hello, Santana."

She jerked at the sound of the voice. Looking around, she watched a feminine shape come closer. The bright light behind her cast her face into shadow. She shifted, and the spotlight fell across her features, cleaving them from the dark surroundings.

"Abuela?"

"Shh," she said, reaching out to feather a touch across Sloane's brow. She stroked, fingering the hair out of her face. "It's all right, pequeña."

"Where are we?" Sloane asked. Her mouth was bone-dry. The corners of her lips cracked as she moved them. "What are we doing here?"

"Santana," Abuela murmured. "I need you to remain calm."

What was this place? The raised rows of seats made it look like an amphitheater of some kind. The spotlight shone dully off windows on the walls high above. As if this had once been an observation room of some kind. The glass had filmed over and the plain Jane analog clock on the wall was stuck at six fifty-five. No one had used this space for some time. Not for its intended purpose.

Which was what? The table she was latched to looked clinical. Had this room been used for medical training? A shiver passed through her, involuntary and thorough, which made no sense either. It was hot. She could feel sweat crawling from her temples to her ears. Fighting to sit up, she made it halfway before firm hands took her by the shoulders and forced her back to the table.

Sloane cried out as her head banged against the metal.

"Gentle, hijo," Abuela admonished.

Sloane blinked up, trying to discern which of her tíos was pinning her to the table. Her vision wavered. Dizziness took her, and her stomach revolted, the overwhelming smell of the place not helping. "I think… I think I'm going to be sick."

"Here now." Abuela waved something under her nose. "Deep breath."

Sloane obeyed because the combined fragrances of mint and ginger were irresistible. The smells brought back those faraway moments spent in front of Abuela's vanity mirror with her hair splayed over her shoulders, the silver-handled brush caressing her scalp. The essential-oil blend and the memories brought a frisson of calm.

It vanished when she heard Nestor's voice. "We can't uncuff her."

Sloane sought Abuela. "Tell him to let me go. He'll listen to you."

Abuela's fingers interlocked with hers. "I wish I could, pequeña. But not just yet."

Sloane shook her head, trying to think through whatever Abuela wasn't saying. Her mind was too muddied. Frustrated, she bit off, "Why not?"

"First, you will listen," Abuela reasoned.

The truth dawned slowly with devastating effect. "Are you…helping him?" she asked in a small voice.

Abuela looked down at Sloane's hand in hers. "I've told you about our lives in Cuba."

"Abuela?" Sloane bleated.

"Castro took everything. He put my father in jail and let him die there. He took the rum business, the one my father had built for me and my children. Arturo was lucky. He escaped imprisonment. We were able to board a plane. But we had nothing. Our family legacy was lost."

Sloane had heard the story dozens of times before. She shook her head. "Why are you telling me this now? Why are we here? What are you doing?"

"Santana, listen to me," Abuela said firmly. "I'm trying to tell you. Arturo and I worked to the bone to build something here in America. A lasting legacy. Soon, the Escarra name meant good rum. Our sons had everything they could want. We thought they could live their lives without fear or recrimination. Then the government started poking around. Taxes started to take more and more. We watched our savings dwindle. And still they took more. Arturo and I knew if our sons were to pass our legacy on to our grandchildren—to you—that something must be done. We had to seek security elsewhere."

"I don't understand," Sloane said. But she did. She just refused to open her eyes to the truth. It would destroy her entire world.

"We bought Carnival Antiquities," she said. "We worked to erect what Gretchen Guidry had built. It was easy with contacts like Sebastian LeBlanc, who knew a network of people who were interested in things they couldn't get through legal means."

"Stop," Sloane demanded, shaking her head. "Abuelo wouldn't! You wouldn't! Not after what I went through."

Abuela nodded. "After you came home to us from Mexico, Arturo saw how broken you were. He didn't have the stomach for the business anymore. Not the kind we were doing with LeBlanc. So, for a while, we handed the reins of the organization over to him. But then Escarra Cuba went under. Your abuelo died. We had little left but the house and some minor assets. I had no choice but to go back into trafficking."

"You did have a choice," Sloane told her. "You had every choice. This is why you wanted me to stop doing my job. This is why you didn't want me to be an FBI agent." Abuela had known she was close. She hadn't just wanted Sloane to give it all up, marry Miguel and keep her head down and her nose clean. She'd *needed* her to.

Sloane's tear ducts stung incessantly, and bile thickened her throat, but there were no tears. It was unbearably hot. She needed water. The nausea wasn't going anywhere. After the revelations, it was worse. "Who else?" she made herself ask, trying to keep her mind clear. "You. Nestor. Abuelo. Who else was in on this?" *Not Papá. Please, not Papá.*

"It is a family business, Santana. We employ many. We put food on dozens of tables, roofs over families' heads—"

"You think what you've done is noble?" Sloane blasted. Her eyes burned now. She was forced to squint. "You think that makes everything okay? How many children have you kidnapped? How many have you transported across state lines? How many have been violated or traumatized or *killed*?"

"We do not kill."

"Esther Fournier died in Abalone in one of *your* brothels."

"She took her life into her own hands when she ran away," Abuela said, her voice even.

"Your man, Booker, hunted her down like an animal and killed her."

"His methods were regrettable," Abuela admitted. "But he's dead now, too. A life for a life."

"His death does not absolve you or Nestor or whoever else you've involved in this." Her tías... Her primos...? *How many?*

"The world is not black-and-white, Santana," Abuela chided. "We must navigate our way through all the shades in between to do what is best for ourselves and our family."

"If you're asking me for forgiveness or understanding, you won't get it," Sloane warned her. "I will never understand how you could hurt so many children and so many families, and I will never forgive you or Abuelo or any of the rest of you for what you've done."

Disappointment sank into the lines of Abuela's face. "That is your choice. But I will tell you one thing. You will stop this investigation," she ordered. "You will call off any inquiries you have made into Carnival Antiquities. You can place the blame on someone else if you like. Booker. McBride. Le Fe..."

"Le Fe," Sloane repeated. She'd been wrong. Sebastian LeBlanc hadn't killed Ray de le Fe. "You ordered the hit. And you had Gretchen Guidry killed, too." The time frame, the puzzle pieces, Guidry's slaying, the Escarra takeover of Guidry's organization, the MO that matched in both the Guidry murder case and le Fe's... It all fit. "You and Abuelo knew you would take over her organization even before her death. You had her removed from the picture so you could seize her assets, just as the government seized yours."

"Ama," Nestor said from the head of the table. "She's done listening. She was never going to listen."

"It was you," Sloane said, tipping her chin up. Nestor looked down at her. The way the light hit his face, his eyes unclouded by questions or remorse…she barely recognized him. "Wasn't it?"

"Don't answer that, mijo," Abuela instructed.

"You would be wise to agree to our terms," Nestor told Sloane.

"Or what?" Sloane challenged. "You'll slit my throat, too?"

"You think I'm so godless as to murder my own sobrina in cold blood?" he asked.

"Sounds like a gray area to me," she sneered.

He shook his head slightly. "We have no problem holding you."

"You've kidnapped a federal agent. Do you know what will happen when they find me?"

"They won't find you," Nestor said with chilling finality.

Remy, Sloane thought. His face wavered through her mind. She grabbed on to it tightly. Remy would find her.

Unless he'd disappeared already.

A scream wanted to break loose from inside her. She closed her eyes, turning away from the light.

"Perhaps," Abuela murmured, "what she needs is more time."

"I'm *not* going to change my mind," Sloane muttered.

Nestor released her shoulders, and she felt him back off.

Sloane pushed herself up onto her elbow. "Abuela. Let me go. Por favor."

"Only if you agree to what I have asked," Abuela said.

"I can't do that. You know I can't do that."

"Then it's true," Abuela said. "Your badge has come to mean more to you than us."

Sloane hissed at a sharp pain above her hip. Looking around, she saw Nestor and the needle. "No…" She struggled against the cuff. The table shook. "No!"

"You'll think on it," Abuela said, backing away. "I have faith in you, Santana, even if you no longer have faith in me."

Sloane fought a losing battle. The fight drained out of her, inexorably. Just as she collapsed again to the table, the light went out, and a door closed, the sound echoing emptily through the chamber.

It wasn't Remy's first raid. The towering art deco facade of the abandoned charity hospital downtown may, however, have been the largest building he'd ever breached. Originally built in the eighteenth century, the edifice had reached its twenty-story height in the 1930s. It, too, had been a casualty of Hurricane Katrina in 2005 and, like Six Flags New Orleans, had been considered too damaged and too large to either be refurbished, reused or demolished.

Horatio stood at Remy's right in a bulletproof vest. At his shoulder was Sloane's boss, Special Agent in Charge Brick Houghton.

"I'm sorry, Senator," Houghton said. "I can't allow you beyond this point."

"She's my daughter," Horatio explained. "They're my family. If anyone can reason with them, it's me."

"Who said anything about reasoning?" Remy asked.

"I don't want her to be held as a hostage," Horatio told him.

"She's already a hostage," Remy informed him. "I told you I'll find her."

"Where do you even begin looking?" Horatio asked, shielding his eyes from the sun as he took in the building's sheer breadth and height. "She could be anywhere."

"She's likely being held in the basement or subbasement," said Sloane's partner, Agent Pelagie Landry. "If the building's breached, they'd be able to hold either more easily than they could secure anything above that."

"Remy!"

He looked around. At the sight of Torben, his feet started moving.

Torben met him halfway. "We checked the Escarras' homes and offices. Nestor's missing, as we suspected. Juan, Vincente and Ramon are, too. Their wives claim they don't know where the brothers are. I sent officers to The Roosevelt. When they arrived in the presidential suite, the door had been breached. They found LeBlanc alone inside, packing for an extended trip abroad. We wouldn't have cause to detain him if we hadn't received a tip from your friend, Dr. Rivera, who says a girl in her care was held against her will by LeBlanc. If she doesn't testify, I'm sure the man who brought her there will."

Remy was vaguely surprised to hear that Othello hadn't taken a leaf out of his book and disappeared altogether. "He's willing to talk?"

"It seems so." Torben nodded to Horatio. "I hear the senator is as well."

"If we can get Sloane out safely," Remy said.

Torben shrugged off his suit jacket and reached for the riot vest on the hood of his car. "Let's get to it." At Remy's silence, he said, "What? You didn't think I'd sit this one out, too, did you?"

Remy didn't care how many people were watching. He swept his friend into a hard embrace. "Thank you, brother."

Torben gave him a hearty rap on the back before they separated. "What's the plan?"

"Hostage crisis entry."

Torben lifted his chin. "High risk."

"Exactly."

"The S.W.A.T. team will breach the front and back bays. They'll spread out and work the first floor, clearing rooms along the way. They'll move up from there."

"And what will you be doing?" Torben asked, seeing the look Remy had exchanged with Agent Landry.

"Sloane's partner and I will go down to subbasement level," he explained. "Our best guess is that she's being held there.

If they're down there, Nestor and his brothers will respond when they hear S.W.A.T. enter the building."

"What if they use Agent Escarra as a hostage?" Torben asked. "I've seen more hostage fatalities than I care to remember during massive search operations like this one."

Remy knew the percentage of hostages killed by their captors during those operations. He also knew that hostage negotiation marginally increased the chances the hostage would get out alive. "Landry worked in hostage negotiation before she joined the Crimes Against Children unit," Remy said.

"You saw the autopsy photos of Guidry and le Fe. If it was Nestor Escarra who killed both, you know he doesn't play around."

"Apparently, he's a good hound who attacks only on Abuela's orders. I don't believe she'll want Sloane dead, even if it means she and her sons are apprehended."

"We'll get her out," Torben replied. "I'm with you all the way."

"Fontenot."

They turned as one to see Houghton approach. "S.W.A.T. team's ready."

Remy nodded. "We're ready, too, sir."

Houghton's look was hard and imploring. "Bring her back alive."

Chapter 22

The team breached the door. The noise was incredible. S.W.A.T. filed past into what had been the emergency room entrance. Remy let Landry lead and followed. He felt more than heard Torben on his six. Keeping a two-handed hold on his weapon, he wove through the hallways, listening to the shouts of the team.

"Clear!"

"Clear here!"

"Next room!"

They'd cleared most of the lower floor before they heard the first gunshots.

Landry put her back to the wall as S.W.A.T. responded. Remy and Torben did the same. She pressed her finger to her ear, listening to comms. Then she exchanged a glance with Remy. "Basement. Just like we thought."

"Are they drawing them out?" Torben asked.

Landry listened, trying to hear above the noise. "One suspect down," she reported.

Remy tried to calibrate his breathing. He felt himself easing back into fight mode. However, the tension in his body threatened to overwhelm training and experience.

Sloane. It was Sloane down there. He closed his eyes for a brief second, trying to anchor himself in the echoing chaos of the hospital's corridors.

Landry nudged him. "If we wind our way through the old radiology wing, we could get to the subbasement level and possibly circumnavigate Nestor and the others."

It was better than standing against the wall. "Let's move," Remy said.

Landry reported their new position through comms as they detoured under the sign for radiology.

The rooms along this corridor hadn't been cleared, so they took their time doing so. There were no windows here. The light fixtures had been removed.

Remy switched on his flashlight, holding it underneath the barrel of his gun as he swept an old MRI room. The machine was gone, leaving behind a steel circle that looked like a hobbit-size portal to another realm. As they wove through the department, Remy knew they were approaching the riverside of the building because of the creeping waterlines along each wall.

If this part of the hospital had flooded, then the basement level would have been completely submerged. How much water had been pumped out? Would Ezmeralda keep her granddaughter in a chamber where mold and God knew what else had been festering for twenty years?

"Morgue," Landry announced as she backed out of a room. "It's clear."

Remy's flashlight passed over the giant pentagram someone had spray-painted in red outside the door. A roach skittered across its center, shying from the light.

A gunshot close by brought the three of them up to their toes. "We should be approaching the subbasement stairwell," Landry whispered as their backs met the wall again.

"There's the elevator," Torben pointed out, nodding to an opening in the wall. The doors and car were gone, leaving the long, upward shaft and its metalworks exposed.

Landry held up a hand. She listened for a moment, pointing her light at the ground. Then she motioned for them to go ahead.

They shuffled forward. Remy saw the sign for the subbasement. His heart hitched into his throat, and he locked down the urgency tearing through his blood. If Sloane was where they thought she was, she was close. The heat of the corridor swelled, and the smell of rot made his nostrils flare.

The door to the stairwell swung open.

Their weapons swung up, their feet braced in unison. "Hands up!" Landry shouted when the figure reached for his waist.

A curse. Hands reached for the sky.

"Turn," Landry ordered, stepping forward cautiously.

Vincente Escarra squinted against the bright beams as he circled around. "I'm not armed," he told them.

Landry grabbed his arm and turned him against the wall. "Search him."

Torben did so, patting his hands over Vincente's person. When he found the weapon at the small of his back, he lifted it to the light.

"Not armed, huh?" Remy asked. His back teeth ground as he glared at Vincente. "Tell us where she is."

Vincente continued to squint. "It's not your job to protect her anymore. You should have left that to us."

"Where is she?" Remy asked, drawing out each word. They felt like sandpaper.

"With Ama. Down at the bottom."

"Where are Nestor and the others?" Landry wanted to know.

Vincente said nothing. When Torben gave him a shove, he bit off a frustrated groan. "Juan and Ramon are holding off the breach team."

"And Nestor?"

"Downstairs."

Remy fought a curse. He looked at Landry. "I'll lead."

Landry eyed him for a moment, uncertain. "If he uses her as a hostage…"

"You can take the reins," Remy granted readily. If they met Nestor on the stairs, however, and he wasn't using Sloane as a shield for him or Abuela, Remy wanted to meet him first.

She gave a nod. "Lead on."

The dank smells of the subterranean level swamped the stairwell. He heard Landry hiss in reaction. It smelled like the deepest, most untouched parts of the bayou, where mud was fetid when disturbed by intruding feet and the bodies of prey moldered as the earth took them back.

Something else lurked in the air, the pungency of water trapped underground for too long. Altogether, the potency of the subbasement atmosphere threatened to make Remy's eyes water.

He heard the distant sound of a cough and didn't know he'd quickened his progress down the stairs until Torben tapped him on the back. Forcing himself to slow again, he measured each spare bit of graffiti on the walls.

His flashlight reflected off windows. They were filthy, covered in the remnants of old sludge. The waterlines were drawn along the ceiling here, everything below streaked in black and green.

Remy hit the last stair before cautiously stepping down to the concrete floor of the landing. He swung around, illuminating the space.

The flash of a knife as it arced had him dancing back. A gunshot rang out from behind him.

Nestor's figure seized. He grunted.

Remy disarmed him quickly, then caught him before he could sink to the floor. He eased the man down against the wall.

A door opened. Remy circled around, gun clamped between both palms again, ready.

Abuela blinked at him. "Remy?"

The muscles in Remy's jaw twitched. "Abuela."

Nestor groaned from the floor.

Abuela's gaze fell to him. She went to her knees. "What have you done?" she asked, prying Nestor's hands away from the wound just below his ribs. Her dark eyes winged accusation as she looked up at Remy again. "What have you done?" she asked again, louder.

"She needs to be searched," Landry indicated.

Torben moved forward.

Abuela rose. Remy saw the small pearl-handled pistol clutched in her hand. She raised it, aiming it at his chest. "Come closer," she dared.

Remy heard Torben's feet shuffle to a halt. Remy didn't take his eyes off Abuela's face. "You're going to shoot me?" he asked.

"How do you think Arturo and I got out of Cuba in the first place?" Abuela asked. "My father gave me this pistol. When Castro's men came for my husband in the night, I knew what I had to do to protect what was left of my family, just as I know what to do to protect my family now."

"Protecting Sloane means holding her prisoner?" he replied.

"Sometimes, we protect our loved ones from themselves."

Torben moved in.

"No!" she shouted, and the pistol trembled as she raised it higher, aiming at Remy's forehead. Torben froze in answer. "You've hurt my Nestor, and I believe reparation should be made to those who've been wronged. You take one step closer, and I'll put a bullet in this one."

There was something foreign about Abuela's eyes, Remy saw. A dark light that hadn't been there before. Though her hand continued to quiver around the pistol's grip, her eyes told him she believed every word out of her mouth. She would use the weapon if provoked.

"Drop your weapons," she told them all.

Remy crouched slowly to set his gun on the floor and then raised his hands as he came back up. He heard Torben and Agent Landry mirror his movements.

"Down on your knees," Abuela instructed.

"If you're going to pull the trigger, I'd prefer to meet my death on my feet," Remy informed her.

Abuela shook her head. "Why didn't you stay away, Remy? You should've left my Santana well enough alone."

"She didn't need me to hunt down the truth," he told her. "You realize how badly you've hurt her with this? How betrayed she must feel?"

"She betrayed us the moment she took her oath," Abuela said. "The only oaths we take should abide by family. I hardly expect a man like you to understand. In all the meals we shared, in all the days you spent under my son's roof, I never heard you once speak of who or where you come from."

He'd been careful never to speak of his mother, his father or his sisters—the one he'd lost and the one he'd left. It wasn't until he lived as a guest under the umbrella of the Escarra family that he'd felt the loss of his own family less like a hole in his heart. It was the first time he hadn't felt that rootless feeling that followed him everywhere he went.

The betrayal Sloane must be feeling…he felt it, too. Because, for a time, the Escarras had felt like his own.

Abuela lowered her chin. "A man without family is as good as a ghost. How could Santana grasp at smoke all these years and call it love?"

He wouldn't blink, he told himself. No matter how close to home Abuela's words struck. As a runaway, then a SEAL and Loup-Garou, he'd kept his steps light. He'd made a living fading into shadow. Smoke and lies weren't a life, but he'd made them his.

"You don't have to listen to this," Torben told Remy.

Then there were those who'd made him feel seen since he'd left New Orleans.

His brother stood at his back, his hands in the air, a breath away from a bullet. He'd walked into a firefight knowing he had a wife waiting for him at home. And Sloane...

Remy spotted the door behind Abuela. He saw the combination lock. He breathed carefully before his heart could beat through his skin. Sloane was in the room below, beyond the dark, filmed-over windows, a hair's breadth away. He visualized her beyond that door. He imagined getting her to safety.

"You can stand here and throw insults at me, but your son's bleeding out, and there's not a doctor to be found in this hospital," Remy pointed out. "You've got two options. The first is you lower that weapon and Agent Landry here will see to it that Nestor gets the medical attention he needs."

Abuela's eyes went to slits. "The second?"

"The second is I go through you both," Remy said. "Like *smoke*."

The muscles around her mouth quivered. The pistol shook violently in her hands now. The light of challenge in her eyes flickered like a faulty incandescent bulb.

He could all but feel Torben and Landry holding their breaths behind him, ready. He was tensed, fight flooding him in welcome waves.

Nestor gave a pained groan.

Abuela froze, then turned halfway toward him.

Remy gripped her wrist, crowding her against the door behind her.

The door shook, and a wild scream tore through the stairwell as the gun, caught between his and Abuela's grip, went off.

Chapter 23

Sloane confronted the dark as she woke slowly. Her breathing thickened as fear crashed through, spidering across her skin.

She heard the scrape of metal on metal, felt the restraint at her wrist. It all came flooding back. Abuela. Nestor. The strange amphitheater-like chamber with the table at its center. And her on top of it, like an anatomy presentation spread before the watchful eyes of ghosts.

Her lips trembled. She heard her own sob echoing off the walls. The darkness felt claustrophobic.

It's the drug, the small voice of reason whispered from somewhere inside her head. She could still feel the pinch of the needle. Her hip ached with phantom pain around the injection site.

She'd been drugged before. Not just the roofies from the club when she was younger. When she'd failed to comply with her traffickers' demands in Mexico, they'd subdued her with opioids. After her leg had been surgically repaired upon her return to the United States, the doctors had prescribed oxycodone. The deep-seated numbness she'd felt after taking her first dose had been distressingly familiar. She'd begged for something else, anything else, to fight the pain.

This felt all too similar to that. She struggled to snap herself out of the sedate, seductive haze of nothingness that coiled around her, dragging her back toward the brink of unconsciousness.

She tried and failed to sit up, fighting the pull like the drowning sweep of a deadly current.

She pushed herself halfway up on her elbows but felt her head loll back to the table. Propping her chin on her collarbone, she breathed through a powerful wave of nausea. The smells of the chamber made her want to vomit. *Focus*, she told herself. Gripping the table ledge, she pulled against the lure of gravity.

She sat upright, wavered and then tucked her knees up to her chest to cradle them with her unrestrained arm. She put her head between them and fought through the roiling of her stomach. Dizziness tossed her perception around like a pair of sneakers caught up in a tumble-dry sequence.

Cursing, she listened to the oath bounce back to her. It sounded sure.

It sounded like herself.

She tugged on the restraint and felt no give. She fumbled until she found the cuff fastening her to the rail. She shook it, feeling for the locking mechanism. She cursed again, reaching up to slick the damp hair back from her brow. The heat felt immense.

Ignoring the fear skating up her limbs again, she gripped the rail on either side of her and wiggled from side to side.

The table legs gave slightly, rocking back and forth. It wasn't bolted to the floor. She heard sloshing when she wiggled again, harder this time.

There was water on the floor.

How deep? How could she find her way out of it in the dark, especially if she was trapped against the rail of this godforsaken table?

She hadn't waited for a rescue in Mexico. She'd clawed her way out, located Pia. She'd paid for it with Jaime Solaro's cruelty. But she wasn't going to wait for Abuela or Nestor to come back. She wasn't going to wait for her fate, whatever it was, to come crashing down on her like hurricane waves, and she sure as hell wouldn't be kept in the foul-smelling dark forever. She'd only ever known how to fight her way out, gun or no gun.

She could reach the floor with her legs, but she would still be attached to the damn table. In order to break the restraint on her wrist, she would need a solid impact of some kind.

Her pulse wouldn't level, not with the drug in her system, so she laid flat on her back, gripped the arms of the table once more and rocked violently from side to side.

The table lurched. Water splashed as the legs fought the imbalance.

She gritted her teeth and rocked some more, throwing her weight into it.

Finally, it tipped. She felt herself falling and tucked her arms to her sides.

The water wasn't cool. Nor was it soothing. It felt thick and slimy. She retched, pushing herself up onto her arms. It washed around her wrists as the table flipped off her back.

She felt the cuff loosen. It had shattered with the impact to the floor.

She scrambled to her feet, lurching as her dizziness swamped her.

Her palms connected with something. A low wall. She planted her hands on it as the tepid water flooded her shoes. The effort it had taken to upset the table and haul herself to her feet made white spots dance before her vision. She clung to the wall, not wanting to fall into the water again as her knees shook.

The weakness… It pissed her off. She gripped the answering anger and let it spread clean through her, chasing weakness off.

Her hands fumbled over the low wall. Her feet shuffled through the water as she sidestepped, looking for an opening.

She found it and dragged her toe over the edge of a step. Bracing her arms, she pulled herself up, fighting the heaviness of her own limbs. She reached out blindly, clawing through empty air.

The back of a chair firmed under her hand. She groped in the opposite direction with her other hand and found another. She was in an aisle of stadium seating. Pulling her other foot out of the water, she took the next stair.

She crawled up another row of seats. Then another. She wished she'd counted them when the lights had been on before. How many to the top? Ten? Fifteen?

Her heart beat at her ears with enough force to split her head open by the time she reached the twelfth row. She could feel sweat crawling down her face. It stung her eyes. She reached out for the next row of seats…and pitched forward when her hands met nothing.

The impact of concrete sang up her knees and through the heels of her hands as they connected with the floor. Still, she felt around, finding the wall in front of her. Success coursed through her, enlivening her, even as fatigue threatened to crush her like an aluminum can.

"Come on," she bit out and forced herself up to feet, her back against the wall. Taking a moment to brace her hands on her knees, she filled her lungs with filthy air once, twice, three times. The wall curved inward, circling the amphitheater. It was rough and unfinished under her palm. She touched something, and it skittered away.

Gritting her teeth, she kept going.

When she finally found the handle of the door, her heart skipped a full beat. She turned it. It didn't budge.

She was locked in.

Oh hell, no. Drawing herself back, she willed strength into being, imagined it flooding her. Then she dove at the door, shoulder forward.

It didn't give.

Her shoulder ached, but she did it again. She drove her fists against it, screaming.

She could hear a struggle on the other side of the door. Someone screamed.

She threw her weight against the door again, sobs flying free from the dry passage of her throat. She beat at it. She'd beat at it until it gave.

The door swung open just as she lunged at it again.

She fell through the open air, putting her hands out to catch herself again.

Someone caught her instead, hauling her to her feet. Arms tangled around her, pulling her up against a hard chest.

The smell of gunpowder singed her nostrils. Then another smell. This one familiar. Steadying. It was the smell of freedom and temptation and home. "Remy?" she choked out.

Hands framed her face. A light flashed. His marble-hard profile cleaved the darkness in two. "Sloane. Are you all right? What'd they do, boo? Talk to me."

She couldn't string a sentence together. Not with relief wrapping her in a cosseting embrace.

He was here.

The edge of his thumb traced something on her cheek that stung. She winced. "You came back," she managed.

He gave a single shake of his head. "I never left."

"You didn't?"

"I couldn't," he said. "I need to know. Did they hurt you?"

The tremors wouldn't stop. They gripped her. "I'm standing, aren't I?" *Sort of,* she thought.

Something like a smile touched his face. She'd never have called it soft, but his eyes were some version of it as they passed over her, his arms tightening as they went around her again. She let herself be held because it felt so goddamn good. It shoved the dark further away. All the cracked glass pieces of her soul on the verge of shattering seamed, shoring up the foundation.

He'd never been far away. When she needed him, he'd always answered the call. It didn't matter where he came from or who he'd been.

He'd come for her, just as he had all the times before. He'd never stop coming for her.

"Santana?"

She stiffened. Turning slowly, she faced Abuela. Pelagie was cuffing her hands behind her back. The pearl-studded pistol she knew belonged to her grandmother lay broken on the floor. "Nestor needs a doctor," Abuela said. "He needs one badly."

Sloane saw the tears in her grandmother's eyes. She saw her chin wobble. On the ground, another man in a riot vest had his hands clasped over the bleeding wound in Nestor's midsection. Anguish painted her tío's face. He looked pale in the semidarkness. Sloane gave a nod. "He'll have one."

Abuela's tears flowed down her cheeks. The drops sluiced to her chin. "None of this would've happened if you'd just looked out for us. Why couldn't you have agreed to our terms—to back off your investigation? To redeem us in the eyes of the law?"

The fear of the dark…the claustrophobia that came with it…the effects of the drugs… They were too fresh for Sloane to offer her forgiveness, much less comfort. With her family now involved in the case, Pelagie would have to build it from here on her own and then the courts would decide her grandmother's and tíos' fates. "It's out of my hands now, Abuela." Sloane swallowed the apology that wanted to jump out when Abuela lowered her chin and sobbed.

Remy's hand passed over her shoulders. "Let's get you to a medic, too."

For once, Sloane let herself be led. She took great pride in knowing that her legs were steady enough to take the next flight of stairs, but the sound of her grandmother's crying echoed after her, chastening her even in Abuela's defeat.

Grace, Remy and Sloane's father worked their magic over Sloane and convinced her to remain in the recovery ward overnight for observation. She'd been tapped for an IV and pumped with hydrating liquids. Her cuts and bruises had been seen to. She hadn't mentioned the considerable amount of pain in her hip from the crash from the table for fear they would have whisked her off for an X-ray.

She refused pain meds. No morphine. No NSAIDs. Remy never left her side, even as Houghton, Pelagie and other law enforcement officials breezed in and out of her room. When visiting hours were over, she still found it difficult to stay asleep for more than a few minutes at a time. She felt ridiculous insisting that the light for the connected bathroom stay on, but she didn't want to wake up in the dark again. She wondered if she ever would.

She insisted Grace depart for the night. She'd seen the bags under her friend's eyes. Between her hours in the OR and dashing back and forth between there and Sloane's room, Grace was worn down. Her father also said his goodbyes, claiming to need a good night's sleep before his interview with Pelagie the next day at FBI headquarters.

Sloane couldn't pretend that she wasn't unperturbed that her father had hidden what he knew of the family's wrongdoings. The twinge of betrayal was hard to face. As he'd sat next to her hospital bed, watching her struggle for rest, she'd seen how much conflict and remorse weighed on him. He looked as if he'd aged ten years in a few days.

The media was going to come after him, her and the members of her family. She couldn't think about it without a headache pulsing at her temples. There would be an investigation, too, into whether Sloane herself had been involved in any of it. Whether or not they took her badge, it would be a mark on her service record.

She expected Remy to drift off as the night wore on, but he didn't. His eyes remained open, onyx, fixed on her.

She wanted him to sleep. She needed to release some of what was inside her. If she had to cry to do that…fine. But she wouldn't do it in front of him. He'd seen too many of her weaker moments. She'd fallen apart one too many times in his arms.

By contrast, his secrets lived in the silence. Long hours had passed, and he hadn't offered any more explanations about what had led him to become Loup-Garou, about the Guidrys or life as a LeBlanc.

The longer the quiet between them went on, the weightier it became.

Still, he said nothing as he continued his vigil at her bedside into the early morning hours.

A knock tapped against the door just after six o'clock the following morning.

As the door opened, Remy stood. Sloane sat upright, watching the man enter the room—the same one who'd tended to Nestor in the stairwell of the charity hospital the day before. A badge gleamed on his belt. The flash of the NOPD emblem made her nod in acknowledgment. "May we help you, Detective…?"

"Ballard," he said, inclining his head toward her. "I'm sorry. We weren't formally introduced yesterday. Torben Ballard, Missing Persons." He glanced at Remy.

Sloane watched something pass between the two men. "You know each other," she surmised.

The corner of Ballard's mouth quirked. "As well as brothers."

Remy had never mentioned Ballard to her. "Thank you for your assistance yesterday," she said. "It was a risk, joining Agent Landry and Remy in the raid."

"I'd do it again," Ballard said graciously. "If it's all right, Agent Escarra, I'd like to speak with you." To Remy, he added, "Alone."

Remy shook his head. "I don't think so."

Sloane sensed something unspoken between them. She glanced from one to the other, trying to grasp what they weren't saying.

Ballard proved just as hard to read as Remy. "Please," he added.

Remy frowned deeply. He looked at Sloane.

She understood his question and nodded her answer.

Remy arched a brow in Ballard's direction before he exited. The door closed behind him.

Sloane eased back against the pillows stacked behind her. It was difficult to feel dignified or professional in a hospital gown. Raising her chin, she gestured to the vacant chair.

Ballard muttered his thanks and lowered to it. He sat forward, over his knees. "I've known Remy since we were kids."

"Have you?" she asked.

"I'm one of the few who know him as both Remy Fontenot and Baz LeBlanc."

"He's never mentioned you before."

"Because he was protecting my secrets. Not his own."

"How many secrets do the two of you have?"

"He's told you about his connection to the Guidrys."

"He has."

"What he didn't disclose is how he and I came to know

each other," Ballard said. He shifted, uncomfortable. "I was another one of Gretchen Guidry's favorite toys."

"I see," she said carefully.

"I don't have to tell you how going through something like that with someone else forges a bond. Often, people who hold victims against their will try to break that bond. They take pleasure in breaking it. But Guidry soon found that some bonds can't be broken. I could only get out from under Guidry's roof because Remy made that possible. He wasn't the only one who escaped her clutches before their contract with her was over."

Amazed at his candor, Sloane struggled to clear her throat. "He's never mentioned you before because he's been protecting you. Your name. Your involvement with the Guidrys."

"It's more than that, Agent Escarra," he explained. "That's what I'm here to talk about. I'm sure you're aware how seriously Remy takes friendship and brotherhood. He's not just covering for me where the Guidrys are concerned."

Sloane tried to think ahead. She braced for whatever bombshell Ballard was going to throw forth next, but her head hurt. Closing her eyes briefly, she concentrated on gathering herself before opening them again. "He didn't want you to say any of this. That's why he was reluctant to leave the room."

Ballard gave a faint, wistful smile. "He'd stand in front of me—and, I suspect, you—until he draws his last breath. Love. Honor. Loyalty. He has them in abundance. Which is why he was never willing to let me take the fall for Loup-Garou."

Sloane gawked at him. "You're Loup-Garou?"

"The two initial raids in Mississippi and just over the state line," he said carefully. "That was me. Remy and I had discussed someone taking matters into their own hands. I'd told him how someone could do that. Trafficking underage victims is becoming increasingly common. My and Remy's story isn't unusual anymore." He gestured to her. "Neither is yours,

Agent Escarra. When Remy heard about Loup-Garou initially, he came to me, furious."

"Why?" Sloane asked.

Ballard dropped his gaze to the ring on his left ring finger. It was a titanium band. Though only a few shades darker than his skin, it stood out. "I have a family of my own. If I got caught, I wouldn't be risking my job alone. I'd lose the life I've built since I wiggled my way out of Guidry's hold. The way he put it, I had everything to lose, and he had nothing. If I needed someone to take on traffickers, he said I'd either let him do it or he'd tell my wife I was involved."

Ballard's frown deepened. "I love my wife, Agent Escarra. I loved her through chemo and everything that came before and after. The idea of letting her down like that…of her knowing that I'd risked my integrity and our marriage so I could chase my demons…it didn't settle. I should've let it all go—my anger and bitterness with the system and those who kidnap and sell people under the law's nose every day. I should've let the job stay the job, let Remy live his life. But he did what I asked. He did it better than I did."

The first two Loup-Garou raids hadn't been as clean-cut, Sloane remembered. She had chalked it up to the vigilante learning his MO. But those first two hadn't been Remy at all. It had been someone else.

Remy had taken up the mantle of Loup-Garou not because he wanted to live outside the law, but because he'd been determined to protect his own. That was why he couldn't tell her any of it, even when she'd thrown the truth in his face outside The Roosevelt and all but begged him for an explanation.

It was so like him. She struggled to take into consideration anything other than what kind of loyalty that took.

She felt her forehead crease as she contemplated the angles. Raising a hand to it, she scrubbed her temple. "When I was investigating the Loup-Garou case, I came across a credit card transaction. Remy bought the Loup-Garou mask."

"He thought the wolfman mask I purchased at Halloween was cheesy," Ballard said with some resentment.

"Did you know he had his wolf mask custom made by his mother's shop in Baton Rouge?" she asked.

He shook his head. "I did not."

"The credit card was in the name Sebastian LeBlanc II," she revealed.

"Dammit, Remy."

"For a man so desperate to keep his identity hidden all these years," Sloane considered, "that seems a great risk."

"Remy left his father's house when he was sixteen," Ballard acknowledged. "In the physical sense. But he's been looking for home ever since."

She sighed. "He wanted them to find him."

"His father knew it," Ballard pointed out. "That's why whenever someone got closer—whether it was Célestine or the private investigator she hired—obstacles always presented themselves. Remy's reemergence and the truth of what happened to him would have been damning for his father. Far more damning than the evidence against him. Some people may ignore charges of child exploitation. But it's far more difficult to set aside wrongs against one's own family."

She nodded in understanding.

"What will you charge him with?" Ballard asked with measured curiosity.

"I'm afraid when I return to work, I'll be facing a lengthy review period to determine whether I was associated with my family's trafficking ring."

Ballard's gaze was probing. His stillness was unnerving. "Would it not be simpler to keep what you know of Loup-Garou and Baz LeBlanc quiet for the time being?"

She stared back, just as directly. "Long enough for him to develop a new identity?"

Ballard acknowledged this with a nod.

"What about your...your wife?" she asked gently. "What happens if I'm reinstated and bring charges against you?"

"I got him into this mess," he weighed. "I'll face whatever consequences I must."

It seemed love, loyalty and honor went both ways. Sloane thought about what she would have done for Grace and Pia to free them from the Solaros' grasp—to free them from their trauma, their own demons...

Ballard was right—some bonds were forged in fire and lasted forever.

"You don't have to answer right away," he ventured. "I would be grateful, however, if you spent your time away from the field office to consider it."

"I will," she replied.

Relief struck his face. "Thank you." Standing, he reached for her hand to shake. "I'm grateful."

She obliged him, letting him grip her hand, and had trouble bringing her eyes up to his. "You're not the only one who loves him."

"No," he said after a moment's pause. "I told him to disappear when le Fe was found. He chose to stay. I'm starting to understand why."

He circled the bed for the door. Before he could reach it, she said, "Detective."

Ballard turned back. "Ma'am?"

She chose her words carefully. "The hit-and-run accident that killed his sister, Gabriella."

"Yes."

She nodded, gleaning what she already knew from his expression. "It wasn't an accident."

"I suspect not. I've always suspected."

"Does Remy know?"

Ballard shook his head. "I don't think so. He finds it difficult to speak of Gabbie."

"LeBlanc laid the blame at his door to cover his own culpability," Sloane explained. "He put that burden on his son's soul."

"Someone should lift that burden."

"I agree," she said.

"I'll use my department's resources to look into it," Ballard promised.

Sloane nodded and said nothing more before the man saw himself out.

Chapter 24

Remy had questions. For instance, why hadn't he been arrested? Sloane had handed over her caseload to Agent Landry for the time being. He knew what the pending investigation cost her. She'd fallen into a brooding silence since he'd returned her to her maisonette on Bourbon Street.

He hadn't left her there alone. The walls were as thin as ever, so he knew when she turned in her sleep. He knew when her feet had hit the floor in the morning. He heard her crying softly over the sounds of the shower shortly after. It took everything in him not to break down the door to get to her.

If she'd wanted his comfort, she wouldn't have waited for the masking of falling water to do so.

He wanted to know how her debrief had gone with Houghton. He wanted to know how she felt about the members of her family who had been arrested. He wanted to know how she felt about her father's home being searched, about the calls that kept coming from media outlets for comment.

His father had once made a spectacle of his family life. Remy had watched him fall from grace, and the fallout that had taken place had swept his mother and Emmie up in the surge. They'd retreated far from the prying eyes of public life. Would Sloane be forced to do the same?

Most of all, he wanted…no, *needed* to know what she wanted from him. If she wanted him at all. Because the idea of a life without her was inconceivable. He was anchored to her. She was where he belonged. And yet he didn't know if she'd forgiven him or would ever forgive him.

Her own grandmother had broken trust with her. Her faith in her family was wrecked. Was it the same with him? Had the lies he told her and the obfuscation broken her conviction, reliance and certainty in him completely? Would she let him repair those things?

She knew him now, past and present, and he was willing to break his back until she could look at him like she had the night they'd spent in her bed. It didn't matter how long it took.

She'd told him she loved him. He was in love with her, too, and had been for some time. He just hadn't thought he had a future to offer her.

When she came down for breakfast, he had strong chicory coffee, poached eggs on crab cakes and strawberries and cream waiting for her. He'd made her a bloody mary, too, because she was off duty and nothing said *I've been through hell and back* like a bloody mary for breakfast.

She looked subdued in an all-black linen jumpsuit. She wore gold leaf earrings, strappy-back sandals and bags under her eyes. "You didn't have to do all this," she said, gesturing to the table.

He pulled out her chair and waited wordlessly for her to sit.

She came forward reluctantly and lowered to the seat. He got hit with a wave of her summer scent. It curled his toes and made longing fist in his navel. It didn't help when he caught her dipping the tip of her pinkie into the cream. She brought it up to her mouth and sucked.

She ate slowly, almost methodically. He couldn't decide if she was savoring each bite or lost in thought. The scrapes of cutlery over her flea market china were the only sounds in the room until she swept the last of the cream from her plate with a finger.

Reaching into his pocket, he unraveled the chain he kept there. He laid it out for her.

She stared at the Our Lady of Charity pendant, unreadable.

He wrestled with his wants and needs, bracing his arms on the table's edge. "You should have it back."

"Remy."

"Wear it," he said before she could speak another word. "Whether or not you want me, it was made for you."

She released a small sigh. Pulling her hair over one shoulder, she looked up at him with guarded, dark eyes.

He picked up the necklace again, unclasped it, then draped it over her neck. He secured the chain and refrained from touching the exposed skin of her shoulders.

She touched the pendant, holding it fast against her heart. "Remy…"

He braced. "Yeah, boo?"

Reaching into the pocket of the jumpsuit, she pulled out a slip of paper. Pushing it across the surface of the table, she placed it in front of him.

"What's this?" he asked apprehensively.

"An address," she told him. "It's not far. You don't have to go, if it's not what you want. But I think you owe it to yourself. More, I think you want to."

It was then that he saw the name *Emmanuelle* written above the location. His heart wrenched. "Will you go with me?" he asked after some thought.

"You'd like that?"

"Yes," he whispered.

She nodded slowly. "Okay."

They took her car and drove out of the city. Nine miles upriver, they crossed into Harahan, tucked into a bend of the river. They drove through streets with old live oaks and historic houses.

The neighborhood the address led them to was neither cookie-cutter nor pretentious. When Sloane eased to a stop in front of a white house with a sprawling green yard and a red door, Remy eyed the bicycle in the yard with trepidation. "It's nice," he observed. The street was quiet. He thought of his farmhouse and the semblance of peace he'd found in snatched moments there. It was peaceful here, too.

He and Emmanuelle had been raised together in chaos. It was no wonder they'd sought the opposite as adults.

"They're inside," Sloane stated. "All of them."

"You've spoken to them?"

She nodded mutely.

He didn't know what to think. He was adrift, his pulse a dull drumbeat in his ears.

Her hand slid over his. He looked down as their fingers intertwined. It was the first time they'd touched since he carried her into the emergency room, demanding she be seen immediately.

"I'll wait here," she murmured.

He shook his head. "I don't know what to say to them."

"You don't have to say anything," she whispered. "Just be with them. Enjoy the moment. You've needed this for a long time."

She was right. He'd always needed his family. Would they still want him in return? Scrubbing a hand over his face and the growth of stubble there, he popped the door handle. Before her hand could slide out of his, he brought it to his chest. "Thank you," he said. Fastening his eyes to hers, he brought her hand up to his mouth and kissed the center of her palm.

Her lashes lowered, curtaining her emotions. "Go."

He unfolded from the car to stand on the curb.

Someone had come out on the porch. She stood tall and straight like him, midnight black curls falling over her shoulders in thick waves.

Her name came to his lips faster than a prayer. "Emmie?"

Her hand lifted to the base of her throat. She stumbled forward and broke into a run.

Sloane thought about joining Remy inside. But he needed this time with his sister, his mother and his nephew. The three of them had spilled out of the door of the house to embrace him. They'd invited him inside, and he'd gone willingly.

Sloane wanted this for him. Remy had earned the right to have his family around him.

The attention and scrutiny her family was going through would be nothing compared to the media frenzy that would descend on him, his mother and sister if she revealed his true identity.

Perhaps Abuela had been wrong about one thing. There may be something she was willing to go against her oath for. She'd disclosed everything in the debrief with Houghton with one exception. She hadn't named Remy as Loup-Garou.

An hour passed before the door to the house opened again and Remy stepped out, his sister Emmanuelle beside him. The woman's arms circled his neck. Remy held her for a moment, his closed eyes and furrowed brow saying more than words. He then turned to Célestine. She cupped his cheek in her hand before going up on tiptoe to touch her lips to the other cheek. She stroked his face, motherly.

Sloane's chest expanded. As Remy descended the porch steps and the women waved goodbye to him, she twined the chain of the pendant around her first finger.

He opened the passenger door and lowered himself into the seat beside her. His silence wasn't heavy this time. It felt reverent.

She tipped her head to his shoulder and felt his come to rest on top of hers. "Are you okay?" she asked.

"I missed them," he said simply.

"Did they tell you about Gabbie?"

"Yes."

"Her death wasn't your fault. LeBlanc never should've put that on your conscience. The blame was never yours to carry."

"You did this," he murmured. "All of it. I can't tell you what that means to me."

"Don't," she told him. "Just sit with me."

He turned his nose into her hair, seeking solace and forgiveness and everything else she had to give.

"I need to say something else," she explained. The words erupted from her, broken and precarious. "Don't go." Absently, she traced the rendered snake shackled around his wrist. "You asked me to come with you at The Roosevelt, and I walked away."

"I shouldn't have asked. It was selfish of me."

"Now I'm the one who's selfish. I'm asking you not to run. I don't want you to disappear. I want you with me." She tipped her chin up. When he brought his mouth to hers, the kiss was a whisper. "Stay with me."

"Does this mean you've forgiven me?"

"I've carried you inside my heart for so long, there's no turning back. Not for me."

His lips grazed her temple. "There's something I should've told you before. I've been yours since the moment I laid eyes on you. You are the only home I've known, the only home that's mattered, since I was a lost boy. You may not have known it, but all the time we've spent together, every moment, I felt found."

"I know the feeling." She knew it exactly. "Let me be your world, Remy Fontenot. I'll love and protect you all the days of your life."

"Is that a proposal?" A smile touched the creases of his eyes.

She laughed in a breathless burst. "I never said I was conventional."

"One of the many reasons I find you fascinating. One of the reasons I love you—with everything I have."

She melted. "I'll never make you breakfast, but I'll always have your back."

He touched her chin, bringing her face up to his. His nose nuzzled hers as his breath fluttered across her cheek. Butterflies wheeled around her stomach, batting into each other. He made her feel such beautiful chaos. "I'll never keep you from your work, but I'll always be waiting for you when you come home. Let me be the place you land when the world's unjust. Let me be your constant."

"You already are," she told him.

"And, boo?" he added, smiling fully now. "I'm going to enjoy every second of making up for lost time." He swept her up in a breathless kiss, and she clung to him, kissing him back with every ounce of need and love she possessed.

Her lone-wolf renegade had come home to her at last.

Chapter 25

Four months later

"Uncork the champagne."

"I can only have a sip," Pia cautioned. She stood before the full-length mirror in the bedroom of the beach house she and her fiancé, Sam Filipek, shared with her daughters, eleven-year-old Babette, and newborn Myla. Smoothing her hands over the hips of her white lace wedding gown, she looked calm and serene. She was the picture of grace. "I'm breast-feeding, remember?"

"Just a taste," Grace promised, hoisting the bottle. After several tries, a satisfactory pop rang through the room. She held it up as gas escaped from the neck in a sinuous plume. Then she tipped the bubbly liquid into three waiting flutes and passed them around. "What should we toast to, ladies?"

"To Pia," Sloane said, raising her glass to the bride.

"Yes, to you, chère," Grace echoed, clinking her champagne against Pia's. "The best of us."

Pia blinked rapidly. "Careful. If I spring a leak, this eye makeup's going places."

Grace lifted a paper fan from the dresser and waved it in front of Pia's face. "No tears. At least not before cake."

"Cake," Pia murmured. She closed her eyes and uttered a dreamy, "Mmm."

"That's right," Sloane encouraged. "Think about triple decker cake and what Sam may or may not be wearing under his tux."

Pia gave a startled laugh. Since Myla's birth, she practically glowed with motherhood bliss. Add to that a Christmas wedding on Flamingo Bay and a soldier groom who adored every inch of her, and that glow reached supernova proportions.

Sloane was ridiculously happy for her. "Bottoms up," she said, touching the lip of the champagne flute to her mouth.

"Wait, wait," Pia said. "I'd like to make a toast to us. To my free girls."

Grace sighed. "Look how far we've come."

"To my chicas," Sloane returned.

"Salud," Pia added. She took a sip. "You brought the good kind."

"I had to," Grace explained. "It's not every day one of us is a bride, is it?"

"Lately, I'd say the odds haven't been against us," Sloane drawled, pointing out the wedding ring on Grace's finger.

"Is this your way of announcing you and Remy are engaged?" Grace asked, eyes widening.

Sloane didn't miss the way Pia pressed her lips together in barely contained excitement. "I told you. We're not rushing anything."

"But you're happy with him," Pia asserted.

Sloane felt a sigh float from her, unbidden. She stared into her champagne and watched the bubbles rise to the surface. Just the thought of him made her feel all sparkly and bubbly, too. "He makes me very happy, yes."

Grace beamed. "You'll get no complaint from us if you decide to take his last name."

Sloane pursed her lips. There would be no taking Remy's true last name. The whereabouts of Baz LeBlanc were still a closely guarded secret. "Perhaps he'll take mine."

"That's the spirit," Pia said conspiratorially. "Grace, did Javy get in on the morning flight?"

"He'll be at the ceremony," Grace confirmed, checking the clock on Pia's nightstand.

"Why did he have to take a flying trip back home to New Mexico again?" Sloane asked.

Grace's expression sobered. She set her glass aside and took one of Pia's hands, then Sloane's. "Let's sit down."

The champagne didn't go down easy at the suggestion. "What's going on?" Sloane asked bracingly as she lowered to the edge of the bed next to Pia.

The bride merely locked her hands together in her lap and waited.

"Everything's fine," Grace said. "I'm fine. Javy's fine. Together, everything's going great. He's the love of my life, and I plan on keeping him for the rest of it."

"But…" Sloane prompted, knowing bad news was coming.

Grace's nerves were all too apparent as she looped one hand around the wrist of the other. "We're going back."

"Back where?" Pia asked.

"To New Mexico," Grace announced.

Sloane gawped. "Why would you do that?"

"Javy doesn't belong in New Orleans," Grace told her. "He belongs in high desert country with the horses and cattle and wide-open spaces. It's who he is."

"What about you?" Pia asked. "New Orleans has always been your home."

"After Mexico," Grace explained, "I only came back to the city because the noise and the crowds and city life made me forget all the bad things that were going on inside my head. That's gone now. I got a glimpse of the quiet in the desert when Javy and I went into hiding there. I want it back. There's a hospital there, too, on the reservation that needs surgeons."

"You're serious about this," Sloane observed.

"I am," Grace insisted. "I'm going to miss you both and Sam, Remy, Babette and sweet baby Myla, and I'll come back to visit as much as possible. But I feel like I'm being pulled elsewhere. Like I'm being called."

Pia shook her head, as if she were at a loss for words. "I would love if the three of us stayed close," she said. "But I want you to have everything you want in life. Both of you. You've earned it ten times over."

"If you were doing this for him," Sloane added, "I wouldn't let you go."

"I know," Grace said with a nod. "But it's not just about Javy. I want this."

Yes, Sloane could see that—and it broke her heart a little.

"When?" Pia asked.

"In the spring," Grace answered. "After Mardi Gras."

"I don't know what New Orleans is without you," Pia murmured. "Either of you. You're more home to me than the city ever was."

Grace pulled them both into an embrace. "It doesn't matter how many miles there are between us. We're connected. I refuse to do life without you. Prepare to be inundated with video chats, photos, phone calls, messages…and I'll want you both out for a visit once we're settled."

"I can't picture Pia in the desert any more than I can picture myself there," Sloane mused.

"You just wait, chère," Grace murmured. "That first sunrise over the mountains… It's a heartbreaker."

Pia fanned her face once more. "Flash flood warning."

"Hell," Sloane said, sniffing furiously. "We may as well cry and get it over with."

"It's the hormones," Pia sobbed. She accepted a tissue from Grace, who took one for herself.

"Might as well get it all out there," Grace said, dabbing at her cheeks. She spread her arms wide. "Javy and I want to start a family once we get settled in New Mexico."

Pia squealed and hugged Grace once more.

"These hormones better not be catching," Sloane pointed out. Being a tía to Babette and Myla was more than enough for her.

Grace laughed. "What's your excuse?"

"Something in my eye," Sloane lied, touching her finger to the corner of it delicately.

Grace wrapped her arms around Sloane's shoulders. "Tears or not, you're still a total badass."

Sloane gave her a squeeze.

"We better redo Pia's makeup," Grace noted. "Sam's going to come looking for his bride soon."

"Should we fight him for her?" Sloane wondered. "We could take him."

"We could," Grace agreed. "But they need each other, every bit as much as Javy and Remy need us."

Sloane couldn't argue with that. "You touch up her makeup. I'm going to find an enormous bottle of rum."

"Ça c'est bon," Grace cheered. "Tipsy bridesmaids for the win."

The wedding went off without a hitch. The weather stayed mild, despite the proximity to the new year. Baby Myla barely made a sound as Sam's mother cradled her in her arms in the first row. In the Filipeks' Ukrainian tradition, wreaths were placed on the bride and groom's heads, deeming them king and queen of their home, and they each took a swallow from a cup of wine to signify that in marriage all things were shared.

Babette came forward in her bronze dress, matching Grace and Pia's bridesmaids' gowns, to read Maya Angelou's "Touched by an Angel."

Sloane looked out over those assembled. Her gaze snagged

on the navy-suit-clad shoulders of the man on the bride's side of the aisle. One corner of his mouth lifted, and he sent her a nearly imperceptible wink.

Remy had been holding those shoulders a little higher lately. After she was put on leave so the inquiry into her family's wrongdoings could be as thorough as possible, she'd joined Remy at his farmhouse upstate. They'd spent weeks there, just the two of them.

Grace was right. There was something to be said for the quiet. Sloane had missed the city and her maisonette. She'd missed her work more. But the time off had done her well. Days and nights spent with Remy were pure bliss.

He had been the one to decide they should return to the Big Easy. *If we're going to have this, you and me, I can't have Loup-Garou hanging over our heads forever.*

When Remy had met with Houghton, Sloane wasn't sure she'd see him again outside of a holding cell.

Houghton had surprised them both. Because Loup-Garou had been cleared in Terry Booker's death and the data chips he had left at the scene of each raid had helped the New Orleans field office gather enough evidence to build a decent case against each of the implicated trafficking cells, he had offered Remy a deal.

Loup-Garou's story was as good as buried, and now Remy Fontenot consulted for the FBI's tech team. The hacking skills that initially led him down a path of destruction had saved him in the end. Torben's role in Loup-Garou's story was never brought to light, and Remy planned to keep it that way.

He visited his mother, sister and nephew regularly, to their delight and his own. In November, he had introduced Sloane to them. She'd been touched by how easily they'd accepted her into the family fold.

His father hadn't fared as well with the FBI. LeBlanc was being held without bail, awaiting his court case in January with evidence piled against him. According to polls, the court of public opinion was questioning his proclivities for the first time since his failed election bid twenty years ago. Buried stories of blackmail and corruption in connection with the Guidrys peppered the headlines. So far, LeBlanc had kept silent about his son's reemergence.

Surely, he knew if he revealed Baz's whereabouts that Remy would tell his new colleagues at the FBI how he had been separated from his family.

At the beginning of December, Houghton visited Remy and Sloane on Bourbon Street to inform her that she had been cleared of all complicity in the case against the Escarras. Her exemplary record had held up, and her partner, Pelagie, and everyone else she'd worked with at the New Orleans field office had vouched for her integrity. Her active agent status was reinstated, and she was eager to return to work the first week of January.

Other members of her family hadn't been exonerated. Her father was currently under house arrest, pending an investigation into his culpability surrounding the family's affairs. The black mark on his reputation as a public servant was nothing to his shame over how far his mother and brothers had gone to cover up their large role in sex trafficking, endangering Sloane along the way.

Sloane hadn't visited her tíos in prison. While Houghton had advised her not to make contact with Ezmeralda, either, she had made two trips to the women's penitentiary to see Abuela. She did it in large part to see that her grandmother's well-being was intact and because her father couldn't come himself.

Abuela expressed little remorse over what had taken place over the course of her illegalities, including Sloane's abduction. She'd broken down into tears, however, when Sloane had told her that Nestor was recovering from his gunshot wound and would live to see a lengthy prison sentence.

How the justice system worked was no mystery to Sloane. She knew her grandmother would likely be released sooner than later based on age and good behavior. She'd live out her years in quiet disgrace, raking up the pieces of the all-important family legacy she and Sloane's grandfather had sought at all costs.

As Babette finished her reading, Grace passed Pia the tissue hidden in her bouquet. Pia touched it to each eye before bringing Babette into the circle of her arms. She held her daughter tight.

When it was Sam's turn, he, too, looked misty-eyed. "I love you," he murmured.

Babette kissed his cheek before returning to her seat, where she took her baby sister into her lap, content to hold her through the rest of the ceremony.

At last, the celebrant pronounced Pia and Sam husband and wife. Sam gathered Pia in close, and they shared a tender, sweeping kiss to a chorus of applause.

The balcony of their beach house had been cleared for a reception. As the band segued into a collection of low-country favorites, the small dance space filled with gyrating partygoers, and the sun dipped toward the horizon, casting the sky in watercolor hues.

Pride struck Sloane when she saw that Remy had secured a table for two near the open bar. He stood at her approach, his brows hitched high, admiring her long bronze dress with its high slit.

"Hot damn," he said simply as he handed her a longneck bottle.

"Look who's talking." She knew he was uncomfortable in the tux, but he looked like a million dollars. "I'd love to see you in uniform."

"I have pictures."

"Por favor," she drawled, batting her lashes.

His warm smile took his gaze all around her face. "Later." He closed the space between them, laying his mouth on hers.

She closed her eyes. The kiss skimmed the surface of desire that simmered whenever he was around. But the promise of it took her breath away.

His hand found its way into the dip of her spine. It stayed there, anchoring her to him as he lifted his head. His brow furrowed. "Have you been crying?"

"Don't pretend there was a dry eye on that beach," she said. "And yes, before the festivities, there may have been weeping. Pia's married. Grace is flying off to God knows where in the American West…"

"Is she?"

"Remind me to kick Javy's ass later," she told him.

"Leave Javier to his own. It was you who saved his life last winter."

"She's happy, dammit," Sloane said, looking across the balcony to where Sam, Pia, Grace and Javier laughed and danced side by side. Pia bounced Myla in her arms, earning a wide smile from her daughter that made her and Sam beam at each other. "They both are."

"It does you well to see it," Remy observed.

"Part of me has always wished we were still who we were before we went to Mexico," she contemplated. "Back when I protected them from mean Catholic school girls and the city that was our home. But even after everything they went through, I see the women they are and the lives they've made, and I realize everything turned out fine. We made it right."

"You did," he agreed. "Strong women run in your circle."

"They do," she said with a smile. She spied Sam's father

twirling Babette so her skirt billowed and her laughter winged into the air. "In the next generation, too."

He cleared his throat. "Speaking of, Sam's mother tells me we've agreed to watch Babette and Myla while Pia and Sam are away for their honeymoon."

She made a face. "It was a moment of weakness brought on by a large bottle of rum. Besides, it's not for more than a few days. Grace and Javy will pick them up from the farmhouse after three nights to spend another two in the city with them." When he only stared at her, she canted her head. "You're Remy frickin' Fontenot. Don't tell me you're afraid of a couple of kids."

"You're going to make me change diapers, aren't you?"

"Tía's rules," she stated, deadpan.

"They leave for their honeymoon tomorrow," he pointed out.

"Yes."

"So tonight it's just the two of us."

She caught his meaning. In the guise of straightening the knot of his tie, she feathered her fingertips across the cords of his throat. She ran her palm down the length of the tie. Her hand disappeared beneath his jacket to rest on his back. "What'd you have in mind, amor?"

She would never get enough of the affection in his eyes or the heat that flashed behind them at her touch. He set down his drink, then took hers and did the same. Holding out his hand, he asked, "Join me?"

Without hesitation, she placed her hand in his. When he led her away from the table, excitement ran through her.

He didn't lead her in the direction she was expecting. Instead, he diverted her onto the dance floor.

"Um," she said, "what are you doing?"

He dropped his head low. "I've been watching you dance

with other people for over a decade." The words whisked intimately across her ear. Using the hand he still held, he raised it and spun her in a dizzying circle.

She whooped, tripping on her heels, and stumbled against him.

He caught her in his arms, the intent of his face spurring her heart into a gallop. "It's my turn now."

"Are you saying Mr. NavySEAL-Bodyguard-Vigilante Fontenot can *dance*?" she asked, delighted.

"You're about to find out."

The band kicked the music up a notch. He dipped her low, grinning widely as her laughter burst freely into the night. He brushed his mouth across hers before pulling her upright once more and leading her into a lively zydeco that kept her feet busy and her smile wide.

The party went well into the night. Sometime near dawn, Sloane found herself on a blanket near the surf with Pia on one side and Grace on the other. Sleepiness clutched her, luring her eyes to close. "You know," she drawled, "I was certain you'd want to spend your wedding night with your husband."

Pia's smile warmed her voice. "He was up early this morning with Myla so I could rest before the ceremony. He crashed on the hammock. I didn't want to wake him."

"I'm partially there," Grace admitted, sounding groggy. The wineglass perched next to her was empty. The breeze scattered the coils of her hair across her face. She didn't brush them off. "I love weddings. I love the music, the dancing, the cake…"

"The cake," Pia hummed. "Wasn't it divine?"

"Whose idea was it to hide the Mardi Gras baby in the layers?" Grace asked.

"Babette's," Pia said. "I thought it was a nice touch until Javier nearly swallowed it."

Grace chuckled. "Poor Javy." She lifted her bare foot to nudge Sloane's calf with her toes. "It's no wonder you're no longer on your feet. You and Remy tore up the floor."

"We did," Sloane said, not willing to hide her smugness about that in the slightest.

"He's got more moves than a can of worms," Pia noted, amused. "Who knew?"

"Not me." Sloane's grin turned soft. "He keeps surprising me."

She didn't see the look her friends exchanged over her head, but she felt it all the same. Pia rolled onto her side and propped her head on her arm. "I think we've all found the right one."

Sloane considered that. "I found mine first. It just took a while for both of us to see it. We had our own journeys to complete first."

"Sam and I did, too," Pia replied. "It was worth the wait. I know you can take care of yourself. But I'm glad he's with you. Not just to look out for you, but to make you smile and laugh like you did tonight."

"I second that," Grace chimed, raising her empty glass.

"After everything that's happened over the last year," Sloane said, "we all wound up exactly where we should be."

"I was just following your example, chère," Grace pointed out.

"Me, too," Pia echoed.

Sloane grasped both their hands. She held onto them as they watched the stars wink out.

She thought she would feel rootless after her family's collapse. But, for her, family went beyond those who raised her. Grace and Pia made her feel steady on her feet. They bolstered her, and they'd be there through every sea change.

Remy was, without doubt, the one. She couldn't wait to see what the future held with him.

No matter what it brought, she'd have him and her girls, and that was all she needed to get her through.

As the sun peeked over the horizon, Grace tipped her head to Sloane's shoulder. "So. Cake for breakfast?"

Pia beamed. "You took the words right out of my mouth."

Sloane folded the blanket. Grace picked up her glass. Pia linked arms with both of them, and they walked back to the beach house, united.

* * * * *

Harlequin® Reader Service

Enjoyed your book?

Try the perfect subscription for Romance readers and get more great books like this delivered right to your door.

See why over 10+ million readers have tried Harlequin Reader Service.

Start with a Free Welcome Collection with free books and a gift—valued over $20.

Choose any series in print or ebook. See website for details and order today:

TryReaderService.com/subscriptions